the summer it started

CAROLINE HOPKINS

ISBN 978-1-961878-13-6

ONE

MY MOM WAS late as usual.

She was always three minutes late to everything, the kind of precision that you could set a watch to. I leaned against the wall of the coffee place, starting to scroll through my phone. A couple of my classmates had already posted pictures from the beach, celebrating the last day of the school year.

I kept scrolling, then hit a picture of Hunter Lowen, the soccer and lacrosse captain in our year. He was pushing his hair back, looking out at the lacrosse field. He looked incredibly hot.

My stomach pulled together slightly. I shut my phone and stuck it back in my bag.

"Kins!" Finally, my mom. She was walking up the street, waving to me with one hand and stuffing her phone into her purse with the other. She always seemed like she was about to become unbalanced and fall over from her multitasking, but she always managed to stay upright. "Happy last day of school!"

"Thanks," I said, my voice muffled by the giant hug that she had pulled me into. She smelled the same as ever, a combination of her deodorant – she used the hibiscus flower one, and I used the pomegranate and vanilla one, and we'd used the same two scents as long as I could remember – and the laundry detergent we had at home.

It should have been comforting. Like things were the same as ever.

"You're getting to be such a grown up. You're probably going to go ahead and order coffee, and I'm not going to be able to say caffeine stunts your growth," my mom said, taking a step back and looking at me. "I'm so proud of you, Kinsey."

"Thanks," I said, looking down at the ground. "I mean, it was just sophomore year. I haven't cured cancer or anything."

"But it's high school, right?" she said, raising an eyebrow at me. It was one of the many skills that we shared, the ability to raise just one eyebrow in the perfect expression of disbelief. "High school can be awful. You should absolutely celebrate. Want to split a ginger cookie?"

"Of course." We both loved ginger cookies, to the point where we'd had to boycott them after we started skipping dinner to eat cookies. We'd swapped out Christmas tea instead and now had twenty backup boxes of it at home.

We walked into Starbucks and got in line. Ahead of us, a group of freshmen ordered frappes, and my mom stared at the menu. "I always think that I'm going to try something different here, and I always get the same thing. The latte really is the pinnacle of coffee perfection."

"I might just get a black coffee," I said, nodding at the menu. I couldn't get the same thing as all of the freshmen ahead of us.

"Nope. You're not allowed to be that much of a grown up. Go back to having your sugary drinks without coffee in them. My mom brain cannot handle this much growing up at once," she said, shaking her head enough that her sunglasses came dislodged from her head. She grabbed them in one swift move and stuffed them into her purse.

"Maybe I'll finally try one of your iced lattes. Since you claim that that's the pinnacle of coffee perfection," I replied as we reached the front of the line. My mom fished around in her purse for her phone again.

"Do that," she said, looking up at the barista. "Hi! One venti iced latte with two extra espresso shots, and for Kinsey, one with half an espresso shot. And please label them so we don't get them mixed up."

The barista just nodded. "See," my mom continued, shoving her phone back into her bag, "this is why ordering ahead online is a good idea. There'd be labels on the drinks, so there wouldn't even be a chance that I would kill you with caffeine."

"I don't think you're going to kill me with caffeine," I replied. My mom didn't know that I snuck coffee ahead of finals just like everyone else. I'd started this fall ahead of my biology midterm.

We moved to the end of the line to wait for our drinks, and I scraped the toe of my flats along the floor. It was a nervous habit that I had picked up from somewhere, and now it meant that I destroyed my flats within a month. My mom had tried all kinds of creative ways to get me to stop doing it, and when they hadn't worked, she'd given up and started buying the cheapest used flats that she could find online.

We grabbed our drinks and found a table outside. My mom pushed her sunglasses back over her eyes and took a long sip of her drink, sighing. "I don't know what it is about these, but they are absolutely the best."

I took a sip of mine. It wasn't bad, but it was nowhere near as good as the frappes. I should have just gone for the basic choice. "So are you excited about this summer?" my mom asked.

"I guess, yeah," I replied. Better to not have school than to have school, all things considered. Even a boring summer was better than the school year.

"Are you disappointed that Jenna's heading out for the summer?" she asked, taking another slurp of her coffee.

Jenna was going to Los Angeles for the summer to spend time with her stepfather and stepsister. Jenna and her mom spent the school year in Connecticut, something about her custody agreement with her dad. Her mom had been planning on the Los Angeles trip for a long time, and Jenna didn't complain.

"I mean, yeah." I glanced at my mom and took a deep breath. My friend group in middle school had splintered, and Jenna had stepped in as my best friend. She was the outgoing one of the two of us, the one who always had a comeback, the fun one. I was the boring one, the loyal sidekick.

"Everything's okay between the two of you?" my mom asked, pushing her sunglasses back onto the top of her head so that I could look her in the eyes.

Normally, this would have been the time that I would have told my mom everything. Something had started to change with Jenna. Maybe she was just too grown up now. I didn't look at pictures of Hunter Lowen and take hot pictures of myself in my spare time. I was still a kid in comparison to her.

But that would have been hard to say to my mom at a normal time. Now it was impossible.

"Of course," I said, staring down at my drink and wishing I had brought my own sunglasses. "Obviously, it's just weird that she won't be here for the entire summer, you know?"

My mom nodded, looking relieved.

For some reason, that hurt more than I would have thought. Last year, if I'd had the same conversation, my mom would have leapt in and demanded to know exactly what was going on. She would have told me how she felt about Jenna a long time ago.

"At least you'll have plenty of time to hang out with Lily," my mom said, taking another sip of her coffee. Lily had been my best friend in elementary school, but she lived a fifteen minute drive away. That was enough to put her four school districts over, so we barely ever saw each other during the school year. Her family is going to the beach this year, right?"

Lily's family rented a house by the coast every year for the summer, so that her mom could sit in peace and write the manuscript that would be published the next year. Lily's mom was a famous child psychologist who had a devoted following. She spent the school year flying around the country, assuring everyone that it was okay that it was okay that their children weren't violin prodigies at the tender age of six.

"It's really great for my self-esteem that my mom's whole thing is convincing parents that it's okay if they have dumb children," Lily had grumbled on more than one occasion.

"Yeah. They're going to the beach for most of the summer. I guess her mom has a new book coming out," I said. Lily wasn't around for the summer either. I was on my own.

"I love her books," my mom said, stirring her drink with her straw. "And please don't take that to mean that I love them because they have convinced me that it's okay that you're dumb."

"No offense taken," I replied. Well, maybe a little.

"Society spends most of its time telling moms that they've somehow screwed up all of the things," my mom continued, pointing her drink at me. "And Lily's mom says the opposite."

"Not everyone can be the Gilmore girls," I replied.

"Okay, you say that, but you were clearly not paying

attention in the follow up season. They all screwed up their lives and showed themselves to be selfish pricks at the end," my mom replied. "Don't get pregnant and stuck in Connecticut, please."

"Definitely not on my list for this summer." As someone who had never kissed anyone, the chances of that happening were zero. A negative number, in fact. I'd never been on a date, never held hands with a boy, never really had a crush.

"If you get into Yale, though, I get to passive aggressively brag to everyone who made fun of me or bragged about their kid, though," she continued, then shot me her widest grin. "Kidding. You absolutely should not do anything with the goal of pleasing your parents."

"I wasn't worried about that." My mom was too chill for that, and my dad probably couldn't tell you what grade I'd just completed.

"You're committed to mid-July this year, right?" my mom asked.

"Yeah. That's the Mandatory Two this year. Or at least one of the Mandatory Two," I said, taking another sip of my less than great coffee.

My dad was entitled to have me visit for two weeks every year. If I didn't do the Mandatory Two every year, my mom would be cut off from child support. That money was what paid for our house and for Betta, my nearly twenty year old Honda Civic. My mom worked in the state public health department. She loved it, but it wasn't paying for college on its own.

So like every year, I was going to serve part of the

Mandatory Two over the summer. I had never quite been clear why my dad's lawyers had put that term in the agreement. My dad never seemed to have any interest in having me there, and most of the time, I would just be alone in his apartment. I usually saved all my summer reading for that week, so it was okay enough. "Maybe this year he'll actually speak to me."

My mom smirked. She had tried for the longest time to avoid saying anything about the divorce, but once I'd become a teenager, she'd given up on that. We, and probably everyone had ever met my father, could agree that he was an asshole.

"I was thinking about seeing if the town has any more spots for coaches in their tennis program," I said, changing the topic away from my father.

"The town tennis program?" my mom asked, tilting her head slightly to the side.

"Yeah." I was sure that we had talked about this already. I told my mom everything. I'd been thinking about signing up to coach because I didn't have other plans, and coaching would at least look good for college. I wasn't excited about it, but it was at least something.

"But when was the last time you played tennis?" she asked.

Middle school gym. "I don't know what else I'm going to do this summer," I said. I could hear the edge in my voice and I tried to swallow it back, probably without luck. "Nobody's in town."

"Don't you have things to do for cross country?" she asked, pulling her sunglasses back down over her eyes.

She should have known this. I did cross-country because it was the chillest sport with the fewest practices. Our coach was off in Colorado, and she'd told us to just not do anything stupid. "No. I have to work out on my own, but there's nothing planned this summer."

"Oh." Mom's voice was smaller, and I swallowed. "I'm sorry. Well, I do think that you should look into coaching tennis then. It would be a good way to meet people this summer."

My mom and I hadn't always been like this. For most of my life, it had been me and my mom against the world. My mom lit up every room she stepped into, the person who would go on late night ice cream runs and sneak onto the beach to watch the sunrise.

My mom and I were a team against the world. We didn't have my dad, but it didn't matter. I hadn't needed a best friend for most of my life, because I'd had my mom. She had always been there, always been in my corner. She was the person who I could text to see if a skirt looked good or if I was bored.

But then Brian came into our lives.

I wasn't stupid enough to think that my mom was never going to get remarried or start dating. I didn't want to imagine her living by herself after I went off to college and started my life. But I had always imagined it as just being the two of us, dancing through our tiny condo.

Sure, maybe she'd start dating again once I went to college. Because before that, she had me, and it wasn't like she needed to have anyone else in her life. And if she started dating, it'd be because she'd fallen for the king of a small European country or some dashing public health hero. He'd maybe show up at college visit days, but otherwise, things would continue as normal.

Instead, we got Brian Day. He was as boring and plain as the name would suggest.

I wasn't able to figure out what made him so special. He was an average looking, average sounding, middle aged white guy. If you went to any high school soccer game, you'd be able to find fifty of him sitting on the sidelines, alternating between checking their phones and getting overinvested in what the ref was doing.

He was sweet enough. For one of their first dates, he'd give her a stuffed plushie of the Ebola virus, which she had written her master's thesis on. He was kind and thoughtful. I could at least give him that.

But I had absolutely no idea what else she saw in him beyond that.

Their relationship, which I thought was just a few casual dates, had turned into a whirlwind courtship. All of a sudden, it was all about Brian. She went with him to his company Christmas party, accompanied him on a business trip to Miami, and told me more facts that I ever wanted to know about this man.

I'd assumed that things would fizzle out after a few months, but nope. No such luck. It wasn't that she couldn't date anyone. It was just – not yet. My mom was mine, not his. No boring old Brian Day deserved to have my mom paying that much attention to him.

Logically I knew that my mom deserved to have

another adult in her life. But it could have waited until I went to college. Instead, we'd jumped from her having a few drinks with this guy to getting engaged this spring.

I couldn't say anything, because I was supposed to want her to be happy. I wasn't supposed to complain and make everything about me. I was supposed to be supportive, not selfish.

So I just nodded and didn't say anything else.

"GOD, I don't know why I agreed to let you take your car for this," Jenna said, looking up from her phone.

I glanced over my shoulder and made sure that the left hand lane was clear before I eased Betta into the next lane. She grumbled slightly but moved over smoothly. "I like my car," I said, and it wasn't like Jenna had offered hers.

Jenna looked up from her phone and glanced over at me. She was slouched in the passenger seat, her feet up on the dashboard. "Your car is twenty years old. It's like a wonder that it hasn't broken down on the side of the road."

I bit my lip and turned my head again to make sure that the lane was clear. Betta was a seafoam colored Honda Civic that my mom had passed down to me when I started driving, and she was everything that I could want in a car. Mostly, she drove. "There's a lot of traffic on the way to JFK. I have to drive carefully."

Jenna grumbled and turned back towards the front, staring at the traffic ahead of us. "At least I'm not going to miss my flight."

"It's reasonable to leave three hours early when you're driving to the airport. you never know what kind of traffic you're going to run into," I said. Jenna was going to have some kind of comeback to that, a snippy remark to remind me that I drove like an elderly person. "And I don't want you to miss your flight to Los Angeles."

She looked back down at her phone, turning on the front camera to check her lip liner. "God, it's going to be so much this summer. I have to put up with Emberleigh all summer. It's going to kill me."

There were many things that Jenna liked to complain about. She hated the way I drove, she hated the size of the mirrors in the girls' bathroom, she hated the selection of food in the school cafeteria. But of those things, the thing that Jenna hated the most was her stepsister.

Jenna's stepsister was Emberleigh – Emberleigh, the full spelling, as tragic as it was. She'd become moderately famous for nothing other than being moderately famous, and she lived permanently in Los Angeles with Jenna's stepdad.

Jenna hated her. Jenna's favorite game was to watch Emberleigh's latest videos and loudly critique them, telling everyone that she thought that her stepsister was attention seeking, or ugly, or something. Every time Jenna opened her phone, there was always another post from Emberleigh staring back at her, and she always reacted.

I didn't think Emberleigh was particularly bad. Her posts were mostly her at the beach, her cockapoo, her almost as famous friends. She wasn't eminently hateable like so many other people. But I didn't argue with Jenna about it, because I knew I was going to lose that argument. In Jenna's mind, Emberleigh was public enemy number one.

"I hope she's not too annoying. But I guess if you do get too annoyed with her, you can always come back for the summer," I offered. I regretted it as soon as the words were out of my mouth. Not that I didn't like Jenna – I had to like her, she was my friend – but maybe it would be nice to have a break from her.

Jenna shot me a look. "You really think that I would rather be stuck in the suburbs for the summer than hanging out in L.A.?"

From how my mom had described Los Angeles, I pictured it as a giant parking lot, not that dramatically different from the suburbs anyway. "No, you're right."

"You need to make sure to keep me updated on everything that happens," she said. I glanced over at her, but she was looking down at her nails now, inspecting her cuticles. "Not that I expect that you'll do anything interesting. I don't care about the Netflix you watch."

I swallowed. That was harsher than I had expected. "I'm not really a party person," I said, my voice sounding too small.

"Oh trust me, I know," she said, glancing over at me again as we pulled into the departures section of Terminal Five. "You're so boring it kills me sometimes."

Time to change the subject. We were almost to the door where I could let her out, but the traffic had slowed to a crawl. I cleared my throat. "You'll have to tell me about all of the cute boys that you meet in Los Angeles. I'm sure there are tons of attractive guys out there."

"I can't meet that many guys. It's not like I'm going to get myself into a long distance relationship before I come back in the fall," she replied, rolling her eyes at me and then going back to her phone. "And what, do you want me to bring one back for you?"

"I didn't mean that," I said, checking the rearview mirror. "I just know that you're going to end up meeting a lot of cool people this summer."

She gave me half a laugh, not looking up from her phone. We'd finally made it up to the curb where I could drop Jenna off. I inched into a parking spot and put on the brakes.

One of the benefits of driving a twenty year old car was that all of the scratches had already been put on it, and so I didn't have to worry about scratching it up any more. It was much less stressful to drive Betta's than my mom's new car.

"I guess I'll go kill a few hours in an airport now," Jenna said, getting out of the car and striding back to the trunk. She tapped on it a few times to remind me that I had to open it up.

I stopped myself from rolling my eyes. I got out of the car and walked to the back, reaching in and helping pull out her massive suitcases.

Jenna had clearly prepared for everything. I was surprised that she hadn't just bothered to ship her entire closet. "Have a good flight!" I said, waving to her as she grabbed the handles of her bags.

"Keep me posted on all the gossip," she called, flipping her hair over her shoulder as she started the march into the terminal. She didn't look back as the doors slid open. She marched through, vanishing into the mass of people checking in for their flights.

I waved again, then sunk back down into the driver's seat, pulling out of the spot as carefully as I could manage. Behind me, a car blared its horn. I slammed on the brakes, whipping around in my seat to see that they were just being a jerk. People really shouldn't use their horns unless there was going to be an accident. It was just too stressful otherwise.

I hated driving in New York. Jenna should have known that before she asked me to drive. But then again, she would have just told me that learning to drive in the city was an important skill and that I should get over it.

That was Jenna's approach to most problems. If it was something that she thought was going to stand in her way, she was going to tell me to get over it and move on with my life. You didn't go to Jenna with your problems looking for a sympathetic ear. You went to Jenna once you had a plan.

The cars behind blared their horns again. I stepped on the gas, trying to merge into the right hand lane. Jenna owed me for this, not that I was ever going to try to cash in a favor with Jenna.

I managed to find my way back onto I-95 heading north. I could feel myself slump down in the seat with relief. Highway driving I could do. Thank god I was out of the city traffic and almost home.

I drove a couple of exits past my normal turnoff to go

home, heading over to the Nest to meet Lily. She was already standing outside the cafe, her hair piled on top of her head, holding a dog-eared book in her right hand.

"Hey, girl!" she called as I parked the car. I could hear her through the closed window. Lily knew how to project her voice. "Happy summer!"

"Hey!" I locked the car door behind me and jogged over towards her. "Summer, finally."

She threw her arms around me in a hug. "Summer is just so magical. I swear that it could be this warm during the school year, and I would still not feel like it's summer."

"Couldn't you test that? You could ask someone who lives in Arizona what it's like to live in a place where the weather is always warm," I suggested.

She tilted her head to the side and stared at me, Lily's patented look telling me that I was being ridiculous. "That was meant as a general observation, not a scientific hypothesis that you have to go out and test and tell me if it's accurate."

"Sorry," I replied, shoving Betta's keys in my pocket. "Sometimes I take things a little too literally."

"Sometimes?" She shook her head, some of her hair escaping from her top bun. "You're the queen of being too literal. You are literally no fun to be around sometimes."

I rolled my eyes at her. Lily and I had slightly different views on life. Lily was a hopeless romantic, one of those people who believed that she had one true love hiding around the corner somewhere. I was a realist, who understood that true love probably didn't exist, and even if it did, you weren't going to find it in high school. True love was something for your twenties, if it existed at all.

"Not to be the hopeless realist throwing water on your plans or anything, but can we get a snack? I'm so hungry," I replied. I hadn't had time to grab breakfast before driving Jenna this morning.

The Nest was our favorite snack place, a café that sold overpriced salads and the most delicious egg sandwich that I had ever had. It was one of those places that I dragged my mom to.

At least, I had dragged my mom there every time until she had found out that they had a food safety violation in their latest inspection. My mom knew all about communicable diseases, so she had steadfastly refused to eat anything here. I loved my mom to pieces, but sometimes she did take certain things a little bit too seriously. I would risk a few food safety violations for the world's best egg sandwich.

"So where were you this morning?" Lily asked, rummaging through her tote bag.

"I had to drive Jenna to the airport this morning," I said, pushing open the front door to the Nest. The smell of fresh baked cinnamon rolls hit me in the face. Those were also worth risking some food safety violations for.

"But you hate driving in the city. You hate driving downtown here, and we have like a thousand people who live here," Lily said, walking up to the counter.

"Yeah, but she asked me to. So I did," I replied, following her up to the counter.

"Did she at least bring you breakfast?" Lily asked, her

eyebrows shooting up further. "Because if she didn't effusively thank you and bring you breakfast, she's a jerk."

"She's my friend. If she wants me to help her out with something, I'm going to help her out with stuff. If you asked me to drive you to the airport, I would do it," I replied, fishing my wallet out of my bag.

"Maybe we have a different definition of friends here, but I also wouldn't ask a friend who I knew hated driving in the city to drive me to JFK," she replied, throwing her hands out to the side. "Are you kidding me?"

"It wasn't that bad of a drive," I replied, ignoring the fact that I had literally sweat through my shirt due to anxiety. "You're on the highway for a lot of it, and the Whitestone Bridge is a little bit tricky, but I figured it out. And it's Saturday morning, so traffic isn't as bad as it could be."

"You are over-rationalizing," she replied.

"You are using your mom's words on me." One of the problems of being friends with Lily was that she would sometimes drop ridiculous therapy words into the middle of a conversation. Lily had spent most of her life talking through her feelings rationally and saying things like "I need some space to process this."

Unfortunately, Lily had also learned that my arguments would fall flat against an onslaught of her mom's talk. In first grade, she'd gotten me to admit that I'd farted in front of everyone in our class. I now got suspicious as soon as a single psychologist word came out.

"So other than your fun trip down to JFK, what have you been up to?" she asked, grabbing our drinks as they came out.

"I don't know," I said, picking up our orders from the counter and looking around for a seat. I could already smell the egg sandwiches in my bag, and my stomach rumbled. "Avoiding my mom and Brian."

Lily rolled her eyes. "Why even bother avoiding Brian? You just have to tune him out. Like radio static."

Ooh, radio static was a good analogy. Slightly annoying, but you could tune it out if you tried. "I don't understand what my mom sees in him," I replied, pulling out my chair and sitting down.

"Maybe they have really great sex?" Lily volunteered. "That's always it in the movies."

"Please never talk about my mom having sex with someone like Brian ever again." I shook my head, closing my eyes and trying to scrub that image out of my brain. "I can't even imagine having sex myself, and my mom is – "

"Your mom had to have sex with your dad, didn't she?" Lily asked, taking a giant bite of her sandwich.

"Nope," I replied, shaking my head. "I'm sure that was a virgin birth. I mean, you've met my dad. I can't imagine why anyone would have sex with him."

"I'm sure that he just loves all the sex he's been having with that new stepmother," Lily replied, shimmying her entire torso.

How the hell were we still friends? "You are saying all of these things because you know that they're going to gross me out," I said, picking up my iced latte.

"No one would date anyone who sounds as terrible as your stepmother unless the sex was really good." She slurped her lemonade, making awkward eye contact with me over the lid.

"You've never even kissed anyone. What makes you an expert?" I asked, taking a giant bite of my sandwich. This was seriously the world's greatest breakfast sandwich. They even made the English muffins with brioche dough and extra air holes.

Lily grinned and pointed her straw at me before jamming it back into her lemonade. "I watch plenty of rom coms. I am an expert in all things romance from Netflix, thank you very much. That is why you need me around."

"Please stop," I said. It was time for a topic change, before I had to think about Dick and the Evil Stepmother. "Any exciting romantic adventures on the horizon for you this summer?"

"Are you kidding? Nothing exciting ever happens in my life. Ever," she said, slurping her lemonade again.

"It's because you watch too many romantic comedies. You're expecting Mr. Right to just drop down from a ceiling or something." I reached over and passed her a napkin.

"Or stand outside my house with posterboard, or ask me to the prom with a literal horse drawn carriage, or buy the bookstore next to mine so we have competing business, or – "

"Buy the bookstore next to yours? What are you, forty?"

"It's romantic, Kinsey," Lily replied. "I could totally have a bookstore if I had someone competing with me."

"I think that you might benefit from having a model of

romance in your life that doesn't come from bad movies." In fairness, it wasn't all her fault. Her parents had met trying to get onto the subway, where they'd both run for the same turnstile and crashed into each other. Somehow, that had turned into them not getting on the subway to go to the dates that they were supposed to go to and instead finding true love with each other.

I was not a hopeless romantic. When Lily told that story, all I could think about was the fact that the New York City subways smelled like pee. I didn't want to have to meet my soulmate in a place that smelled like a bathroom.

Anyway, my parents had met in what could have been a romantic situation, when my mom had accidentally walked into the wrong party in her apartment building. I had seen how that had turned out. At the end of the day, my mom and I had ended up much happier alone and in our own house, not trying to pretend that my mom had some kind of fairy tale relationship with my dad. Maybe that was the reason that I was so much more grounded about these things than Lily was.

"You have to like someone, Kinsey," Lily said, deciding to change the topic right back to things that I didn't want to talk about. "You have a long summer ahead of you. And you know that if there's any time of the year that you're going to fall madly in love with someone and live happily ever after, it's going to be the summer."

The summer in Connecticut was normally just hot and sweaty. It was the kind of summer where I went to the beach because our house didn't have air conditioning. While my mom and I opened every window and ran fans at full blast, it still got sweltering hot in my room. I loved the summer, but it didn't make me think of romantic love. It made me think of lying around in bed and sitting at the beach and hanging out with my mom.

Not that I got to do that this year. I didn't get any of the traditions I loved this year. Because now we had Brian Senior, and of course, my mom had to spend all of her free time with him.

"I don't like anyone," I replied.

"You have cute guys at your school, though. I don't have any at mine, so don't give me that ridiculous excuse about not being able to find anyone," Lily replied, putting down her egg sandwich and redoing her top bun.

I snorted. Lily was convinced that there was something in the water that made all of the boys at her school impossible to date, and apparently things were very different over on the other side of the town line. I could assure her that it was not, but she wasn't interested in hearing what she referred to as my excuses.

"I have cute guys at my school, but they're all assholes," I replied.

"You mean Hunter?" Lily asked, tying her hair back up and reaching for her sandwich.

Hunter Lowen was a known entity everywhere. He was one of those guys who was apparently so popular and so attractive that it couldn't be restrained to a single town. Everyone in the state, it felt like, knew about Hunter Lowen and what he looked like.

There were Tumblr fan accounts for him. Which was pretty embarrassing that anyone had enough time on their hands to actually make a fan account. Also, creepy if I thought too much about it.

"Yeah, exactly." I wasn't going to mention the fact I wasn't popular or hot enough to date Hunter. I wasn't trying to be cynical about it or dramatic about it or anything. I was just realistic. And that wasn't what I was looking for anyway. I had seen enough from my mom that I knew to avoid any guy who seemed too good to be true.

I wasn't going to find the perfect guy in high school. That was just a fact, and I was going to accept it. I wasn't going to be one of those people who set myself up for disappointment by convincing myself that I could fall madly in love.

"You could totally like Hunter Lowen," Lily said, starting to stare off into the distance. "Did you know that I found a new Tumblr about him yesterday?"

"Why were you looking up Tumblr fan blogs about Hunter Lowen?" I asked, then shook my head. "Why were you on Tumblr anyway?"

"I sometimes do things that are interesting and secret," she replied, staring back at me and then shaking her head. "Anyway. He's so attractive. It's a rom com waiting to happen."

Not one with a happy ending. "He's an asshole who cheats on everyone."

"And how do you know that is true?" Lily asked, raising an eyebrow.

"I just know," I replied. He was too attractive and popular for anything else to be the case. There were plenty of rumors at school about it, and with that many rumors, there had to be a shred of truth.

"You've never dated anyone, Kinsey," Lily replied.

"Neither have you," I said, wrinkling my nose at her. "You're just as guilty."

"We've talked about this. Your school has a much higher concentration of attractive people I'd want to date. There's no one that I'm interested in at my school. That is the problem, and this is why I don't understand why you're not taking advantage of the situation more," Lily replied.

"It isn't a situation." I sighed and leaned on the table. "Can we talk about something other than boys?"

"Jenna?"

No. I'd had enough of that topic. "Nope. Not that."

"Your mom and the most interesting man in the world?" Lily asked, waggling her eyebrows.

That one too. I sighed. "Can we pivot back to talking about your life, maybe?"

"I have nothing interesting going on in my life," she said, pushing her lips into a pout. "Absolutely nothing. I'm going to be spending the summer with my stupid siblings and my family."

"What's in this book?" I asked, reaching for a napkin.

"It's something about thow to talk to your teenager. I know," she said, shaking her head at my facial expression. "Helping your teenager adapt to the change of the teenage years. As a teenager. Something like that."

"I'm sorry. That sounds awful." Hopefully Lily wasn't going to end up in this one too, poorly disguised. That had happened with one about slow starting elementary school students, which Lily had discovered during middle school. It hadn't been great for her self-esteem.

"Don't get me started." Lily shook her head again, then took a giant bite of her egg sandwich. "Before I leave, want to at least help me find a bathing suit?"

At least that was one summer tradition that wasn't changing. "Are you kidding? Of course."

TWO

TWO NIGHTS LATER, I flopped down on my bed and stared at the ceiling.

It was still uncomfortably hot in the house. I had thought that this was going to be okay for another couple of weeks, but apparently Connecticut had decided to turn up the heat early in the summer.

My mom was a big fan of living in what she considered to be the natural environment. "People should know that they have to adapt to the natural conditions around them," she'd explain. "Sitting in air conditioning all the time leads to obesity. You have to be able to live through a little bit of discomfort."

I was only half convinced that she actually believed that and that it wasn't just her long excuse for the fact that we didn't have air conditioning at the house. We lived in a tiny condo downtown, part of a house that had been chopped up into apartments. The people who had built it a hundred years ago had apparently not been able to predict that climate change would mean that someday, we'd really want air conditioning.

I picked up my phone and stared at it again. I wanted something to do. I shouldn't be this bored this early in the summer.

But unfortunately, my mother was out with Brian Senior going to dinner or something. I didn't understand why they went to dinner so much, mainly because I didn't understand what on earth my mom could talk about with Brian Senior.

I picked up my phone again and stared at it. Jenna had sent me something earlier in the day, a picture of her at the beach in California. She looked like she was having a great time if you didn't know her. But if you were a trained Jenna watcher like I was, you could see the slight turndown on the course of her mouth, the way that she was squinting at the camera.

Emberleigh must have been getting to her even more than I expected. I thought about texting and asking, but that wasn't going to get any good answers. She was just going to be pissed that I'd asked and didn't immediately understand why Emberleigh was the worst.

I sighed and stared at my phone, scrolling through Instagram. There was nothing new from the last time that I had scrolled through.

I flipped over to my texts and started to look through them. I couldn't be this boring just because Jenna was out of town. I had to have other friends. I wanted to have other friends, to be someone who wasn't totally dependent on one person who was turning a little toxic.

In my texts, I spotted Ellery Hamilton. I hadn't talked to her much since the end of school, but we'd run cross country together last fall. We chatted on our long runs, and she seemed really cool. I hadn't talked to her as much in the spring after the season ended, though.

Was I actually bored enough to text someone who was basically a total stranger and ask them to hang out with me?

I looked up at the ceiling again. Yeah. I was.

What are you up to? Want to hang out? I texted her, then shut my eyes. It sounded like I was one of those creepy people on a dating app. This was not the most smooth thing that I had ever done.

But fortunately, Ellery didn't seem to notice. *Hey Kinsey! I was thinking of heading over to a party at Max's but didn't have anyone to go with. Want to come over and then go over there?*

Two birds with one stone. I was going to get to hang out with someone, and then I could end up at a party. Excellent. Max was one of the guys on the soccer and lacrosse team, one of the popular guys at school. So when Jenna asked me what I'd been doing, I was going to have something to say that wasn't just lying in my bed. I wasn't as boring as she thought I was.

Definitely, I texted back, rolling over and getting out of my bed. If nothing else, I was pretty sure that Ellery's house would have air conditioning. And even if the party was hot, it couldn't be worse than my house. *I'll head over.*

I grabbed a bag of clothes, then headed down and unlocked Betta. I plugged in my phone for music, then manually rolled down the windows to make the car less stifling. As long as I didn't sweat too much on the drive, I'd be okay. Or I'd have to ask Ellery if I could shower at her house, which felt too awkward.

I drove through town, turning the music in the car up, then pulled my car up in front of Ellery's house. "Hey," I said, parking and getting out of Betta.

"Hey!" Ellery said, bounding out the front door and waving to me. She was already wearing her party outfit, a sequin covered halter top and jean shorts. "Thanks for texting. I wasn't sure what I was going to do tonight."

"That makes two of us," I said, grabbing my duffel bag from Betta and following her inside.

"No plans for you either?" Ellery asked as I followed her inside. The house was all glass in the front, one of those super modern homes that my mom always slowed down the car to look at. "It's ugly, but it has so much character!" she'd always say.

"Jenna's out of town, and she's usually the person I go out with," I said, then immediately regretted it. Great going, making Ellery think that she was just a backup person. I wanted to be friends with Ellery. I needed more friends.

"I forgot that she was going to Los Angeles for the summer," she said finally. "I don't know how I forgot, given how much of a big deal she made about it all year."

I snorted slightly, then stopped myself. I wasn't supposed to say mean things about a friend, even if they were true. I swallowed. "She is excited about it. I guess it's a chance to get out of Connecticut for the summer."

"Yeah, but all of her friends are in Connecticut," Ellery

said as I followed her up the stairs to her room. She pushed open the door to her room, and I followed her in. It was one of those amazingly modern rooms, with a wall full of glass looking out over the backyard.

"Are you ever worried that someone is going to be able to see into your room?" I asked, glancing out at the backyard, which was covered in giant pine trees.

"I don't do anything exciting enough that someone would want to spy on me," she replied. "You'd have to be really bored to spy on me. Mostly I just do homework and sleep."

"But still." I walked over to the window and looked out. I could still see the tops of the trees around the house in the fading light. It was more beautiful than I expected.

"Literally, no one can see in unless they're hiding in my backyard. And I promise that I didn't invite you over so that people could spy on you. You brought party clothes, right?" she asked, leaning down towards her computer and turning on music. "Unless you weren't planning to go to the party. Which is totally fine, if you don't want to."

I nodded towards my duffel bag and started to unzip it, pulling out a halter top and shorts that I had pulled out of my closet. I held them up, looking at them for a second. Would it be weirder if I changed in front of Ellery or asked for the bathroom? Probably the latter. I pulled off my athletic shorts and stepped into my jean shorts.

"Cute," Ellery said, nodding towards the top that I was holding out. "I like the ruffles."

"Thanks." I said. It was a navy top with a giant ruffle on the front, high necked in the front. Jenna had had a different opinion, so I'd avoided wearing it out in the past. She'd told me that there was no way that I could pull off ruffles.

Oh well. If she saw pictures from tonight, she'd just get to feel superior about the fact that I was making questionable fashion choices while she was hanging out in Los Angeles with her far cooler friends. I liked the shirt.

"I heard a rumor at school," Ellery said, flopping down on her bed and turning to look at me.

"What?" I asked, finishing zipping up the halter top and leaning forward to check myself out in her full length mirror. I looked pretty good. I ran my fingers through my hair, trying to get the frizz out. Connecticut summers did not agree with me.

"I heard there's a rumor that Hunter Lowen likes you. He's chasing you with his big stick hoping to score," she said, pausing in applying foundation to look directly at me.

I stopped, turning towards her. My stomach pulled together at Hunter's name. "There's no way that that's true," I said.

"I heard it from Max. And you know that Max is one of his closest friends," she replied.

"No way," I replied. If I said it enough times, I'd stop feeling queasy. "There's no way, because there's no way that Hunter would actually like me." Hunter wouldn't even know my name.

"Why not? You're cute enough," she replied, putting down the foundation and reaching for her lip liner.

"That was such a backhanded compliment." I could feel

my stomach flipping at the thought of Hunter Lowen. Not that I had a crush on him, but if I was going to have a crush on someone, it would be him. Not that I was thinking about that.

"I didn't mean it like that, obviously," she replied, starting to put on her lip liner. "I meant to say that I feel like you're one of those people who doesn't go around thinking that they're so attractive that the world owes them something. You're just cool."

"I still think that feels like a very backhanded compliment," I replied. I had to keep talking so that I wouldn't show how much the idea of Hunter Lowen liking me was freaking me out.

He was cute. Obviously, he was really cute. But he didn't seem like someone who would actually like me. Maybe he would hook up with me if he was bored. But actually like me? No way.

She rolled her eyes at me, putting her makeup back into its bag. "Just take it as a regular, non-backhanded compliment. That's what I meant, anyway. So, are you going to go for it?"

"Go for it?" I pulled my mascara out of my bag and started to put it on. Not that I normally wore it, but it was giving me something to do during this conversation.

"Hunter. Kinsey, keep up!" She pointed her phone towards me. "I am asking you what you are going to do about the combination of these two facts. First, the hottest guy in school likes you, and second, he is going to be at this party tonight."

"Maybe?" I turned back towards her. The idea that

Hunter Lowen could like me was thrilling and terrifying at the same time.

"Why not at least see what could happen?" she asked, putting away her makeup and rolling onto her bed. "He is objectively the hottest guy in our class, and the universe throws in the whole sports star thing as a bonus."

"You're making him sound like a buy one get one free offer," I replied.

She snorted, propping herself up on a pillow. "Yeah. You're right. But you can't tell me that you're not going to at least try to talk to him."

"You are way overestimating my courage," I replied. Maybe she thought that I was brave and outgoing, but even the thought of a guy having a crush on me made me want to puke. Especially when that guy was Hunter Lowen, who I maybe thought was really attractive.

"Courage is knowing that you're scared to do something and doing it anyway," Ellery replied, rolling out of bed and standing up. "Your makeup looks great, by the way."

"Thanks," I said, sticking my mascara wand back into the tube and screwing it shut.

"Ready to head out?" she asked, punching me lightly in the shoulder. I nodded, pushing my things back into my bag. This party would be fun even if I just hung out with Ellery, I told myself as I followed her down the stairs. This was how you made friends, and I needed friends.

"Do you want to just ride with me?" she asked as we walked out the front door towards her car. "Parking is always such a pain at Max's."

"Do you mind if I crash with you tonight?" I asked, both because it meant I wouldn't have to worry about drinking, and because Ellery had air conditioning. Mostly the second one.

"Of course," she replied. "Are you planning to really get hammered tonight or something?"

I snorted. Clearly Ellery didn't know me. "Not me going wild, just me knowing that my mom will ground me for life if she finds out that I put Betta in danger."

"What?" Ellery turned and looked at me, raising an eyebrow. Right.

"Betta's my car," I said, nodding towards where Betta was sitting in the driveway. Betta looked tiny in between Ellery's family's car.

"That is cool," Ellery said, nodding towards my car. "We'll leave Betta in my driveway to protect her from harm, and we can take my much less fun car. But I do have great speakers. I finally found my aux cord the other day, and I will even let you pick the music."

"That's an honor," I replied, climbing into the passenger seat of her SUV. Based on the stickers on the windshield, it had also been her mom's car before it had gotten passed down.

"I'm assuming that you're going to make good choices for music that will get us pumped up for this part that we're about to go to. If you get on my speakers and play some kind of weird electronic stuff, then I'm going to regret this, and you're going to be banned from my stereo system ever again," Ellery said, turning on the car and pulling out of the driveway.

I resisted the temptation to play opera just to troll her, going for an old party playlist instead. Ellery started to nod her head along to the beat as we drove towards Max's. I leaned back in the seat. This was going to be fun. I was going to be fun and not awkward tonight.

I could hear the music from Max's house before we even parked. The lights were all on in the house, and you could see the people through every window. It was packed.

Ellery unbuckled her seatbelt, then leaned back and stared at the house. "If I start talking to Max, do you mind if you, like – "

Oh, this was going to be good. "If I what?" I asked. If she was going to talk so much about Hunter Lowen, I was going to get her back with this.

"You know." She blushed, not meeting my eyes.

"Is this why you were so excited to have a wingwoman going with you to this party?" I asked, the smile on my face getting wider.

"I was excited to have a wingwoman for this party because I wanted to get to know you better,," she shot back, but she was starting to blush even more.

"You like Max," I said, turning the way towards her.

"Okay, I sort of like Max. He's cute, and we flirted a little bit in study hall at the end of the year, and I wouldn't mind seeing where it goes. Happy now?" Ellery asked, her hand on the door handle on her side.

She wasn't getting off that easy. "I think so. I'll be happier if you guys actually start dating, but – "

"Don't even start with me," she said, staring straight at

me. "I'll be happy if you decide that you're going to talk to Hunter, but I'm guessing that that isn't going to happen."

If Ellery thought reverse psychology was going to work on me, she was wrong. I had too much practice with that from Lily. "There's no way that Hunter could like me," I said again. Maybe she was right, and maybe there really were rumors that Hunter liked me.

But that seemed too good to be true. He was the guy that everyone wanted, and he was kind of an asshole. He wasn't someone I could imagine a happily ever after with.

"We're going to stop this ridiculous conversation, because I can't tell you how many more times I can tell you that you are just wrong," Ellery said.

I unbuckled my seatbelt. "You are still being ridiculous, Ellery. We're focusing on Max and what you're going to do tonight."

"Shut up. Let's both get over ourselves and go hit on the guys who we are convinced don't like us. Deal?" Ellery said, pulling down her mirror and checking her makeup.

"Deal," I said. Hopefully that wasn't a binding deal.

She took a deep breath, pushed the mirror back up, and turned towards me. "Ready?"

I nodded. We got out of the car, starting the walk into the house. I wasn't going to get nervous now. I was here with a friend, so everything was going to be okay.

As soon as we pushed open the door, we were hit with a blast of hot air. I had hoped that it was going to be cooler here than my house, but that was not the case. Maybe it was because there were so many people packed into the tiny space, but I was pretty sure that it was getting close to a thousand degrees here.

"Hey!" Someone over towards the side waved to us. Ellery grabbed my hand and pulled me through the masses of people towards the person who'd called. Gianna, one of the girls on the soccer team, was waving. When we reached her, she wrapped Ellery in a hug.

"I didn't know that you were coming out," Ellery said as Gianna released her from the hug.

"Have you ever checked your phone?" Gianna asked. "Hey, Kinsey."

"Hey," I said back, nodding towards both of them. Gianna had been in my chemistry class with me last year, and she always seemed cool. We'd worked together on labs, but I'd never hung out with her outside of that.

Maybe that was my fault, if I thought about it. I hadn't really made the effort to ever text her. I could have done it. I had been the one to text Ellery tonight, and look where I was now.

"I haven't seen you out much," Gianna said, turning towards me as Ellery hugged someone else.

It was true. I wasn't much of a party person. I always felt like the awkward person left in the corner. I shrugged. "Things were quiet at home tonight, so I thought that I might as well come out and enjoy. You know. First few days of summer and all."

"I know," another one of the girls in the circle said. "My parents have me going to so many summer camps and SAT tutoring and everything. Sometimes I just want to do nothing in my room."

I got the general concept, but there was no way that I would want to be stuck alone in my non-air conditioned room. That sort of thing was the privilege of people with proper AC. "Yeah," I said, agreeing because going into a long rant about air conditioning wasn't really appropriate. I did have that many social skills, at least.

"I'm going to get a drink. You want to come with me?" Ellery asked me, nodding her head towards another part of the party.

"Yeah, a drink sounds great," I replied, waving bye to Gianna and the other soccer girls and starting to follow Ellery.

To my surprise, we walked past the kitchen and then down the steps towards the basement. "Where are we going?" I asked, following her down the steps. The music was much quieter down here, and it was almost peaceful.

"Max told me where all of the good stuff is hidden," she replied, skipping down the last two steps. Things between her and Max were much better than she let on. Boys didn't go around telling you where the good alcohol was unless they wanted to impress you.

"So you weren't just flirting in the study hall, I take it," I said into her ear as we reached the bottom of the steps and rounded the corner towards another room.

"I'm not answering that question," she replied, glancing back over her shoulder towards me. "You'll never let me live it down."

That was as much as I needed to know to give her grief later. I followed her into the room, where there were already a few people gathered. "Hey," Ellery said, nodding towards the group of guys standing around.

Oh god. The guys gathered around were all of the soccer and lacrosse guys, all of the most popular guys in the school. And all of the most attractive guys. I swallowed.

Logan, another of the soccer guys, looked over and raised his eyebrows at me. I swallowed again. I couldn't just talk to these guys. I wasn't confident enough to do that.

If Ellery could do this without acting nervous, I could too. I was being ridiculous. I just had to stop feeling awkward. Because telling myself to not feel awkward had always worked in the past.

"Hey, Kinsey, hey, Ellery," said Ethan, another one of the guys on the soccer and lacrosse team, nodding towards us. "You want something to drink?"

"That'd be awesome," Ellery replied, glancing at the cabinet behind them. "We just got here, and I could use a drink. It was a long run day for me."

One of the other guys snorted, reaching towards the liquor cabinet and passing over a bottle of wine. Ellery unscrewed the top, balancing it on the table beside her, and poured two cups. "Thanks," I said, taking one of the cups from her.

"So what are you guys up to down here?" she asked, pushing her ponytail back over her shoulder. "Everyone upstairs was just complaining about how many things they have to do for school this summer. Not quite a party."

One of the guys snorted. I lifted my drink and took a first sip. It burned my throat as it went down, but better than a lot of what I'd had at these parties. Ellery hadn't been lying about knowing where the good stuff was.

Before I could figure out how to join the conversation, I saw Max sidling up to the group. "Hey," he said, his voice always deeper than I expected. He was one of those boys who almost seemed to be notable because of how normal he looked. He was the goalie on the soccer team, normal height, normal build, normal brown hair. But something about him always seemed friendlier than the other guys around him. He was the only one of the soccer guys I found approachable. The rest of them always seemed too perfect.

"Hi!" Ellery said, her face immediately turning red.

"Hey," I said, glancing up at Max and then down at my drink.

"You went for the white wine. Nice," he said, nodding down at my cup.

"I did," I said, nodding back. Clearly I was great at making conversation.

It didn't help that I was standing next to Ellery. I looked back over at her, trying to tell her psychically that meant that she needed to handle the talking part of this interaction. I was only here for decoration.

"Way better than having the normal stuff," Ellery said, smiling at Max. "We owe you one."

Okay, this was my cue to leave. I had to be a good wing-woman and let the two of them talk. "I'm going to find the bathroom," I said, not entirely lying. I smiled at Ellery and walked away before she said anything else.

Thank god I was out of that conversation. That was so awkward.

I should probably go back upstairs. I couldn't be the annoying person who insisted on getting in her space while she was trying to make a move or something. If I hung around downstairs, I'd end up getting pulled into talking to her again.

I started to walk towards the steps, then spotted a bathroom to the side. This was going to be a better option than going all the way upstairs. It was probably going to be a whole lot less gross, because it didn't seem like that many people had found their way down here.

Hmm. Damn it. I looked down at the cup in my hand and then over at the bathroom. I didn't want to just leave my drink on the floor, because who knew what would happen to it. Making sure to watch your drink was one of the things that came up on a lot of shows that Lily watched.

But I didn't exactly want to take it into the bathroom with me. The idea of peeing next to my drink was gross.

I stared at it for a second, then shrugged. There was no one around to see me have to take my drink into the bathroom, and then I was just going to keep it as far away from me as I could. That seemed like a good compromise.

I shut the door, putting my drink inside the bathroom cabinet. I stood up from the toilet and washed my hands, checking my hair in the mirror before I got my drink back out of the cabinet.

I should have driven Betta. I should have known that Ellery was going to be the kind of person who got sucked into conversations. I was going to be awkward and on the outside by myself, waiting for her to tell me what to do.

Two hours. I could make it another two hours, and this

was how I was going to make friends. I sighed and picked up my drink, unlocking the door and heading back out.

I turned to the left as I exited the bathroom door. "Hey," a voice said in front of me.

I stepped back, splashing my drink over my front.

Then I looked up at who it was.

Oh, shit.

"Did you just have your drink in the bathroom with you?" Hunter Lowen asked me, a corner of his mouth twisting up into a smile.

I swallowed. "I didn't want to just leave it on the floor outside," I said, a wave of nausea hitting me. Oh god. Hunter Lowen was standing right there. "Haven't you seen most of the movies on Netflix? It's asking for something to get slipped in your drink. Or someone to pee in it or something."

"Someone to pee in it?" he asked, the corner of his mouth twisting up into a higher smile. "You think that someone would have done that?"

I was making myself sound stupid. I didn't want him to think that I was a blubbering mess.

Not that I cared what Hunter Lowen thought, obviously. There was no way he liked me, so it was all irrelevant. Obviously.

"Forget that I said that," I replied, taking a deep breath and trying to stop the word vomit.

"I don't know if I can forget that," he replied, taking a step closer to me. I had to lean my head all the way back to look up at him. It felt like he was a foot taller than I was, leaning over me without even trying.

Okay, there might have been some exaggeration in all of the stories of how hot Hunter Lowen was, but there wasn't that much exaggeration. He was *hot*.

I didn't know that I wanted anyone. Or I had thought that there wasn't anyone at school that I was attracted to, but it was like I hadn't stood this close to Hunter before. That if I had been this close before, I would have known that that was a lie, and that I was most definitely attracted to Hunter Lowen.

All of the time that he spent winning state championships had given him an amazing body. I could see his abs through his t-shirt. And if I looked back up at his face, I was pretty sure I'd throw up.

I swallowed and forced myself to look back up at his face. I couldn't just keep staring at his chest without being weird. "I – "

Okay, I was lost for words. I wanted to say something that would get the conversation back to something normal, something that put me on equal footing with him again. "I was heading back upstairs," I said finally. Good. Normal enough. "Ellery invited me down here to find better alcohol."

"Max always offers the best alcohol to the girls he wants to impress," Hunter replied. He took a tiny step towards me. "You're lucky that he isn't making you drink the warm beer from a keg upstairs."

"I don't know if I'd want to do that," I replied. My brain was short circuiting. That wasn't clever or funny. Ugh, brain.

He nodded towards the steps. "I'm also heading upstairs. Let's go check out what's happening."

I stared at him, my brain overloading. Part of me wanted to tell him no thanks, that I was going to go back to the room where Ellery was, where I could sink into the side of the room and not be noticed. I wasn't cool enough to walk upstairs with Hunter and not embarrass myself.

But then again, said a voice in the back of my head, you felt awkward and weird sitting there on the side. And no one is saying that you have to hook up with Hunter. All you have to do is go upstairs with him. Just see what happens.

"Okay," I said finally, the braver side of my brain winning out. "I'll come up."

He grinned at me, this time the grin actually hitting both sides of his face, and nodded towards the steps again. I gripped what was remaining of my drink, the part that wasn't drying on my top, and followed him up the stairs back towards the party.

The upstairs felt like it was twenty degrees hotter than downstairs. The music was so loud the photos on the wall were shaking, and even more people were squished into the living room. Max's parents were going to be pissed.

Hunter turned around and reached for my hand, holding it as we navigated through the crowd towards the kitchen. There were a few fewer people here now, enough space that I could turn around and take a breath.

"I haven't seen you out much this year," Hunter said, leaning down to speak the words into my ear.

"What do you mean?" My heart started to pound, and I swallowed again. It was probably because it was so hot in this room. It had to be that, and not the fact that Hunter was standing so close to me.

I was not getting flustered by the fact that Hunter was so close to me. I wouldn't be flustered by that sort of thing. Obviously.

And wait. Did Hunter mean that he had noticed that I wasn't at the parties? Did that mean that he thought I wasn't cool or something? Not that I was, but I had to defend myself. "And I do go to parties. Maybe I just didn't say hi to you at them."

"So are you saying that you've been avoiding me?" he asked, still leaning down to say the words into my ear. "And you would have avoided me again if you didn't owe me for splashing your drink all over me?"

"I didn't splash my drink all over you!" I protested.

"Want to bet?" Out of the corner of my eye, I could see his slow, steady smile creeping back onto his face. I didn't want to look at him directly. I wasn't sure if my heart rate could handle it.

"There is no way that I actually spilled my drink on you," I said again. "Most of my drink is all over my front right now, so there isn't enough liquid in my cup to have spilled on you."

He took a step back and met my eyes again. "Check it out for yourself."

Oh god. Hunter Lowen seemed to be flirting with me, and even worse, he was asking me to look at his chest.

"I don't see anything," I said, gulping down another deep breath and then looking at his shirt. It was a navy t-shirt, and I couldn't make out anything that could have been a splash from a drink. Not that I was looking too hard.

"Give me your hand," he replied, reaching around and his fingers resting lightly on my wrist. I swallowed again, hoping that he couldn't feel how quickly my heart was beating. He lifted my hand up towards his chest and rested it on his shirt. It was damp.

Oh. Great. I had not just gotten caught coming out of the bathroom with my drink in hand, but I had then covered Hunter Lowen with that same drink. Not my finest moment.

"Told you so," he replied, his smile getting wider and wider. I could feel his heartbeat, steady and slow, through his shirt.

This was a dream. I was going to wake up in a few minutes in my bed and wonder why I was having such a detailed dream about Hunter Lowen, of all people.

I pulled my hand back and pushed it into my pocket. "It's hot in here. Really hot," I said finally. The temperature felt like it was a safe topic, something that I could handle.

"Want to go outside?" he asked, nodding towards the deck overlooking the pool. It seemed much more empty outside, probably because everyone in the house was convinced that it would be even hotter outside.

"Yeah," I agreed. He turned towards the door, and I followed him. He was so much taller than everyone else that I could spot him through the crowd. He reached his hand back towards me for a second, and I brushed his fingers.

Nope. Wasn't going to do that, because then I really

was going to throw up. We reached the back door, and he pushed it open, holding it open for me.

I followed him outside. The night air had cooled down, and it felt like the humidity was finally breaking. I lifted my head up towards the sky and took a deep breath, closing my eyes for a second.

"You were really missing this when we were inside there," he said, raising an eyebrow towards me.

I nodded, looking up at him. "This is my favorite part of the summer, when it gets cold enough at night that you actually want to wear a sweatshirt and be outside. You can still enjoy it and not feel like you're about to die of heatstroke."

"I can see it," he said, standing beside me on the deck. He leaned back against the deck railing and took a sip of his beer, his eyes on my face.

"I live right near the center of town, so I always go try to catch fireflies in the park at night," I said. It was something that sounded stupid almost as soon as I said it, and I glanced away from Hunter, not wanting to see his reaction.

"That's cool," he said, his eyes still on my face. It was like I could feel them burning into the side of my face. Maybe all of this was in my head. It was one of those moments where my brain seemed to dissociate from the conversation I was having, where there was a part of my brain that was sitting outside of me, just repeating *You are talking to Hunter Lowen. You are standing here and having a whole conversation with Hunter like he's just a random person. Keep doing that. Good job, Kinsey. Don't be weird.*

I closed my eyes for a second and tried to give myself a

single moment of freaking out. Then I took a deep breath and turned back towards him, tilting my head up slightly to look at him.

Hunter took a step towards me, and I could feel the warmth from his body radiating towards me. He smiled down at me. "Normally I just think about the temperature and I think about how much it's going to suck to have to go to practice the next day."

"I think that too," I said, pushing a stray piece of hair back.

"You don't play a sport, do you?" he asked. The conversation felt so normal, but at the same time, it was like I was still so aware of him standing next to me, so close that I could smell his deodorant. It was that scent that all of the guys at school seemed to use, the vague scent of pine covering up the scent of sweat and the drink that I had spilled on him earlier.

Okay, I was not letting my brain wander to those places. Those were bad places to let your brain wander. I was going to focus on having a conversation with Hunter. I looked over my shoulder, focusing on the landscaping behind the pool. Focus, Kinsey. "I should, I know, but I'm too uncoordinated. I played tennis for a while, but I wasn't competitive enough. I run on the cross-country team, but it's mostly because they don't have cuts."

"Don't talk yourself down. Running is a real sport," he replied. He shifted his weight against the deck railing, inching closer to me.

"Our team doesn't really treat it like a real sport. Most of us are doing it because the guidance office threatened us with not getting into college if we didn't play a sport," I replied.

Hunter snorted. "The guidance office is good at that, threatening you with not getting into college."

"Oh, come on," I said, turning towards him. "You're Hunter Lowen. There must be recruiters busting down your door."

"Only one recruiter has actually shown up to my house so far, so I wouldn't say that they're exactly busting down the door," he replied.

It felt like he had taken another step towards me, his body closer to mine. The blood started rushing through my ears, and I swallowed again. I wanted to reach up and kiss him, but I knew that that was a terrible idea. I was not supposed to kiss Hunter Lowen.

I thought he didn't like me. Or if he did, he was just playing me.

Oh my god. I closed my eyes for a second. This was real, wasn't it?

His hand started to rest on my waist. I swallowed. "Kinsey?" he asked, his voice softer. I swallowed again, then looked up towards him. "Can I - "

And with perfect timing, someone burst through the sliding glass doors. "Kinsey, you came with Ellery, right?"

I whipped my head towards the side, away from where I was staring up at Hunter. Ethan was standing frozen in the doorway, staring at me and Hunter.

"What's up, bro?" Hunter asked, nodding towards him and then back at me.

It felt like Hunter was looking out for me, like we were

a unit here and not just two random people standing on the deck. My heart gave another leap in my chest. I wasn't going to be able to stand this much longer.

"Kinsey, I think Ellery might have had too much to drink," Ethan said, nodding towards me. Or towards Hunter, more likely, in one of those bro greeting rituals. "Can you make sure that she gets home?"

Right now, part of my brain was screaming that no, I wasn't going to go take care of her. I wasn't going to leave this chance to see what Hunter had been about to ask me. I wasn't leaving Hunter now.

But the other half of my brain was sighing in relief. Even if Ellery hadn't meant to do it, she was coming up with the perfect reason for me to leave this situation and get back to my normal life. A life where Hunter Lowen didn't just start talking to me at parties.

"She's downstairs still?" I asked.

Ethan nodded. "We started playing beer pong, and we ran out of cheap beer, so we were playing with wine."

"You did not play beer pong with Max's parents' wine," Hunter said, his hand still on my waist. "You are idiots."

"We may have done something like that," Ethan replied, looking down at the deck and then back up towards Hunter.

I glanced up at Hunter for a second. The decision was made for me. The moment, whatever it had been before, was gone. I couldn't tell if I was relieved or sad.

I started to walk towards Ethan. Hunter followed me. I could feel his hand brush my back as I walked back towards the sliding doors and into the house. Or maybe I was just dreaming.

"Max is going to kill you all tomorrow when he realizes that." Hunter's voice was lower than I expected, low enough to carry over all of the party noise around us and still be heard clearly.

"Max was the one who suggested it," Ethan protested.

"You should have probably stopped him. You know his parents."

"Dude, he was drunk, and he thought that it was a good idea I wasn't going to stop him. And anyway, we were out of beer," Ethan said, looking over his shoulder towards me and Hunter.

"I can't leave you idiots alone or this shit happens," Hunter replied. He sounded like he was still right behind me as we pushed through the party back towards the steps to the downstairs.

We walked down the steps, and I turned to see Ellery slumped in the corner, looking extremely drunk. There was what appeared to be a white wine stain on her front, and she was staring at me from her chair. "Kinsey!" She looked at me and then at Hunter behind me. "I told – "

Oh no. Oh no. I almost sprinted over to her. "Ellery, have you been drinking?"

"Obviously," she replied, then looked up at Ethan. "Did you tell her that we won every game, and you're a sore loser?"

Hunter snorted, turning towards Ethan. "Even Ellery knows you're a sore loser."

"I'm not used to having to play beer pong with wine, okay?" Ethan said, crossing his arms over his chest. "It's way tougher than beer. Really different bouncing point. That's science."

"Max's parents are really into wine," Hunter said to me, leaning down, his voice still feeling too close to my ear, all of him too close for comfort. "They fly to vineyards to buy wine. They are going to be pissed when they find out that Max was using it for beer pong."

"Wine pong, you mean?" I asked. That might have even counted as flirty.

"Right," he said, his hand brushing my side again.

Ellery gave me another look and started to open her mouth. Before she had a chance to say anything, I ran over to her. "Come on. Let's get you home."

"You can't drive if you've been drinking," she said, very obviously looking in between me and Hunter. "So maybe you should stay here."

"Lucky for you, most of her drink is on me," Hunter said, his voice quiet enough that only I could hear. I blushed again, and I thought I could feel Hunter's arm rest on my back for a second.

Nope. I was making this up. This was pure wish fulfillment action going on. I wasn't going to listen to the hormones that were telling me that hooking up with Hunter might be a good idea. Those were hormones, and hormones were just evolutionary responses to the fact that there was an attractive guy around me.

I reached under Ellery's arms and helped her up. She wobbled slightly. I leaned her against me, letting her rest her head on my shoulder. "Do you need help?" Hunter asked, his eyes traveling over my face.

I looked at him and shook my head. "Ellery, I haven't had anything to drink, so I can drive you home, okay?"

She nodded and reached into her pocket, passing me the car keys. I wrapped my arm around her waist and started towards the steps, her wobbling with every step. We were not wearing the right shoes for this.

"I've got this," Hunter said, walking towards me.

"Seriously, she's my friend, and I'm going to make sure that she gets home safely. I don't want you to think that just because I spilled something on you I can't drive," I said, wrapping my arm around Ellery.

"You are not going to get her up the stairs that way," he replied. "Just let me."

"Let you what?" I asked.

"Can I carry you, Ellery?" he asked. She giggled in response.

Hunter reached down and picked her up in one fluid movement, like she didn't weigh anything. She wrapped her arms around his neck, and he started up the steps, me running behind him to keep up.

We reached the top of the stairs, and Hunter set Ellery gently back down onto her feet. I wrapped my arm around her waist to help her stand. "Thanks," I said, not fully meeting Hunter's eyes.

"I told you, it would have been impossible for you to actually carry her up the stairs," he replied, another smirk starting in his voice. "You would have been stuck down there for years trying to get up the stairs, and I would have had to call an ambulance or something when you came tumbling down."

"I don't appreciate your lack of faith in me," I replied, more crossly than I meant. I swallowed. He was an asshole, but he had actually done something nice. I should probably appreciate that. For whatever it was worth. "But thank you for helping me with Ellery," I said finally, making direct eye contact with him. My stomach flipped again, the butterflies coming back in a giant rush.

"You're totally sure that you can drive?" Hunter asked, his eyes on my face.

"Yes!" He didn't need to worry about me. "As you reminded me, I spilled my drink all over you, so I didn't have any."

"Okay," he said. He reached forward and pushed back a piece of my hair that had fallen in my face, tucking it behind my ear. "I'll see you later, Kinsey."

"Later," I said, my voice barely audible.

Oh no. I was down bad.

I walked with Ellery to the front door, not glancing backwards towards the party. I couldn't look back and see Hunter. I wouldn't be able to do it without dying of embarrassment, or excitement, or nervousness. Or some horrific combination of the three.

We made our way out the front door. Ellery wavered on her feet and crashed into the wall. "Oops," she said as I wrapped my arm around her again.

"I've got you," I said, holding her as close as I could as we reached the car. "Can you give me the keys?"

Ellery nodded, fishing the keys out of her pocket. "And

what's your address?" I asked, opening my maps app and getting ready to type it in.

She grabbed my phone and started entering it, surprisingly well enough that auto correct seemed to figure out what she was trying to say. I helped her get buckled into her seat on the other side of the car. "Do you want me to spend the night?" I asked, not sure if it was more awkward to ask or not ask.

"Yeah. You're my friend now. Spend the night," Ellery said, leaning her head back against her seat. I nodded, then started the drive back.

THREE

I STOOD IN THE KITCHEN, eating an apple that I had fished out of the fridge. I glanced down at my phone, where there was a new text from Ellery Hamilton. *Thank you again so much for saving my ass yesterday.*

"Hunter?" she'd kept asking in the car, turning towards me. "You were hanging out with Hunter."

Fortunately, she'd drunk enough that I didn't have to elaborate. We'd snuck her into her house and then crashed on her bed, sleeping until this morning.

I'd come home before my mom this morning, getting in, showering, and getting dressed. My mom had wandered into the kitchen an hour later and done the same thing. I'd resisted making any comments about the fact that she was sneaking around like she and I were the same age.

Those were the comments that I might have made two years ago, when it was me and my mom against the world. Now it was my mom and Brian Senior against the world, and me on the sidelines wondering when the rest of my team would show up.

I'm always around if you need someone to bail you out of playing beer pong with wine, I wrote back. *Thanks for going out with me.*

Okay, that sounded so stupid. I sounded like the kind of person who didn't have a life and needed to actually thank her friends for deigning to hang out with her. Jenna would have told me that I sounded desperate.

You still haven't told me why you came downstairs with Hunter. Or why Hunter was the one who carried me up the stairs, she texted back.

I was going to ignore that text for now. I didn't have a good answer, and it still made my stomach churn thinking about it.

Hunter had been so much nicer than I had expected. I hadn't asked him to go downstairs and help me make sure that Ellery could get back out to her car, that I could get Ellery home despite her being the drunkest she'd ever been. I would have assumed that Hunter would have just tried to hook up with me and left Ellery in the lurch.

That's what the rumors would have said. That was what the popular guy at school would do in this situation. He didn't need to be there to help me take care of Ellery, because he was going to be too busy trying to sleep with someone. He wasn't the friend you called when you really needed help.

But that wasn't what he'd actually been like. He'd actually helped me and Ellery. He'd been downright sweet.

And he'd been about to ask me something at the end when Ethan had come out.

I took another bite of my apple and looked down at my phone again. *Ethan asked Hunter to help make sure that you got to your car safely. And apparently Hunter doesn't think that I'm strong enough to carry you up the stairs.*

Okay, I didn't need to be carried. I wasn't that drunk, she texted back.

I grinned down at my phone and heard my mom entering the kitchen. "Hi, Kinsey."

"Hey," I said, placing my phone down on the counter and looking up at her.

"Did you have a good time at your sleepover?" she asked, reaching into the fridge and pulling out one of the cups of iced coffee she'd save for herself. My mom was known for ordering too much iced coffee in one go, and then she'd stick them in the fridge so that she didn't waste them. We'd have three or four half drunk iced coffees in our fridge at all times, waiting for my mom to get back to drinking them.

"Mom. No one calls them sleepovers any more," I said, rolling my eyes at her.

"You were sleeping over with a friend," she replied. "It's not like I'm going to say that you were out at a party with your friend, because obviously you would not have gone to a party with your friend, right?"

"Right." I shook my head. A year ago, I might have thought that my mom was joking around, that actually she knew that I had gone to a party and that I'd gone out. A year ago, I would have sat down in the kitchen and told her everything, dissected every one of Hunter's moves, figured out what he could have possibly wanted to ask me.

I wouldn't have had to start the conversation before. My mom would have taken one look at me, sat down across from me in the old rickety kitchen stools we'd bought at a garage sale, and said, "Okay, Kinsey, you've got a story, and I want you to share it."

"How do you know Ellery again?" my mom asked, leaning on the counter and looking over at me.

"We run cross country together," I replied, reaching for a water glass.

"I haven't heard her name much before," my mom said, looking over at me and then glancing towards my phone. "It seemed like you were always out with Jenna."

That was true last year, maybe. I hadn't even really been out with Jenna in the past year, because she'd started to become too popular for me. She'd go to parties and be in the center, leaving me on the sides. "Yeah."

And it wasn't like my mom seemed to remember any of this any more anyway. I had definitely mentioned Ellery many times before. It wasn't like there were that many people in my life that it was difficult to keep up with.

"Well," my mom said, standing back up and taking a drink of her iced coffee, "I was wondering if you wanted to come venue shopping with me today."

"What?" I asked, putting my water back down on the counter.

"Venue shopping," she said again, as though the issue was with my hearing and not with my comprehension. "I was going to look at a few places that have spots for the end of the summer. There aren't that many, so I thought maybe we could check them out and then go get ice cream together."

Nope. I was not interested in this. It was going to be hard for me to overstate how uninterested I was in this. "I can't," I said, looking down at my phone. "I've got plans."

"That's too bad," my mom said. "I was hoping that this would be something that we could do together. You know, go out and enjoy it, for old times' sake."

If she wanted to do more stuff together, she could have also stopped dating Brian Senior, but that was going to be one of those things that I wasn't supposed to say out loud. "I told Lily that I would do something with her," I said. Fortunately, just at that moment, my phone vibrated, making it less obvious I was lying through my teeth.

"Oh, okay," my mom said, glancing down and away from me. "Well, maybe we could get dinner later? Just the two of us?"

"Maybe," I replied, picking up my phone and looking down at it. It was another text from Ellery, sending over a picture that she must have taken last night of the two of us. It was actually pretty cute.

"Okay," my mom said again. And I thought I could see her trying to catch my eye. I looked down at my phone, forcing myself to focus on that and not my mom. I didn't want to have to have this discussion. "Well, I'lkl be back later."

"Okay," I said, staring down at my phone and starting to type out a text back to Ellery. *We look a lot better in the picture than I remember us looking.*

I told you that you looked cute!!! she texted back. I smiled. The ruffles had actually worked out at the end.

It was too bad that I had ended up spilling stuff all over that top. Hopefully it would all come out in the wash.

"Let me know if you change your mind. You can always meet me at one of the later venues," my mom said, turning back to look at me as she walked out the front door.

I waved to her as she left and picked up a banana from the fruit bowl on the counter. The door closed behind her, and I sat back down on a kitchen stool.

Do you want to do something? I texted Lily, praying that the answer would be yes.

I have to go to Costco to pick up some stuff for my mom. Want to come with? she texted back.

That didn't sound fun, but it also didn't sound terrible. Sitting alone in my house sounded much worse, and if I didn't leave soon, my mom might know that I was lying. Plus, Costco had great snacks. *Yeah. See you soon.*

"OKAY, I know that I was sent here to get toilet paper, but we need one of these," Lily said, lifting up a six foot long crocodile pool floaty.

"You don't have a pool," I said, pointing out the obvious.

"Everyone needs a six foot long crocodile in their life. And anyway, my mom did tell me that I could buy anything else that I thought we might need," Lily replied, resting it on her head.

Lily's mom was a huge believer that anything you could buy, you should buy in bulk at Costco because it saved you so much money in the long run. "Girls, you should understand one thing about money," she'd tell us as we drove back into the Costco parking lot for the thousandth time. "You can't always control what comes in, but you can control what goes out. And when you know that you can save money, you should save that money."

That meant that when Lily and I had played soccer together as kids, we'd go to Costco afterwards every single time. Her mom would decide that they needed just one more roll of toilet paper, and we walked out with enough for a small army instead.

I was pretty sure that my mom and I had survived on Lily's family's leftovers for most of elementary and middle school. Lily's mom would suddenly realize that they didn't need quite as much of whatever they'd bought, and it would show up at our front door the next day.

"I don't think you're going to take that six foot long crocodile into the ocean with you. It'll get destroyed," I said, leaning on the cart.

"That," Lily said, turning towards me and dramatically pulling the crocodile off the top of the display heap, "is not the point. This is not the point at all. You should have things in your life that bring you joy."

"And you think that that crocodile is going to bring you joy?" I was pretty sure that Marie Kondo would not approve of Costco.

"How will I know if it brings me joy if we don't bring it home and see?" she asked, waving its little crocodile feet in the air.

I shook my head and started to push the cart forward. "I

am not entertaining this, Lily. Let's go find the toilet paper." I made it halfway down the aisle before Lily finally pulled herself away from the crocodile pool toy heap and started to follow me.

"Think this is good?" I asked, lifting up the smallest thing of toilet paper that I could find and putting it in the cart.

"Maybe we should get two of those. I do have siblings, you know," she said, pulling up her shopping list on her phone.

"We should not get two of these. You will literally be drowning in toilet paper. You will be stuck forever in your house behind mounds of toilet paper. It will be the end of your life. Suffocated by toilet paper."

"Oakay, drama queen," Lily said as I started to push the cart further down the aisle towards the next things on Lily's list. We had once made the critical mistake of coming here without a list, and we'd shown up home with enough olive oil for the entire country of Italy.

She glanced down at her phone as I steered the cart into the foods section. "Damn it. We forgot paper towels."

"Are you serious?" I looked down at the amount of toilet paper that we already had. "Are you sure that you can't just use some of this toilet paper?"

She sighed, shaking her head at me. "Paper towels are for spills, and toilet paper is for your butt. They are different things."

"And I'm just saying, that you have enough toilet paper for several thousand years, and so you might want to think about other uses for it," I replied, nodding towards the toilet paper in the cart.

"You don't have younger siblings. Diarrhea is a real thing in my house," she replied. "We need all the toilet paper that we can get."

"Please stop talking." I did not want to have to imagine any of this. "That's so gross."

"Again, you're just lucky that you don't have siblings," she said, pulling a massive thing of hand soap into the cart. "Younger siblings are the worst. Also, they spill lots of things on the ground, so can you please go get the paper towels and stop explaining toilet paper to me?"

"Fine. But you owe me one for having to haul the paper towels all the way back over here."

"Fine. I owe you one. I will consider getting you a piece of pizza if you don't complain any more. And I'll remind you that you volunteered to come and hang out with me, and I told you that this is what I was doing," she said, crossing her arms and narrowing her eyes at me.

Valid point there. This was still better than going venue shopping for the wedding that I didn't want to happen. I would rather be arguing with Lily about her siblings' bathroom habits any day. "Fine back at you. You owe me pizza."

I walked through Costco, trying to figure out which of the aisles was going to have the paper towels. The whole store felt overwhelming. You never quite knew where you were going or whether you were going to walk out with whatever you had decided to come for. In our case, that was usually because Lily impulse bought lots of random things.

I turned into the aisle that I thought had the paper

products and spotted the paper towels on one side. They were in a container that was almost as tall as I was, and I pulled a package down towards me.

Yeah, there was going to be no way that I was going to be able to carry this. It was bigger and bulkier than I was. I was going to have to go with the old strategy of just dragging it through the store and hoping that the plastic wrap didn't tear.

I grabbed the top section and started the walk back through the store. The paper towels bumped along on the floor behind me. I lifted it up slightly to try to keep the package from tearing.

I stared up the aisle signs. Lily was probably still in the regular food section. There was no way that she would have made it to frozen foods. She would have known that going to the frozen goods section without me was a friendship violation, because that was the section that always had the best samples.

I turned to go right and ran smack into another person.

"Do you make this a habit?"

Oh no. I knew that voice. I swallowed and looked up to see Hunter Lowen standing there, a smile spread right across his face. He was straight up grinning at me.

"No! I just – this is a really big thing of paper towels. And hi Hunter."

He snorted. "Hi, Kinsey." For some reason, hearing my name from his mouth made a shiver run through my entire body, like every single cell in my body was freaking out at the fact that he was there and standing there and looking at me.

God, I was going to have to learn to calm down, or I was just always going to be a sloppy mess when there was an attractive person around me.

He tucked your hair behind your ear last night. He was going to kiss you out on the porch, and you know it, said a very unhelpful voice in the back of my head.

"What are you doing at Costco?" I asked finally. Good job not being awkward, me.

"I could ask you the same thing," he replied, sticking his hands into his pockets and glancing up and down my body. I could feel myself blushing, one of those blushes that seemed to be my entire body, not just my face, where I was so thoroughly embarrassed that all of me was turning red.

This was ridiculous. I wasn't going to be embarassed. I was just getting paper towels at Costco, which was a totally normal thing for anyone to do.

Okay, maybe not people my age, maybe more like people like my mom. But still. It wasn't like he caught me smuggling drinks into the bathroom this time.

"I had to get stuff for my dad after practice," Hunter replied, taking half a step towards me again. "And you?"

Well, at least he was answering the question first. "I came with my friend Lily. I'm helping her get stuff for the house her family is renting at the beach. They're going for the summer, and they have to take a lot of paper towels with them."

"I see," Hunter replied, glancing behind me towards the thing of paper towels. "That's a lot of paper towels."

"That's how they sell them here," I replied, before I realized that I was dangerously close to diarrhea of the verbal type, which was something that no amount of toilet paper was going to be able to help with. I did not need to lecture Hunter on Costco.

"You think?" Hunter grinned at me again, the corner of his mouth tweaking up again.

was getting out of this conversation before I said something else stupid and embarrassed myself in front of him. I saw Lily's cart starting to come around the corner. I was not ready for the explosion when Lily saw me talking to Hunter Lowen.

I had to play it cool. I had to avoid making a fool of myself, at least any more than I'd already done. "I have to go. My friend's waiting for me," I said. "See you later, Hunter."

"Bye, Kinsey," Hunter said behind me. I refused to turn around to see if he was trying to follow me through the store, walking as fast as I could without losing the paper towels. They bumped along behind me.

I had messed that up. I had totally messed that up. I wasn't cool or funny or anything.

"Are you okay?" Lily asked as I arrived back at the cart. I bent down and lifted the paper towels from underneath to throw them in.

"Yeah, why?" I asked, moving in the paper towels in the cart to make sure that they fit nicely. It was easier than looking up at Lily.

"Because your face is bright red, and I don't think I've ever seen you run through Costco before. You literally passed the woman with ice cream samples and didn't even notice," she replied.

Oh. I glanced back over my shoulder to see the ice cream sample woman standing there, holding out little cups to everyone who passed. I never missed the chance to sample ice cream.

"I'm okay," I said finally, looking down at the cart. "It's just more of a workout than you would expect having to carry the paper towels."

"I'm worried about your physical fitness if you can't manage to carry paper towels through Costco," she replied, lifting the world's largest thing of frozen peas into the cart. "You know that they're not that heavy, right? They're just paper towels."

"And there are a lot of them. If you pile anything up enough, it becomes heavy. We learned about it in science," I replied, trying to force myself to calm down.

She snorted and started pushing the cart. We started to walk through the frozen food section. I distracted myself by seeing if I could spy the taquito sample station. Costco made what were in my opinion the absolute best frozen taquitos, and I could never quite find them anywhere else.

My mom had asked Lily's mom to make sure to pick them up for a while, and then she'd made the critical mistake of looking at the nutrition facts. That had ended the frozen food phase for me.

Someone turned the corner, and I stopped, my heart jumping. I glanced back. Not Hunter. I had to calm down.

We walked towards the front of the store to check out. Lily looked at me, narrowing her eyes. "Are you sure you're okay? Because you keep looking around like you're expecting the bogeyman to jump out of the dairy aisle."

I forced the most natural smile that I could. "Of course. Absolutely. No problem whatsoever here." Even if I knew that I was glancing around because there was still part of me that wanted to see Hunter again.

I wanted to see him again and talk to him some more. But I also didn't want that to happen at Costco, probably the least romantic place in the world. And I didn't want that to happen with Lily here.

We walked out to the car and loaded up the groceries. "I can drop you at your house," Lily offered, ignoring the fact that it was the total opposite direction from Costco. I was starting to think that Lily had just wanted someone to validate her feelings while she bought a six foot long pool crocodile.

"Thanks," I said, buckling my seat belt as Lily maneuvered the minivan out of the Costco parking lot. I was pretty sure her mom had given us this car because there was no way to hurt it.

"So this is where I tell you that I still don't believe you that there was nothing going on at Costco. The dairy aisle isn't that scary," she said, drumming her fingers on the steering wheel.

There was no point in trying to hide things from your best friend, was there? "Okay. I ran into Hunter."

"Hunter as in Hunter Lowen?" Her eyebrows shot up so quickly that I thought she might manage to sprain her forehead muscles, if that was even physically possible.

"Yeah. I saw him at a party last night, and then I ran into him when I was dragging paper towels through Costco. And it's kind of embarrassing to be caught with family sized paper towels, so you know. I freaked out a little bit," I said, hiding my head in my hands.

"No, no, no," she said, slamming her hands on the steering wheel. "Back up. The paper towels are not the important thing here. The important thing is Hunter Lowen."

"Thanks, Lil." My heart had already started to pick up speed, as though it knew that this was the conversation that I wanted to have and really didn't want to have at the same time. I wanted to talk about Hunter, to analyze every little thing that he said or did, but that also meant that I was going to have to admit that I might be developing some feelings for Hunter Lowen. If Hunter really liked me –

Nope. I wasn't going to think about that. There wasn't a chance that Hunter would like me.

And even if he did, there were so many reasons that this would never work. I didn't believe in the romance movie where someone fell in love with someone and then everything worked out. I was a realist. I knew that after the first happy ending, there were lots of problems, and for most of those couples, there wouldn't be a happy ending after all.

"You are doing your lost in thought thing. And I'm guessing the thoughts are about how hot Hunter is, which are true thoughts. But you need to tell me more." She slammed on the gas as we hit the highway, and I gave her a look. We weren't supposed to be drag racing in her mom's minivan.

Deep breath. "He talked to me, but I don't know. It just felt like too much."

"He is the hottest guy I have ever met," Lily replied, pulling the minivan into the left hand lane and passing a BMW.

"You've never met him," I said.

"Irrelevant. I've seen pictures." She glanced back over at me, taking her eyes off the road. Someone blared their horn next to us.

"Can you not kill us, please?" I said, gesturing at the road.

"I'm not!" she said, but she did at least turn back to the road. "So are you not into him? Or guys generally?"

"No, I'm into guys," I replied. I was definitely into Hunter. I couldn't speak when he was around. "It's just that – " The good thing about best friends was that they knew how to deal with a stream of consciousness talking. "Everything's changing this summer, Lil. My mom is getting married, and maybe a guy likes me, and you're leaving me and going to the beach, and I don't know what to do."

Just on time, my phone buzzed. A text from my mom. *Isn't this pretty?*

It looked like any other golf course to me. I gave it a thumbs up response and shoved my phone back in my pocket.

Was it bad that I was hoping that it was a text from Hunter? Even though I wouldn't even know how he had my number?

Yeah, that was bad. I was in deep.

"But maybe that's not bad. It can be your movie summer," Lily said, looking over at me for a second. Just for a second, because she was also in the middle of passing a Mustang. We were setting some minivan speed records.

"My movie summer?" I asked. That sounded like something that Lily would come up with, something that belonged to the hopeless romantics of the world.

She nodded, cutting across two lanes of traffic. "It's going to be the summer where you figure out what you want and who you are. Like in the movies. Obviously."

"I know who I am," I said, looking over at her. "And I don't need a guy to complete me or anything."

"You don't need a guy to complete you. But no one's saying that it wouldn't be fun." She flipped on the turn signal and passed another sports car. "This is going to be your movie summer, Kinsey. Just you wait and see."

FOUR

IT WAS THREE DAYS LATER, and Lily had already left for the beach with her family. I was only slightly annoyed and jealous. With Lily's family very obviously not in town, I didn't have an excuse to get out of wedding planning with my mom.

"Do you want to come help me pick flowers?" my mom asked, looking up from the kitchen counter towards me. Since I'd gotten out of venue shopping, she kept trying to pull me back in.

"You know that I have no taste when it comes to things like flowers," I replied. That was an understatement. I didn't get why people were so into flowers at weddings. They were expensive, and then you were just going to throw them away when the wedding was over. At the very least, couldn't you get plants that you could actually keep around afterwards?

"Come over here," she said, signaling towards her computer. I wandered over to see the webpage for one of the local florists. "I was thinking that these pink ones would be the best."

"Pink? Seriously?" I took a step back and stared at her. "You used to hate when I had anything pink."

"Hate is a strong word in this situation," my mom said, tapping her finger on the screen of the computer.

"You used to tell me that the color pink was basically a tool of the patriarchy. I shouldn't think that pink was any more of a feminine color than blue, and that I should feel free to make my own choices. You weren't going to force me to wear pink things just because you thought that I was a cute girl," I replied, walking over to the fridge and pulling out one of the iced coffees that was still mercifully full.

"That might have been a little bit of an overstatement," my mom said finally, tapping the screen again. "I might have been trying to make a point and ended up exaggerating a tiny bit."

"A tiny bit?" I pulled out the fullest looking iced coffee and shut the fridge. "That was one of your favorite rants to go on."

"I have a lot of favorite rants," she replied, turning towards me and grinning.

I started to smile and then stopped. My mom's favorite rant was one of those jokes that belonged in the Before Brian time. I couldn't imagine my mom out at dinner telling Brian exactly what she thought about the pink chiffon and tiara complex, as she'd dubbed it. They probably just sat there and talked about stock portfolios or whatever the hell that Brian did.

"But I'm thinking that pink could look really nice," she

said, picking up the topic again. "And it's a lot easier to get pink flowers than some of the other colors that I was looking at. I made the mistake of suggesting that we get red roses, and then Brian reminded me of the red wedding in Game of Thrones. We don't want that."

Great. Now Brian was going to try to bond with me and my mom by talking about a show that we had already watched. My mom had started it with me because she'd heard that it was a great fantasy show, and no one had warned her about all of the sex scenes. Eventually, she'd just shrugged and told me, "Better that I watch this stuff with you and make sure that I can correct all of the things that are wrong about it, than you watch it on your own and you really think that any of this is okay in a modern relationship."

Actually, if my mom and I survived the red wedding, maybe that wouldn't be the worst outcome. It would make sure that I never had to go through another one. "Yep," I said finally.

"Roses aren't a normal wedding flower," my mom said, looking up at my iced coffee. "Want to pass me one of those?"

I rolled my eyes and reached into the fridge, passing her the emptiest one. "Thanks," she said, taking it from me. "You know, there are so many of these wedding traditions that I had no idea about. It's kind of fun learning about them all."

"Why are you listening to any of those traditions anyway? If you want to have roses at your wedding, you can just have roses at your wedding, and it's fine," I said, taking a long slurp of my iced coffee and turning away from her.

"Just because lots of people do something doesn't mean that it's not fun. We shouldn't dismiss things as not having value just because they're popular," my mom said, finishing off her coffee.

This sounded like it was going to turn into another of my mom's favorite rants. She had both sides of this one, sometimes arguing that popular things were overrated and sometimes arguing that we shouldn't dismiss things just because lots of teenage girls liked them. I suspected that the second rant might have been mostly for my benefit.

"If you want to have roses, just have them," I said again, closing my eyes for a second. This was such a stupid argument to have to have. Nobody cared about the flowers. Just pick them and move on.

"Is everything okay, Kinsey?" she asked, shutting her laptop and staring at me.

"Of course. But I have to go," I said. If I stayed here much longer, I was going to say something that I regretted. I'd go to Starbucks and see if there was anyone there I knew.

"I was actually hoping that we could talk about some stuff – " my mom said, trying to make eye contact.

Nope. I wasn't ready for a deep conversation today. "Sorry. I really do have to go," I said, pulling my phone out of my pocket. "I'm going to hang out with Ellery today since Lily's at the beach with her family."

"Didn't you go over to Ellery's a few days ago?" my

mom asked. "You've been spending a lot of time with her recently."

"And?" I asked. "It's not like I have a lot of friends right now."

"Are you sure that you don't want to go get coffee or something?" she asked, her eyes on my face.

So that we could try to continue this conversation? No thanks. I was done discussing flowers for today. "I really want to go out and hang out with my friends now, okay?"

She stared at me for a second, then nodded. "Okay."

I waved and walked outside, walking up the street. That felt like a fight even if it wasn't, one of those conversations that could have been a fight.

Maybe I was just reading too much into things. That could have been a normal conversation with my mom, where she just wanted to understand who my new friends were. But everything felt more important than that.

I opened up my phone, holding it in front of my nose. Jenna had posted a picture recently, one of her standing at the beach with her feet in the water, her arms spread wide in front of her and her eyes closed, her face turned up towards the sun. *Summer sun feeling fine,* read the caption.

It was such a ridiculous picture. I stared at it for a few seconds before I shut my phone again. There was no way that Jenna lived that close to the beach. I hadn't actually been to Los Angeles before, but from what my mom said, it was all traffic, not all glamorous shots of people at the beach. It wasn't like Jenna was actually spending her time at the beach. She was probably sitting alone in her room pretending that she was having a great time.

I was going to start sounding cynical and terrible if I kept this up. I started to scroll through my phone again. Another text had come in from Ellery, and I clicked on it, glancing at the link that she'd sent me. Some cute video, probably of a wombat, which had been our thing lately.

Do you want to do something? Ice cream? I texted her. *I had to get out of my house. My mom is trying to make me pick wedding flowers, and I'm going to explode.*

Wedding flowers? she texted back immediately. *Please tell me they're not for your wedding.*

I snorted. *Nope, my mom's. Ice cream in town?*

I just finished my long run and I want the better ice cream place. Meet you there? she texted.

I texted back a thumbs up, then went home and got Betta from her parking spot. I parked in front of the ice cream place just outside town, the shack on the beach that everyone in town always went to. It was one of those places that was run by a local family and hadn't really changed in the past forty years, still offering the same selection of things, and still with the same signs in the front door reminding you that it was no shoes, no shirt, no service.

"Hey," Ellery said, waving to me as she walked up to the front door of the ice cream place. She was wearing short shorts and flip flops, her hair wet. She must have been on a run and showered. She was making me feel bad about my lack of training for cross country in the fall. "Did you know that I had a policy of never saying no to ice cream?"

I laughed. "I didn't, but there aren't many people who would say no to ice cream."

"Valid point," she replied, and we walked inside. I

stared up at the flavor selection on the wall, looking for something that was normal. This was a place that had changed over from the normal, sensible selection of ice cream flavors to ones that were too avant garde for anyone to enjoy.

The owner's daughter had become a star chef in the city, and then she'd decided to move back out and take over the store. The problem was that she was so used to serving fancy diners that she hadn't realized that people in town weren't looking for fancy flavors. They were just looking for something that tasted good, like vanilla or chocolate or maybe rocky road.

"I don't know why anyone would want avocado and kale ice cream," Ellery said from beside me. "Why would you put vegetables in ice cream?"

"Fruit works in ice cream," I replied. "Maybe the thought was that avocado is basically a fruit?"

She narrowed her eyes at the menu. "I don't know what to do about this. I think I'm going to just go with vanilla."

The vanilla ice cream had vanished from the menu until there had been a viral Facebook petition demanding its return. There were a lot of people in town with too much time on their hands. "I'll take ginger snap cookie, actually."

A few minutes later, we wandered outside, ice cream in hand. "So what were you saying about wedding flowers? I wasn't entirely following that long series of texts," Ellery said, taking a giant bite of her ice cream.

I stared over at her for a second. "Please tell me that

you're not one of those people who bites their ice cream when they have an ice cream cone."

"I am," she replied, looking me in the eyes and then taking another bite of her ice cream.

"That is such the wrong way to eat ice cream. That should be banned. Like, I don't know if we can get ice cream together at all this summer," I said, licking my ice cream cone like a normal human.

She shrugged. "Some people lick it, some people bite it."

"That sounded so sexual and just wrong," I said.

She snorted. "Okay. Valid point again. On the things sounding wrong and sexual, not on the ice cream point. I prefer to eat my ice cream this way, and I don't appreciate the ice cream shaming that's going on right now." She took another giant bite of her ice cream. "So anyway, wedding flowers?"

I sighed. "My mom is getting married at the end of the summer. And I keep getting pulled into wedding stuff."

"Are you happy about it?" Ellery asked. She passed me her ice cream cone to hold for a second and put her hair back up into its ponytail.

"The wedding stuff? Obviously not," I said, passing her back her ice cream cone. "I'm not into debating colors."

"I mean about the fact that your mom is getting married to someone," Ellery said. "Do you like him?"

That felt like a deeply personal question for someone I had just started hanging out with. Then again, I'd had to rescue her at Max's party, so maybe our friendship was just on an accelerated timeline. "Not really. She's marrying the human equivalent of soy milk."

"Soy milk?" Ellery asked.

"Yeah. He's white and bland, but not quite self-accepting enough to be normal milk. Pretentious enough to be a milk substitute, but not one of the interesting ones like coconut milk or oat milk or something. Just – original soy."

"That sounds awful," she said.

"I don't get it." I had probably complained about this to everyone at this point, but I couldn't stop myself when I got started on a good Brian Senior rant. "My mom is a really exciting person. She used to tell me that as soon as I leave for college and she doesn't have to worry about bringing infectious diseases home, she's going to go find the cure for Ebola or something. And then she decides to get married to Original Soy instead. I don't get it."

"I'm sorry, that sucks," Ellery said.

"Thanks." It was the first time that I felt like someone had said exactly what I wanted to hear. The situation sucked. I was going to lose my mom to the most boring man on earth, and there was nothing that I could do about it.

"So how are things going with Max?" I asked, leaning against the beach railing next to her.

She stared out towards the water for a second. "Nothing there. I mean, not that I was expecting anything after I epically messed it up last weekend."

"You didn't epically mess it up," I protested.

She shook her head again, this time taking the final bite of her ice cream cone. "I drank all of his parents' fancy wine, and then I threatened to throw up all over myself, and then Ethan had to go find you to rescue me. It wasn't like I made a great impression."

"Everyone goes to a party and messes up sometimes," I replied. Better to be Ellery than to be me normally, standing on the outskirts of the party and hoping that no one noticed me.

She turned back towards me. "That's what you think. I know exactly how bad I looked, and I don't want to think about it."

"You didn't look bad!" Okay, maybe a little out of it, but Ellery managed to look good no matter what. The pictures of us from that night were actually really cute.

She reached over and punched me gently on the shoulder. "I know you're lying, but that's what friends are for."

I wasn't going to admit it, but it felt really good to hear the word friends there. "That's what I'm here for," I agreed.

FIVE

"PART of this plan is going to me that I am actually going to go to a party."

I lifted my phone up closer to my face and squinted at it. "You're going to a party?"

"Yep," Lily said through the phone. It was a little hard for me to actually understand what she was saying, because she was doing her usual, which was to video call me and then point the phone at the ceiling. I could now tell exactly where she was from the ceiling pattern.

"Explain how you're going to a party." Lily didn't know anyone at the beach where she and her family spent the summers. I was pretty sure her parents secretly liked it like that. They thought it was good family bonding. Lily thought that it was suffocating pretty quickly.

I was on Lily's side in this dispute, but there was no way that I was ever going to say that to her mom.

"I have not figured that part out yet," she replied. I could see her shaking her head from the hair that was fluttering around the screen. "But I can tell you that I will have the clothing for this party when I find it."

"Got it. So you're focused on making sure that you have the clothing for a party that you may never go to," I said, flopping onto my bed and propping my phone up on my nightstand.

"You are not getting the point, Kinsey. You are supposed to dress for the job you want, not the job you have."

"I'm pretty sure that that's not a relevant saying in this situation," I said, propping myself up on a pillow.

"My job is to be cool. Because that is the thing that I have decided that I am going to do this summer. So I need to dress for being cool," Lily said, finally putting her phone down so that I could actually see her and not the ceiling.

"I don't think that's how it works. I think the whole thing about being cool is that it happens when you're trying not to do it," I replied.

"It's how it's going to have to work," she replied, her voice settling into what I recognized as her very stubborn tone of voice. "I want to be cool, remember?"

I rolled my eyes at the phone. "And I want to be the richest person in the world, but that's not happening. Manifesting doesn't work, Lily."

"I really don't appreciate the implication there, if you can think about that comment there for a little bit longer," Lily said, finally turning the camera so I could see her and not the ceiling.

"Right. Sorry," I replied.

Lily turned the camera around to show me the dresses

that were in her room. They all appeared to be very glittery. "I found this great boutique down the road," she said, nodding towards the dresses. "It's called Seabreeze, and they have clothes to die for. Like, I cannot believe how amazing some of these clothes are."

"They seem very – sparkly." Not that that wasn't Lily's aesthetic, but it was a lot of sparkles. She'd look like a disco ball.

"So I was thinking about that. I think that sparkles are sort of a nineties and prom thing, but if I wear them now, it's ironic sparkles. Who says that glittery dresses are only for New Year's and the holidays? I'm making a statement that they should be all the time," Lily said, picking up one of them and spinning around with it.

"That seems like a lot of statement for a single piece of clothing." I checked my nails, then looked back up at the phone.

She sighed dramatically. "Okay, fine. I thought they were cute, so I bought them. Can you stop raining on my parade?"

Of course I was being too logical for Lily. "I'm sorry that I said that the sparkly dresses weren't a statement. They're a great statement."

"Thanks. I'm glad that you appreciate them. And me," she replied. In the background, I could hear someone starting to yell. "Gotta go. Talk to you later."

"Bye," I said, clicking off the phone and hearing the silence of my room. Through the open windows, I could hear the noise from the highway at the bottom of the hill below us.

It was another surprisingly hot day for this early in the summer. My room had to be eighty degrees already. I stood up and stretched. Climate change was the worst.

My mom was at work, giving a presentation about the importance of early detection of disease to a room full of people somewhere.

Ellery was probably running. She actually cared about doing well at cross country in the fall. I should have gone for a run, but it was too hot.

Well, that left me hanging out by myself. I really didn't have all that many friends when it came down to it.

I wandered downstairs and opened the fridge, looking for something cool to drink. It was definitely a day where I deserved iced coffee. Shockingly, my mom hadn't left any half finished ones in the fridge for me.

It was time to take a walk, then. I let myself out of the house, locking the door behind me, and headed down the street.

My mom and I lived in a random enclave of town, right downtown and only a few blocks from Starbucks, but in a series of houses that were all small and normal looking. They weren't the big houses further back, with gated driveways and in Jenna's case, fake fountains in the front. Instead, they were cute and normal, houses that had little gardens in the front and lots of decorations in the winter.

I loved our little neighborhood. If you turned your head just right at the end of the street, you could see all the way down to Long Island Sound. My mom and I used to go on walks down there at night to catch the breeze off the water. Nature's air conditioning, my mom called it.

I turned right at the end of my street, starting the walk down towards Starbucks. There were already a ton of people out on the street in the center of town, probably looking so put together because they were running from one air conditioned store to the next.

I turned into Starbucks, pushing open the door and getting in line. I leaned my head back to enjoy the temperature for a second. I obviously wasn't going to get carried away with how much I liked the air conditioning. I was tough enough to survive the summer without it, unlike all those other people in their fancy houses.

I shifted my weight in between my legs, digging my phone out of my pocket. My mom had given me access to her Starbucks account last year. It was one of the things that we'd almost started as a bit of a tradition in between us, texting the other person to let them know that we were getting something to drink.

"A venti large iced coffee, decaf please," I said, scanning my phone at the register. I didn't totally believe the claim that caffeine stunted your growth, but I wasn't going to risk it.

I headed to the end of the line, leaning against the table in the middle of the room and staring at the parade of drinks that were coming out ahead of mine. I had arrived right after some office decided to do their coffee break.

"Hey." There was a voice next to me, and I turned to see who it was.

Damn it. Hunter.

My heart started fluttering. Oh god. "Are you following

me?" I blurted out, the words escaping before I had a chance to stop them. Great going, Kinsey.

"I wasn't planning on it, no," he replied, raising an eyebrow at me.

Okay, so I was just embarrassing myself in front of Hunter. Again. "I just – I feel like I keep running into you," I said, swallowing.

"Literally, yeah," he replied, his eyebrow still raised.

I should have realized that that was where he was going to make that comment. I should have known better than to say that. "Yeah, I – " I swallowed again, glancing down towards the floor.

He took a step towards me. I looked up towards his face, and my stomach pulled together. He was wearing a t-shirt that looked almost the same as the one he had been wearing that night at the party.

Okay, he was hot. I was attracted to him. Just putting that out there.

"You don't have a friend hiding around here, do you?" he asked, running a hand through his hair.

"A friend? I mean, no?" I replied, glancing up towards his eyes and then back towards the floor.

"I wanted to talk to you at Costco," he said, taking another half step towards me. "Why'd you bolt out the door?"

Oh my god. My heartbeat was too fast now. I was going to pass out at Starbucks. I was going to faint and have to be taken to the hospital, because I could not handle talking to Hunter. I was going to embarrass myself so badly that I was going to have to move to Alaska and never come back.

I swallowed. "Kinsey?" the barista called.

Before I could walk around to pick up my coffee, Hunter reached behind me and picked it up. "Decaf?" he asked, turning the cup in his hands.

"That's my coffee, if you could hand it to me, thanks," I said, blurting out the words.

He looked at me for a second, his eyes grazing my face, then passed me the coffee without a word. "Can you answer my question, though?" he said finally.

In the list of things that I wanted to do right now, answering that question was towards the bottom. I took a deep breath. "Sorry. I wasn't trying to be weird." Well, I had done that anyway. He should have expected it by now. Okay, better excuse coming. "I just didn't have that long to talk. I was helping my friend's family buy stuff."

Hunter ran his hand through his hair again. "Okay, so what if this time, I skip all the small talk and ask you to get pizza with me on Friday?"

It appeared that Hunter Lowen was asking me out. Not sort of asking me out, not asking me to duck into a bedroom at a party, but like, actually asking me out.

I was dreaming. I had to be dreaming. I pinched myself in the elbow. Nope. Not dreaming.

I stared up at him for a second, my eyes meeting his. It felt like he was standing so close to me that I couldn't focus, that all I could do was stare up at him. "I like pizza," I said finally.

Behind him, the barista called out his name, but he didn't move. His eyes stayed right on mine. "So you're saying yes to pizza with me?" he asked, taking half a step towards me again. He was close enough now that I could smell the soap he used.

"Yeah," I said. I wanted to say something funny and maybe a little bit cutting, something that would make Hunter think that I was too cool for him.

But that wasn't happening. I wasn't cool in the first place, and right now, I was trying not to throw up all over Starbucks from nervousness.

"Cool," he said, a small smile starting on his face. He picked up his drink, his eyes not leaving my face.

It was hard for me to pay attention to anything through the rush of blood in my ears. It was going to be impossible to think about anything else.

But Hunter seemed like he might be kind of nervous, too. He was gripping his drink tightly enough that there was a little bit of it spilling out the top, coming out and dripping down the sides.

"I'll text you later?" he said, still standing there next to me. "I actually have to go now. My mom is waiting for me, and I'm not saying that because I'm avoiding you."

"That sounds - that sounds really good," I said, staring up at him still and swallowing. I was supposed to say something interesting and funny here, not just freak out about the fact that Hunter was talking to me and I didn't have anything interesting to say.

"Cool," he said, his hand brushing my side as he left the Starbucks. "Bye, Kinsey."

I stared after him as he left the Starbucks. I could see him walking down the street through the windows, his stride the same jaunty and confident stride that I always watched him do.

Just before he turned to cross the street, he glanced back over his shoulder towards me. Our eyes caught for a second, and I just stared at him. My stomach contracted again, and I swallowed.

He gave me a nod, then vanished across the street. I stared out the window for longer. God, this was so weird.

I was pretty sure that Hunter Lowen had just asked me out.

Another wave of nausea came through me. Hunter Lowen had asked me out.

"Are you okay?" asked a woman in front of me, staring at my face. "You look like you're a bit queasy."

Yeah, I'm fine," I said, quickly, holding up my iced coffee. "Just – yeah. Momentarily lost in thought, you know."

She didn't look convinced, so I headed towards the door. I wasn't going to hang out in Starbucks and risk embarrassing myself further. I turned and opened the door, walking out into the monstrously hot day. The weather wasn't doing anything to descramble my brain.

I could go out with Hunter. I would do it and see what happened. And anyway, ignoring the fact that my heart was still racing in my chest, my hands still feeling like they were trembling, it wasn't like this meant all that much anyway.

This was Hunter we were talking about, after all. He was Hunter Lowen. He could go out with anyone he wanted.

It just didn't make sense that that person was me.

I stopped abruptly at an intersection, forcing myself to lessen the grip on my coffee before I forced the lid off and spilled coffee all over myself. I had to calm down.

Well, it was only pizza. I was going to have to get pizza and just see what happened.

I managed to make it back to my living room before I let out a scream.

SIX

THE WATER GLASSES in the restaurant clinked, and I forced myself to not look around for an escape from this conversation. I could manage to be polite for another twenty minutes.

With the impending wedding, my mom had decided that I needed to spend much more quality time with her and Brian Senior. She'd caught onto me and told me that hanging out with my friends was no longer an excuse that was going to work for me to get out of it. Instead, she'd move around her schedule to make sure that I had a time that worked for me to get to know Brian.

The whole relationship had been like this. My mom had always wanted to make sure that I had my own space, that I didn't feel like she was dropping Brian in as a new dad. When they'd started dating, she'd pulled me aside. "I'm seeing Brian, but I want you to know that I'm not expecting you to think of him as your dad. But I do want you to know that I am always here for you, and I'm always going to support you. No matter what happens, I'm your mom, and I will make sure that you feel like you're first in my life, okay?"

Which had been a nice thought, but it didn't exactly feel like it was coming true. Now my mom was over at Brian's house all the time, and I was alone in ours.

I realized that this was a situation that most of the people I knew would have killed for. My mom trusted me so much that she didn't care what I did. I could have thrown a giant party in the house, and she would have never noticed. Not that I could have fit a giant party in our house anyway, but the thought was there.

"Have you been up to anything interesting this summer?" Brian asked, pulling the bread basket in the middle of the table towards him.

"Should you be eating that? That seems like it has a lot of carbs," I replied, nodding towards the bread basket. Brian had recently done keto, and he was a big fan of telling everyone how he'd lost so much weight on it.

He chuckled, although I was pleased to note that it sounded quite a bit forced. "I've gone off keto because I'm training for a half marathon right now. You have to make sure that you have enough carbs for your fast twitch muscles, you know. But they have to be high quality carbs. No sugars."

Maybe I was misremembering biology, but I was pretty sure all carbohydrates were sugars. "I didn't know that," I said, deciding that this was not the time to re-argue my biology final. "That's really fascinating, Brian."

Brian nodded, looking over at my mom as though he

was hoping that she would bail him out of this conversation. There was an awkward pause for a second, and then he nodded. "It is actually really fascinating. I've learned all about this kind of stuff so that I can always be at peak performance."

Oh god. Apparently Brian Senior had a broken sarcasm meter, and I was going to be stuck talking about his running diet.

My mom cleared her throat gently, her way of telling me that she heard and understood the sarcasm, and wasn't particularly happy about it. "We missed you at venue shopping for the wedding, but we think that we've picked a location."

My stomach turned. I reached across the table, pulling the entire bread basket towards me. This better not be a lunch where they were planning to spring more bad news on me. I needed something dramatic to happen, something that would knock the wedding off its course and let everything go back to normal.

Maybe the wedding could go so spectacularly wrong that my mom and Brian Senior would break up, and then everything could go back to the way it was. I'd be my mom's best friend, instead of that title going to the loser who was sitting in front of us, and my mom and I could go back to laughing about boys and having ice cream in the kitchen.

My mom didn't eat ice cream any more, because Brian Senior thought that too much dairy wasn't good for his training for his half marathon. Because like every other middle aged man in town, he was convinced that he would suddenly be attractive again if he started running. And he couldn't just do it casually to try to get in better shape. Nope, he had to take that one thing and make it his entire personality.

Unfortunately, he'd stopped by the house one time in the spandex that he apparently thought was appropriate running gear, and I still hadn't been able to scrub that image out of my mind.

"You really should have come shopping with us," he said, nodding towards my mom. "It would have been fun girls' bonding, you know?"

"Not if you were there. We don't invite boys to girls' bonding," I replied, tearing off a piece of bread and stuffing it in my mouth.

"Well, since you had plans with Lily when we were going to go shopping, I invited Brian," my mom said, her voice measured. "You were my first choice to come with me, to be clear."

Oh great. Here went the guilt trip about how I wasn't a good daughter, that I should have gone with my mom to go look at wedding locations. I should be happier for my mom and over the moon to do all of the stupid wedding stuff.

"Cool," I said finally.

"Well, we picked a venue," my mom said, smiling at Brian and then turning back towards me. "After all of that work shopping and checking out places, we realized there weren't a whole lot of options willing to work on our timeline."

Oh thank god. They were going to push back the wedding. I was going to have a few more months, or if I could play this right, hopefully the rest of high school before Brian Senior entered my life. I sent up a note of thank you to the wedding industrial complex that demanded that people book venues years in advance. I never thought that I would want to thank the wedding industrial complex, but there was a first time for everything.

"So rather than having to wait another year to get married, we decided that we're going to do a simple ceremony on a weekday," my mom continued, wrapping her fingers around her water glass. "We thought that would be more meaningful for all of us, because we could celebrate as a family sooner."

I stared at her for a second. "Celebrate as a family?"

"Yep," she nodded, smiling at me in a way that I could only describe as seeming slightly drugged. My mom wasn't the kind of person who smiled like that. My mom should be making sarcastic comments about weddings and how it was better to save your money for something fun. "Our family. We're building a family together."

"Are you sure that you want that?" I said, the words rushing out. "Because you could always wait another year, and then you could get one of the venues that you liked. You don't have to skip out on your dreams just because the venues aren't available. That's so not you."

Not that I knew who my mom was any more, but I was pretty sure that she would listen to that argument. She smiled at me, then shook her head. "Brian and I are really excited about this, Kinsey. And it's more important that we have the chance to be together as a family than to have a special location for our celebration."

"But you shouldn't give up on your dreams," I said.

Especially if it meant that I could keep my dream of a Brian Senior free life for longer.

My mom shook her head. "My dream is that we're all together as a family, Kinsey. I know that sometimes we joke about things, but at the end of the day, that's the most important to me. That we're all happy and spending time together."

Right. Yeah. Because this was family. It wasn't like that I already had a family, which consisted of my mom and me. Not Brian Senior.

"Okay," I said finally, looking in between the two of them. I couldn't win this argument if that was where we were starting from.

"Brian and Elise are going to be at the wedding as well," Brian Senior said. "Isn't that great? We're all going to be there."

Brian – to be clear, Brian Junior, Brian Senior's just as bland son – and Elise were Brian Senior's kids from his first marriage. They spent their time with his ex-wife, who seemed to be a just as boring person who lived in a nearby town, worrying about whether her hair was properly dyed and whether she was being charged extra for guac.

"Brian and Elise aren't my family," I said, looking in between my mom and Brian. "I don't care if they're there."

My mom closed her eyes for a second and tilted her head back towards the ceiling. "Kinsey, Brian and Elise are becoming your family, too. I know that it's difficult, and that you haven't had the chance to spend much time with them yet, but I'm sure you'll love them."

"You'll have a lot in common with them," Brian Senior

said, further proving his uselessness. "They're going into the same year that you are."

Because apparently all that you needed to have in common with another person was being in the same year as they were. And then you magically became best friends. That was definitely working well for me with all of the people in our year.

This was one of those things that I would never understand about parents. They had this idea that all you needed was to have an age in common, and then, best friends. It was like adults seemed to forget that not all of us were the same.

It shouldn't have surprised me that Brian Senior would say something like that. "Yeah, we can talk about taking the SATs and stuff, I guess."

My mom shot me another look, but Brian Senior didn't seem to catch on that that was sarcasm. "I thought you'd have plenty to talk about. There are so many things that you kids have now. I read this great article about how –"

Oh god. Brian Senior's new favorite bonding technique was to read articles about teenagers in the Wall Street Journal and the New York Times. He'd read them back to me as though they were telling me things that I didn't already know. As a bonus, he'd always manage to find the articles that were the most patronizing and unnecessary.

Before, my mom and I would have laughed about it, about how out of touch and ridiculous he was. But now, she was on his side, and she would tell me that I should appreciate that he was making an effort to try to bond with me.

The waiter came over, putting our planets in front of

us. Brian Senior appeared to have ordered a salad with only grilled chicken on top of it, probably to make sure that he didn't eat anything that would interfere with his training for his half marathon.

"You know that I want you to be my maid of honor, right?" my mom said, leaning forward towards me, her fork threatening to topple over from its mound of spaghetti. "It's really important to all of us that you feel like this is your celebration, too."

Nope. No thanks. "I don't think you're supposed to make your kid your maid of honor."

My mom and Brian Senior exchanged looks, and he leaned over and rested his hand on top of hers. Gag me. "You were just telling us how you don't want us to be constrained by tradition too much," my mom said, raising an eyebrow towards me. "And it would mean a lot to me if you would agree to do this."

Ugh. She was pulling the card that I couldn't do anything about. It wasn't like I could just look at my mom and refuse to do something that she cared about. She knew that, and I struggled so much with that.

"Great," I said finally, hoping that my voice didn't sound completely as unenthusiastic as it felt.

My mom smiled at me, one of those smiles that was half relief and half warning me that she could tell that I was getting close to stepping out of line. "I want to make sure that you feel included, and that you know that we're adding Brian to our family, not taking anything away."

I swallowed and looked at her. There was suddenly a lump in my throat. "Great, Mom."

The server came over and put down our plates. I started digging into my pasta immediately. Brian decided to enlighten us by telling us lots of facts that he had read about the nutrition of all of our various dishes. "There's research that shows that you should actually make sure to have a healthy fat alongside your salad," he said, dumping olive oil over the top of his pile of lettuce. "If you don't have healthy fat alongside your vegetables, it's much harder for your body to absorb all the nutrients from your salad."

"That's really fascinating," I said, blinking twice at him.

He didn't get the sarcasm. "Yep. There's so much that you have to learn about nutrition when you become a runner. There are so many things that you wouldn't guess actually make a huge difference to your overall health."

"Kinsey, isn't this helpful for your cross-country season to know all of this information?" my mom prompted, smiling at me.

That was rich coming from the woman who I normally caught eating ice cream out of the container. "I'm sure at some point in my life I'll care about the benefits of healthy fat."

"Peak nutrition will definitely help you to run faster," Brian Senior said cheerfully, nodding towards me and pointing at me with his fork, a piece of lettuce dripping olive oil on the end. "It's never a bad idea to make sure that you're in the best position for your training."

"Brian's son also plays sports, as does Elise," my mom said, reminding me of another piece of trivia about two people I did not care about. "That's another thing that you have in common."

My phone vibrated next to my plate. Thank god, something to distract me from this conversation.

My stomach twisted as I saw the message on the front screen. Hunter Lowen: *So before tonight, the important question – are you one of those people who eats pineapple on pizza?*

I caught myself starting to smile and forced myself to stop. I was not going to smile at lunch with Brian Senior. I needed to make sure that my mom knew exactly how I felt about this whole nonsense. *Absolutely not. Pineapple is fruit. Fruit doesn't belong on pizza.*

So what do you think of tomato and basil pizza?

Was he already picking out the pizza for tonight? That was a little bit extra, but also super flattering. I forced myself not to smile too much at my phone and give away that there was something exciting going on. I Didn't want to have to answer questions from my mom about why I seemed happy all of a sudden. *A classic. An excellent pizza choice.*

Really?

Yes, really! I typed back. *Isn't that like the original pizza from Italy?*

Because I have heard that tomatoes are fruits, and I thought you had a no fruit rule on your pizza.

Okay, I was going to take back everything that I had thought about Hunter Lowen. He was clearly a jerk, and also, not very smart. *Nope. Tomatoes are not fruits.*

My phone buzzed again, this time with a link to Wikipedia. I shook my head at my phone, reaching for my water glass.

"Do you want to share, Kinsey?" my mom asked. I looked up to see her staring at me, her head slightly bent.

I glanced back down at my phone. *I have a date with Hunter Lowen later,* I wanted to say, *and it is the single most exciting thing that has happened to me in a very long time. And he's literally texting me about tomatoes right now.*

"Nope," I said, clicking off the front screen of my phone and staring back at her. "Nothing."

SEVEN

I WAS STARING at my closet when my phone buzzed. It was Ellery. *Want to get ice cream?*

Normally the answer would have been hell yes. Today it was a little bit more complicated. *Normally yeah, but I sort of have a date tonight?*

I didn't even think that I'd hit the send button before I had an incoming video call. I answered, propping up my phone on my dresser. "You have a date? With whom?" Ellery demanded.

I was nervous enough that I didn't even make fun of her for the *with whom.* "Hunter?" I said, my voice ending up in a question.

"I knew it!" Ellery threw up her hands. "I told you he liked you!"

I couldn't even think about that. I'd throw up. "Focus, Ellery. What the hell am I supposed to wear?"

She sat down on the edge of her bed and leaned towards her phone. "I cannot believe you weren't immediately going to tell me. I told you so! Kinsey. I cannot believe it."

This was not helping. I clapped my hands together. "Ellery. Focus. What am I supposed to wear?"

She bit her lips together, narrowing her eyes. "What are you doing on this date?" she asked.

"Getting pizza." Where? Would we be sitting inside or outside? I had no idea. And not that I was normally someone who got worried about what I was going to wear, but this was Hunter Lowen asking me on a date. I was allowed to spiral.

"I wish I was there. Do I have time to come over?" she asked, leaning forward towards her phone.

I should have thought of that earlier, but it was too late now. "I'm meeting him in fifteen minutes."

"And you still haven't picked an outfit? What are you even doing?" she demanded. "Okay. You look good in dark colors. What do you have that's not black but dark?"

Now we were getting somewhere. I reached into my closet, pulling out a navy sundress and a romper. "These two."

She nodded, leaning even closer to her camera. "Put the dress on. That looks cute."

I stepped off to the side and pulled it on over my head. I stepped back into the frame, and Ellery stared at me, tilting her head towards the side. "Yeah. That's cute. You can definitely wear that."

"Are you sure?" I asked, looking down. It was cute but maybe not the sexiest thing I could wear.

"It's very you," Ellery said. Which was funny, because I

almost never wore ruffles. I liked them, but Jenna had told me that they made me look frumpy.

My phone beeped with a text. *I can pick you up, not sure if you have your license yet.*

"Try the romper, though. I bet that would also be cute," she said. She looked up at me and clapped her hands. "What are you doing? We have limited time here. Get the romper on."

"Hunter's texting," I said, staring down at the text. Before I had the chance to figure out what I should say, another text came through. *Don't want you running into me while you're driving or anything.*

"Okay, valid. What's he saying?" she asked, putting her elbows on her knees and leaning all the way into the camera.

"He wants to know if he can pick me up?" I was guessing the answer was supposed to be yes.

"Say yes. He has an awesome car," she replied. "And okay. I need to let you go get ready. Wear the romper. It's cute. You have to text me tonight and tell me everything. And you owe me ice cream because I told you so."

If this date went well, I'd get her all the ice cream she wanted. "Okay." I took a deep breath. "You're awesome. Thanks."

She clapped again. "Kinsey. I am so excited for you. You're going to have an amazing time, and you're going to tell me everything tomorrow. Right?"

Hopefully there would be something to tell. "Right," I said, waving and hanging up the call.

Oh god. I was going to do this. I took a deep breath and

stared at myself in the mirror. I looked pretty good. Maybe I could have done more with my hair, but it wasn't like I had time now. And it wasn't frizzy.

Lip gloss? No, I couldn't pull it off. And I didn't normally wear that much makeup, so it would be weird if I showed up with it now.

But it was Hunter, said the other side of my brain. You should absolutely look your best. It didn't matter if it wasn't you normally.

Yeah, but there was no way that I was going to pull it off, so no. Deep breath. I picked up my phone. I could waste a little bit of time until he showed up. I needed puppy videos to calm me down.

Outside, a car horn beeped. I jumped up. How was he here already? I grabbed my phone and headed downstairs, pushing open the front door.

"Hey," Hunter said, standing there with his hand on the doorbell.

"Hey," I said quickly, glancing from him back to the black sports car that was idling in front of my house. "Um –"

"I swear I wasn't the one who honked my horn. I wouldn't just sit in my car and honk at you to come outside. I'm not that much of an asshole," he said, sticking his hands into the pockets of his shorts.

I smiled and glanced down towards the ground. He looked awesome, and I felt underdressed now. "Just a coincidence?"

He smiled at me, meeting my eyes when I looked back up. "Yeah. You look great."

I was pretty sure that I had turned so red that it would be possible to see me from outer space. "Thanks."

I followed him down the front porch steps to the car, and he opened the car door before I had a chance to reach for it myself. I glanced up at him, my brain not able to form words, and sat down in the car. He closed the car door behind me, then walked around towards his side.

Oh god. It was cold. What was it with people and keeping their cars so cold? This car was so cold that I was going to have trouble doing anything but shivering. "All good?" Hunter asked, slipping into the front seat and glancing over towards me.

"Yep," I said, glancing down at my legs and seeing goosebumps forming.

"Let me know if the car's not cold enough," he said, taking the car out of park and driving down the street. "I left it running so that the car wouldn't get warm while you were waiting."

Right. That was a very nice thought of him, but also, this was awful. "I have a small question," I said, glancing over at him. "Is this the normal temperature that you keep your car?"

He looked at me, raising an eyebrow. "Are you complaining about the temperature in my car?"

I swallowed. Eye contact with Hunter was something that I was still not used to, and I wasn't sure that I was ever going to be used to it. It was just too much for my hormones.

It would have been so much easier if I was going out with someone who wasn't so hot. It would have been great if he could have been totally average looking, not the kind of person who looked like he should be on a billboard. "Yeah. It's freezing."

One side of his mouth turned up in a smirk. "I pick you up from your house, and the first thing that you do is complain about the temperature of my car."

"It feels like you're trying to freeze me to death," I replied. The contrast between this car and my house was a lot.

"Or you're so hot that I have to keep the air on to make sure that the car doesn't overheat," he replied, grinning at me.

My face flushed bright red, and I closed my eyes for a second. I was pretty sure that Hunter Lowen had just called me hot. Before I had a chance to say anything in response, not that I could have thought up a clever response anyway, he reached over and flipped on the set heater for me. "Compromise?"

"Thanks," I said, turning and staring at him for a moment too long, his silhouette in the driver's seat.

"I don't want you to be so cold that you decide that we can't get pizza," he replied as he turned down the street and headed towards the highway.

I glanced over at him and then back at the road. I had assumed that we were just going to the place a few blocks away from me, and the only reason that I had accepted the ride was so that I didn't get there late and disheveled. I didn't think that this was a situation where I was going to be driven somewhere.

To my surprise, we pulled up to an Italian restaurant in

the town nearby, hopping off the highway and pulling into their parking lot. "You decided to go for fancy pizza," I said, nodding towards the restaurant ahead of us.

He parked the car and then grinned at me. "I wanted something nicer than the pizza in town. And you said you liked pizza."

"I do," I said, my face turning red again as I unbuckled my seat belt. My hands were trembling slightly. He hopped out of his seat and walked around the car, opening the door for me. He held his hand down towards me. I grabbed it, and he pulled me up, helping me out of the car.

We walked to the restaurant. He opened the door for me, holding it as I walked in. "After you," he said, motioning me inside.

I walked in, the hostess taking us to a table in the back. It was set aside in between a couple of giant fake plants, and I could hear what was supposed to be waterfalls in the background. This was a lot fancier than I had been expecting. I should have probably thought more about what I was going to wear. I was dressed for normal pizza, not adult pizza.

"So I'm guessing that you're getting the pesto pizza without any sauce on it?" Hunter asked, glancing at me over the top of his menu.

"Look, I don't agree that a tomato is a fruit. A tomato is a vegetable." I shook my head. "Like, olive and mushrooms and even broccoli are acceptable on pizzas. Because they are vegetables. And if you make the dividing line between fruit and vegetables whether it's good on pizza, then you realize that a tomato is definitely a vegetable."

"So then, by my standards, pineapples are vegetables, because they are good on pizza, and actually, you know what, so is pepperoni. My favorite vegetable." He grinned at me again, the corners of his eyes crinkling slightly.

I might have taken things too literally sometimes, but Hunter was doing it on purpose now. I shook my head. "Obviously pepperoni is not a vegetable. You can't make up things like that."

"I'm just following your rules," he replied, grinning at me again. My stomach pinched together. The waiter came over and brought us glasses of water and a giant bread basket in the middle of the table.

Hunter apparently hadn't heard all of Brian Senior's warnings about carbs, because he pulled the bread basket towards himself and immediately took the largest piece. "So what are you up to this summer?" he asked finally after he'd swallowed the half a loaf of bread that he had stuck into his mouth.

There was probably an answer here that made me sound cool and funny and sexy and everything else. But I wasn't sure what that was, and I didn't honestly have any plans. "My mom is getting married," I said finally.

"You don't sound excited about that," Hunter replied, in what had to be the understatement of the year.

I took a deep breath. I couldn't believe that I was telling this to Hunter Lowen of all people, but it wasn't like I could stop a rant about Brian Senior once it started. "She's marrying the most boring man in the world."

"That's a high standard," he replied, taking another piece of bread. "Worse than my dad?"

"I don't know your dad, but there's no way that Brian Senior is more interesting. He doesn't eat carbs or dairy, and everybody knows. It's like he thinks he's a champion athlete, and people want this information from him."

"He's one of those guys who has to tell you everything about his diet and his training program?" Hunter asked, taking a long drink of his water to wash down the second giant piece of bread he'd eaten.

I shook my head. "Worse. He's one of those guys who has to tell you everything, and then he has to ask you whether you've done the same thing in your regime."

"Ouch," Hunter said, leaning back in his chair. "He sounds like my coach but worse."

"He gave me a lecture about how I should make sure that I eat right for cross country this year. I wanted to tell him that I'm about ten times faster than he is, but you know. My mom would have been pissed." Also, I hadn't really trained this summer, so I needed to be sure that I could beat him first. Maybe I could rope Ellery into it.

"I mean, if he's going to be annoying about his training, he deserved it," Hunter replied, resting one of his arms on the table. "It's like the first rule of fight club is that you don't talk about fight club. The first rule of training is that you don't talk about training."

I snorted. "I don't know if he has anything else to talk about. He's one of those people who might just be doing it because it's all that he has."

"Oh, that's the worst," Hunter agreed, leaning forward towards me. "Have you challenged him to a race yet?"

"Wait, me challenging him to a race?" I asked, leaning

forward to match Hunter. My hands crept towards his in the middle of the table. I had to resist the urge to reach forward and entwine mine with his. "What if he thinks that I'm doing it because I want to bond with him or something?"

"Or you completely kick his ass, and then for the rest of his life, you get to remind him that you're not interested in what he has to say because you already won," Hunter replied, smirking at me. "Better idea."

"I have to be able to beat him for that to work." Brian Senior was very into his running. The few times that he'd stopped by my house, it was usually because he was in the middle of a training session. He'd show up in his dumb Spandex bike shorts, telling us all about his pacing so far.

"Pretty sure I could beat him," Hunter replied. The waiter came over and refilled out water glasses.

"You're offering to challenge him for me?" That was — wow. Not what I had been expecting.

"I mean, I'll eat a pint of ice cream and a Chipotle burrito. Then I'll go beat him and then you'll never have to hear about any of this ever again," he replied, grinning at me again. There was a fleck of rosemary from the bread caught in his teeth, and it made him so much cuter, like he needed that one little imperfection to make sure that he was normal at the end of it all.

I stared at him for a second, my breath catching in my throat. Before I had a chance to think too much about what I was feeling and what I was thinking, the waiter arrived again. "What would you like?"

Hunter glanced at me. "A pepperoni and a cheese

pizza?"

I glanced down at the menu again, and then stared at the choices. "I'll get the vegetable pizza."

"Oh no," Hunter said, a smile starting at one side of his mouth. "You are not going to do this to me."

"I heard that you like vegetables on your pizza," I replied, resisting the urge to stick my tongue out. If Hunter was going to be literal, I was going to be literal right back at him. "Can we get double vegetables on that one too?"

"Of course," the waiter said. "And an order of garlic knots?"

"Oh yeah," Hunter replied, grinning up at the waiter. "Thanks so much."

"So, what are you doing this summer?" I asked. I didn't want to keep talking about Brian Senior, because it didn't seem like there was much to gain talking about Brian Senior and his diet.

"Practicing for soccer in the fall," he replied, taking another piece of bread. I grabbed one before he had a chance to finish the entire basket.

I dunked my piece of bread into the olive oil container. "I heard that you're the captain next year." There had been a big piece of gossip around the school – the fact that Hunter, despite only being a rising junior, was already being considered for captain. Normally that was always given to seniors to polish up their college applications, but Hunter was so much better than all of the other players, the rumor went, that he had gotten the position without a question.

He snorted. "Not really." He rolled his shoulders and

glanced away from the table, then back at me. "The rumors at school weren't great. Coach was super pissed for a while, because he was worried that I was trying to make it happen by just spreading a rumor until everyone else quit."

"Oh," I replied. I had been one of the people who had heard it and repeated it, because of course it was going to be a fact that Hunter Lowen was the captain for next year. It wasn't like there could be another captain for the soccer team. It just wouldn't be possible.

He drummed his fingers on the table. "The deal ended up being that I have to prove that I deserve to get the captain position at the end of the summer, or it's going to be given to someone else. Or we'll just have a team without a captain."

"A team without a captain?" There was no way that the school would do that. They weren't going to deny someone the ability to put being the captain on their college transcript.

He nodded. "Coach is going to make all of the seniors co-captains if I don't earn the spot. So that all of them can claim it for college. "

"But shouldn't it be obvious that it should be you?" Not that I knew a creepy amount about Hunter or anything, but he held the state record for goals scored in a single season. And we lived in a state with a lot of people who got really into sports.

"Coach doesn't see it like that. Nobody wants to play with the asshole who spends the entire time reminding them that they scored more points or whatever. People want to know that they have someone who cares and trusts them and everything," he said, reaching for another piece of bread. "The problem is that the seniors all hate me."

"I bet," I said, the words sounding totally inadequate. My cross-country capitan for next year was a senior, Luisa, who kept putting up the fastest times in the state, and on top of that, was just a nice person. There was no way that I could ever compete with her, and I wouldn't want to. It was her turn to be captain.

"I don't know. I mean, it's easy enough for me to be the best player on the team. I can just work harder than everyone else, and then I'm the best. But getting everyone else to follow me is tough sometimes. Our year is really good, and I love the guys. But some of the seniors are assholes," he said, tearing the crust off another piece of pizza.

It wasn't what I would have expected Hunter to say. Hunter was supposed to be the kind of guy where you couldn't complain about him. Of course he was going to get the captain position, because he was Hunter.

"Do you like it?" I asked. "Soccer, I mean. All of the stuff that you have to do for college and everything."

He smiled, a slower smile than before, one that started in one corner of his face and then crept up to his eyes, lighting up his whole face as it went. "I love it. Like, when I go out on the field, I get to leave everything on the field. It's not like I have to worry about the normal stupid shit that happens at school. It's me and my team, and we have a game that we're going to win. There's none of the stupid politics, none of this worrying about stuff, it's just the game. And it's great."

"It's not too competitive?" I asked, taking a sip of my water. "I mean, you literally play for the state championship every year."

"That's the best part," he said, leaning forward towards me. "You get to do what you love and take it to the next level."

"I don't know. I get so nervous before races," I said. I hated race day. I hated the thought that I was going to screw up and all my training would be wasted.

"Me too," he replied, tilting his head slightly to the side. "Of course you get nervous. It's that rush of adrenaline right before you start, getting you ready to get out there and do it."

"That's not quite it for me. For me, it's more like – when I think about trying to beat my time, half the time I just want to throw up. I don't want to be out there beating people. I tried sports other than cross-country, and it was always about beating someone else, and I just never liked it. At least now it's like I'm trying to beat myself." I could win against myself without feeling bad.

"You don't want to win?" he asked, leaning forward again.

"I want to win, but the thing is that I'm kind of used to losing things. I don't want to put someone else in that position, you know? Like, I know how much it sucks to lose at something that you really want, so I don't want to be the person who steals the victory from the other person at the last minute," I said, glancing down at the table.

That was my thing in watching competitive sports. When we watched the Olympics, my face always lingered a little too long on the silver medalist, the person who was standing there happy to be on the podium but secretly wondering what they could have done to have that first spot. I hated watching the clips of the losing team leaving the field, because I knew their thoughts. If only they had played a little harder, tried a little more, left it on the field.

I compulsively cheered for the underdogs because I wanted them to feel what it was like to win something. Maybe I saw myself in them too much.

The waiter came to the table holding four personal sized pizzas, one with so many vegetables on it that for a second I wasn't sure if we'd just ordered a salad. "Wow," I said as the pizzas were set down in front of us, the vegetable pizza dropping a couple of onions onto the table. "This is impressive."

"I'm starving," Hunter said, pulling the first piece of pizza towards himself.

"How? You literally ate the entire bread basket before we even ordered pizza," I replied, pulling my pizza towards me and taking the first piece. It smelled amazing, although I had a low bar for pizza. All pizza was good pizza. You could not mess up pizza. Unless you tried to make it carb free and dairy free, but you ruined all food that way.

He looked over at me, where I was starting to scoop the vegetable pizza onto my plate. With the sheer number of vegetables, they were starting to fall off and drop onto my plate.

"Enjoying all those vegetables?" Hunter asked, looking over at me and raising an eyebrow.

"Don't be a hater." I wasn't actually enjoying these

vegetables, but I was going to make a point here. I wasn't going to lose to Hunter.

"You look like you're looking over at my piece of pizza and want it," he said, starting to grin.

I did. I very much regretted this choice. I had an opportunity to have all the carbs and dairy in the world, and I was eating uncooked vegetables instead. But I had to show Hunter somehow. "Here," he said, taking one of the pieces from his and sliding it over towards me. "You look sad looking at that pizza."

I looked down at the massive piles of vegetables that were on mine. They hadn't even been cooked, just straight added to the pizza. It was so aggressively healthy that it was not very good. "Thanks," I said, looking at the much more delicious slice of pizza that he had given me.

"Were you really trying to prove me wrong so badly that you managed to get a pizza that doesn't taste good?" he asked, leaning back. His eyes ran up and down my body, and I swallowed. He was checking me out. Hunter Lowen was checking me out.

"I'm not going to admit that," I said, looking down and then deciding that I would eat a garlic knot to buy myself some time.

Hunter laughed. "You know the guys used to do this all the time to me. They'd try to prove me wrong, and I always got them back at the end."

"Really?" I tore off a piece of garlic knot. Carbs. Carbs were delicious.

"My freshman year, one of the senior guys on the team spent an entire season trying to get me with a super soaker after every practice. I couldn't do anything without getting shot by that thing. And he'd always aim so that it looked like I peed myself," Hunter said, leaning forward.

I started to laugh. Hunter's eyes went right onto mine, staying there. "I waited until the end of the year, and I rigged up a water bucket over his locker in the locker room. He'd been bragging about how he was going to ask this girl to homecoming, and I knew it was that afternoon. He went to open his locker, and boom. Completely soaked."

"That's brutal," I said, shaking my head. "And you even knew that he was trying to impress someone?"

Hunter smiled at me, his eyes on mine. "I think it was hazing freshman year. Coach put me on varsity right away, and the guys hated it. I was so happy this year when the rest of the team came back."

"You played varsity freshman year?" I had totally missed that. That would have been a huge deal, because our school was known for being very competitive about sports.

He nodded. "It honestly kind of sucked. I mean, I was more than good enough to be on varsity, but the seniors were all pissed that I got so much play time. My parents kept telling me that I was going to have so many friends from sports, and literally, everyone on the team hated me for being a show off. The seniors tried to drive me off the team, and it was not fun. It didn't get better when we switched over to lacrosse season, either."

I would have never thought that could happen to Hunter. He was clearly so good at soccer that they should have all just embraced him. "I'm lucky," I said. "The cross country team is so nice. I only started running because my counselor told me I needed to do something for college, but they're the nicest."

"No embarrassing stories?" he asked, his hand reaching towards the middle of the table.

I shook my head. "The closest is that Luisa, our captain next year, made us all cupcakes freshman year to celebrate the end of the season. But she put way too much dye into the frosting, and my tongue was blue the entire day. I had to give a presentation in history with a bright blue tongue."

Hunter laughed. "That's seriously the most embarrassing thing that's ever happened to you?"

I couldn't believe that I was talking about this with Hunter. I was about to admit my most embarrassing moments to the most attractive person in school. Well. "During my first practice, I was wearing a pair of my mom's old shorts. I didn't know that they were too big and falling off. This random woman biked up next to us and told me that everyone could see my butt crack."

Hunter snorted. "You managed to flash your entire team on the first day of practice."

"I almost quit after that. I couldn't bring myself to go back and run the next day." Luisa, again the nicest person in the world, had taken me aside and told me that it happened to everyone and I shouldn't be worried. She was literally the only reason I was still on the team. "I mean, my mom talks a lot about poop, so I guess that's embarrassing. But she's in public health so I'm used to it by now."

Hunter snorted again, this time so hard that water came out of his nose. "Kinsey, you can't tell me this stuff when

I'm trying to drink," he said, staring at me and shaking his head.

"That wasn't supposed to be funny! My mom threatened to skip my kindergarten graduation because she had seen a parent not properly washing their hands after they used the bathroom, and she was worried about E. Coli transmission at the buffet after. My teacher had to calm me down because I was sobbing about how poopy hands were making my mom go away."

Hunter burst into laughter, leaning forward on his elbows. "I can't imagine your teacher's face."

The waiter came back over and looked between the two of us. "Anything else? And do you need a box for that?" he asked, looking down at my pile of vegetables.

Ugh. I hated to be the person to waste food, but I really did not want to eat these. Hunter glanced at me and then up at the waiter. "I think Kinsey needs a box."

"I'm really good without all those vegetables," I said, shooting him a look. He grinned back at me, the grin lighting up his face and making him even more attractive.

Oh boy. I was down bad.

The waiter passed us the check, and Hunter snatched it before I could reach for it. "I've got it," he said, fishing something out of his pocket.

"What do you mean?" I asked. I had my mom's emergency credit card with me, my little way of getting her back for forcing me to have lunch with Brian today. If she was going to make me sit through those awful meals, she could pay for it later.

"I've got it." He passed a credit card to the waiter. "This is a date. I'm paying."

My heart rate had jumped up a thousand beats per minute. I smiled at him across the table and over the remaining pizza crusts. I wanted to reach across the table and grab his hands, but that was too much, too soon. "Thanks, Hunter."

He grinned at me, reaching his hand across the table and brushing it against the back of mine. "You're welcome, Kinsey."

After the waiter returned with the card, we walked out towards his car. The heat had started to break from the day, and I closed my eyes and lifted my head up towards the sky for a second. "You really like the weather at night, don't you?" he asked, walking alongside me.

"I love it. It's finally cool out," I said. Maybe he was making fun of me because I'd done this with him before, but I wasn't going to be embarrassed.

"I don't think I've seen someone as excited about cool weather as you are," he said, looking down at me.

This was because Hunter didn't realize how most people lived. "I don't have air conditioning at home."

"You don't have air conditioning at home?" he asked, his eyebrows flying up. "Are you serious?"

"Why is this such a surprising thing for everyone?" I shook my head. "No, I don't have air conditioning at home, because my mom and I live in an old house."

"And you survive the summer without getting heat stroke every week or something?" he asked.

"Obviously. I wouldn't be standing here if I was dead of

heatstroke," I replied, trying and failing to give him a grouchy look.

Hunter grinned at me again. I thought I could see the lights from the street behind us sparkling in his eyes. I cleared my throat. "It's kind of cool, not having air conditioning. I used to sneak onto the town beach at night so that I could go swimming under the moonlight and cool off. I love being outside at night, and I think it's because I've had to do it so much just to find bearable weather."

"You're really cool," he replied, and my entire body flushed. I was definitely no longer cool. I was much more warm all over.

We walked into the parking lot towards his car, slowly. I didn't want to get in and stop the date. I wanted to keep going, keep hanging out with him, but there was no way for me to say that without sounding desperate.

"I'll drive you home," he said, nodding towards his car. I climbed into the passenger seat again. This time, the car had warmed up from being outside, and it wasn't like climbing into a small ice box.

"You really don't like the fact that I keep my car so cold, do you?" he asked, glancing over at me as I checked for the seat heaters.

"I mean, I appreciate having air conditioning, but when we're talking about temperatures where I'm pretty sure that ice cream wouldn't melt in the car, then – "

"Let's test it."

I looked over at him and wrinkled my eyebrows together in the center. "What are you talking about?"

"You claim that ice cream won't melt in my car. I would

bet you that ice cream would melt. Let's go," he said, putting the car in reverse.

He steered the car out of the parking lot, hopping onto the highway again. We were heading away from town, towards where everyone's favorite ice cream place was. Around us, I could see his face lit through the streetlights.

He parked the car in front of the ice cream parlor. "You're not serious," I said, looking out the window and then back at him.

"Of course I'm serious." He grinned, reaching down and undoing his seat belt. "You told me that you didn't think that ice cream could melt in my car. That was a challenge, wasn't it?"

"It wasn't a challenge. It was just me giving you a hypothetical example of something that couldn't happen," I said, reaching for my own seat belt.

"It was a challenge, Kinsey. And I don't back away from a challenge," he said, looking straight at me.

I caught his eyes again, and my stomach flipped. "Let's go," he said, nodding towards the ice cream store, and I followed him in.

"Two scoops of cookie dough," he said, sticking his phone out over the register.

I never got two scoops of the same. And cookie dough was great, but maybe not what I was feeling. "I was – "

He laughed, his hand resting on my back for a second. "You thought that I was ordering your ice cream for you? Come on, I can't believe that you think so little of me. Ordering someone else's ice cream without asking?"

I glanced up at him. He was still smiling down at me, his eyes bright. "What do you want?"

I was going to win this bet. One of the ridiculous fruit flavors had to be one that was going to melt faster. The sorbets seemed like they'd melt pretty quickly, since they were just sugar and ice. But maybe traditional ice cream was going to be faster.

"Um, I'll do the key lime pie and avocado," I said finally, starting up at the menu. That seemed like one of those two had to be an ice cream that was going to stick together for a long time. Avocados didn't melt, so there was a good chance that avocado ice cream was going to hold its shape too. That was a good idea.

"Avocado?" Hunter demanded as we walked back out to his cast, him unlocking it from the clicker and o[pening the door with one hand. He hadn't started eating any of his ice cream, and he slid into the drivers' seat, holding it out in front of him.

I sat down next to him, looking over at him. He reached down and turned on the car, the air conditioning coming at me full blast. I blinked a few times, my eyes not used to the cold and dry air shooting at them.

I reached down with my empty hand and flipped off the seat heater. "Aren't you going to get cold?" Hunter asked, looking over at me.

"It's not a fair experiment if I have the seat heater on. I'll be letting you win, because I'll be bringing my side of the car up to a liveable temperature," I replied, holding up my ice cream directly in front of the air vents. "That would ruin the scientific integrity of this experiment."

He looked over at me again, the corner of his mouth twisting up. Something formed in the pit of my stomach, something that felt like I wanted him. I apparently wanted Hunter Lowen, of all people.

"And really," I said quickly, tearing my eyes away from him, "it should have gotten the ice cream in a cup and put it into a cup holder. Because the heat from my hand is also going to mess up the experiment."

"Really," he replied, raising an eyebrow towards me.

I nodded. "You know that your hand is adding extra heat to the ice cream cone. And that's going to make it melt sooner, and that's going to prove your point."

"I thought that you said that you weren't competitive. You like to let the underdog win," he replied, turning over in his seat to look directly at me, one hand holding his ice cream cone out in front of him.

"I don't think you count as the underdog in this situation," I replied, not able to keep a smile from starting. My heart rate had sped up, and I couldn't tear my eyes away from him. I swallowed, almost like my brain thought that something was going to happen,

That was ridiculous. There wasn't anything that was going to happen here. I was just sitting in a car with Hunter, talking about nonsense.

"Look!" He pointed over at me.

I looked down at my key lime pie ice cream, which had started to melt, a stream of melted ice cream dripping towards my finger. "No!" I lifted up the cone and tried to lick it off before it could drip down and run onto the leather seats below me.

"I told you!" Hunter said, pointing at my ice cream again.

I took a bite of my ice cream, trying to stop the melting, even though I'd made so much fun of Ellery for this ice cream method before. Desperate times called for desperate measures.

The key lime pie ice cream. It had let me down. "Seriously?" I said, staring at the ice cream in my hands. "This wasn't supposed to happen."

"I thought you told me that my car was going to be so cold that it wouldn't melt," he replied, turning towards me as I took another huge bite of the ice cream, trying to save it before it got all over the leather seats.

"Yours isn't melted!" I said, leaning forward and pointing towards his ice cream, which was still in one shape and holding up just fine. "See?"

"But yours is melting, so clearly my car is just fine," he replied, leaning forward towards me.

And then all of a sudden, I looked up at him, his face inches from mine. And then before my brain had time to process, his lips were on mine.

My stomach was completely turning. Hunter's lips were on mine, moving over mine, one hand gently cupping my face, a finger wrapping around one of the strands of my hair.

His lips pressed against mine again, and I leaned forward towards him, trying to get closer to him. There were so many butterflies in my stomach that I felt like I could have flown away, just taken off and soared through the sunroof.

My first kiss, in Hunter Lowen's car, holding ice cream. He leaned back into him, and his hand cupped my chin. I closed my eyes tighter.

"Shit!" he said all of a sudden, pulling back from me. The ice cream scoop on the top of his cone had fallen off into his lap, landing on the top of his leg right where his shorts ended.

"Oh my god," I said, pulling back and covering my mouth with my hand. My ice cream started to run all over my hand, and I stuck as much of it as I could in my mouth, trying to prevent it from going all over the car. The avocado flavored ice cream had not been a good choice.

Hunter opened the car door and hopped out, throwing the ice cream to the side of the road, trying to make sure that he wasn't going to get it all over the car or something. I tried to wipe my hand on the side of my romer, making sure that I wasn't getting more all over myself.

"Shit," Hunter said again, reaching into the car and pulling out a package of tissues from the center console, passing one to me. "I forgot about the ice cream."

He had a smear from one of the chocolate chips on the side of his face. I started laughing, looking at the bit of mess on his face. "Sorry," I said finally, looking away and grinning "But you have ice cream all over your face."

He laughed, running a tissue over his face. "Not my sexiest moment, that's what you're telling me?"

I shook my head, the tension of the moment before broken. There was still a voice in the back of my head reminding me that I had just been making out with Hunter Lowen. I was going to think about this later and probably have to scream or do a happy dance in my room, but that was a problem for later.

"I should have thought about that whole ice cream situation," he replied, tossing the tissue to the side of the road. "Not my best moment."

I grinned again. I wasn't able to take my eyes off of him. Like he had turned into a magnet, and I couldn't look away, couldn't turn myself away from him.

I was in for it. I was falling for Hunter Lowen.

"I won that, you know," Hunter said, climbing back into the car and settling down into the front seat.

"Oh, come on. You didn't win that." I shook my head at him, not able to wipe a grin off my face.

"I totally won that. You told me that my car was cold enough to keep ice cream from melting, and I proved that ice cream was melting in the car despite me keeping on the AC. I won," he replied. I smiled again, not able to stop myself. He reached over and brushed his thumb along my cheek. "You have an ice cream spot there."

"Thanks," I said, glancing up at him and then back down towards the floor of the car. Then, like a magnet, back up at him. He was still smiling at me, his face soft.

He started the car and backed out of the parking space, heading back towards the highway and driving the ten minutes back towards the center of town where I lived. Beside his leg, I could see the spots where the ice cream had dripped down onto the seat and was forming a stain.

That wasn't going to be fun to get out tomorrow. I looked at it, then back up at Hunter. He was staring ahead on the road, one hand resting on the steering wheel, the other on the gear shift. He glanced back over at me and grinned, catching my eyes. "I still won," he said, his hand reaching over and squeezing mine for just a second.

He pulled off the highway at the exit back towards town, driving through the center of town towards my street. He pulled up to the front of the house and stopped, putting the car in park.

"That was – that was fun," he said. I stopped from where I was about to turn towards the car door, looking back at Hunter.

I smiled, a lump catching in my throat. The blood started rushing through my ears again, and I nodded. "Yeah. That was really fun."

"We should hang out again," he said, reaching towards me. His hand skimmed my face again, and I swallowed.

It was something about the way that he said it. Not the normal confidence that I would have expected from Hunter Lowen, but just sounding like a normal person asking someone else to hang out. Almost like he was nervous about it.

"Yeah. I'd like that. I'd really like that," I said, smiling back at him, my stomach now doing a full gymnastics routine.

"See you later," he said, his eyes meeting mine.

I waved, not sure that I could actually form words, and started the walk onto my front porch. As I reached for my keys, I turned around and saw him still waiting there, waving again before I opened the front door and walked inside.

EIGHT

"OKAY. TELL ME EVERYTHING."

Jenna's tone of voice made it clear that she didn't think that much was happening. "Not much," I said, taking a deep breath and leaning forward towards the mirror, inspecting a zit that had shown up out of nowhere.

Being a teenager sucked sometimes. Everyone talked about acne, and it was like not even my dermatologist totally understood just how humiliating it was to suddenly have your face covered with little hills. I didn't want someone to tell me that this was a normal teenage rite of passage. I wanted them to make it all go away.

"Nothing?" she asked again. "What have you been doing, just sitting at home by yourself? Sounds like you."

My stomach flipped over, thinking of the night before. Thinking of sitting in Hunter's car outside of the ice cream place, of my lips on his, of his hand running up through my hair, of the way he'd leaned towards me and pressed closer to me. I suddenly wanted to throw up.

Nope, I wasn't ready to talk about that. Not with Jenna. She'd tell me all the reasons that Hunter would never like me, and I'd start to believe them, because she was right half the time.

I was keeping Hunter for myself for now.

"Nope, nothing," I replied, trying to keep my voice steady and normal. "You know. It's the normal boring stuff going on."

"It's like there's nothing happening when I'm not there," she replied, and I thought that I could hear something like satisfaction in her voice. Like she had just been trying to get me to say that I needed her.

"I mean, I had to have lunch with Brian Senior again," I offered as an olive branch.

She snorted. "Yeah, I don't care about that. Come on."

"What's going on for you? Come on, you have to have all kinds of exciting things going on in Los Angeles," I replied, turning away from the mirror and starting to do the much less exciting task of folding and putting away my laundry. I had been trying to get myself to stop freaking out about Hunter all morning by doing chores. It was only partially working.

That question was apparently what she'd wanted me to ask. There was a giant sigh on the other end of the line, and then Jenna clicked her tongue. "God, Emberleigh is the worst. She's so self-centered, and it's like I have to spend the whole time just dancing around her and all of her ridiculous demands."

"That sounds awful." The best thing to do with Jenna was always to agree with what she said, to affirm all of her feelings about whatever she was talking about. You didn't get anywhere trying to argue with her about things.

"Don't even get me started. You're so lucky that you don't have to deal with siblings."

Jenna didn't exactly have to deal with Emberleigh. They didn't usually live in the same house, and they only communicated through social media posts that were visible to the entire world. But maybe that was worse for her, having Emberleigh in the back of her head. I didn't have siblings, so I didn't know.

"Well, I should go. I'm meeting with people," Jenna said, tossing it off as though she was half expecting me to demand to know who. I stayed silent, wanting to deny her that tiny little pleasure. After a few moments of silence, she clicked her tongue again. "Okay, talk to you later. Keep me posted if anything interesting happens."

"Will do," I lied. Something interesting had happened, and I hadn't told her. And I wasn't going to.

The connection clicked off, and I sat down on the bed. I stared around the room, my brain spinning. I had kissed Hunter Lowen the night before.

All I wanted to do was sit here and freak out about the fact that I had kissed Hunter Lowen in his car the night before. He had leaned over towards me and looked at me and laughed with me and kissed me.

And maybe I was wrong, maybe I was too optimistic, but it didn't feel like he was just doing it so that he could hook up with me. Because he had taken me out to dinner and talked to me and really made it seem like he cared about what I was saying. He hadn't just met me at a party or something.

Hunter Lowen had taken me on a *date*.

I couldn't tell Lily this over text, because she would kill me for not giving her the full story. I needed either ice cream or a Nest breakfast sandwich for the full story. I took a deep breath and texted Ellery. *Hang out this afternoon?*

Ellery immediately texted back. *I'm so down. You owe me a story. And ice cream. Meet downtown?*

I sent back a thumbs up, then took a deep breath. I was going to get a snack first, and then I'd find my sunglasses. I wanted to tell her everything, dissect everything that had happened, but at the same time, maybe I'd wait to tell her that I'd kissed Hunter.

Oh my god. I'd kissed Hunter yesterday.

Deep breath. No more freaking out. I went downstairs to find my snack before I went out. Maybe my mom would have brought back some more iced coffee, and I could snag that. I didn't hear the noise in the kitchen until I turned the corner. "Kinsey!" my mom said, beaming at me. "We just stopped by."

We? And then of course, I looked towards the fridge, where Brian Senior was busy checking himself out in the window. He turned towards me. "Hello, Kinsey," he said, reaching out to shake my hand.

Seriously? Didn't this guy have a job that he had to go to? What was he doing in my house at lunch?

"So what have you been up to today?" my mom asked.

I shrugged, stepping around her to try to reach the cabinet. I grabbed a glass and started to fill it up with water.

"Hanging out." I wasn't going to tell her about the date with Hunter. Not with Brian Senior here. I mean, I would have wanted to tell her and hear her excitement, but not with this guy.

"Are you still thinking about getting a job?" Brian Senior asked, turning towards me and giving me the widest, creepiest smile. "Your mom mentioned that you were thinking about tennis camp."

"What do you mean?" Getting a job was supposed to be one of those unambiguously good things. I wasn't some kind of lazy teenager who wasn't willing to work. Wasn't his generation the one that always complained about how mine didn't have enough of a work ethic?

"Since your mom and I are getting married this summer," Brian Senior said, "it's really important to me that you are there for her and can support her." Almost like marrying him was such a chore that she needed someone to lighten it up for her. Not that I made that particular comment out loud.

"And?" I asked. I had mentioned tennis camp once and never followed up on it. It had been an idea that I'd thought about for all of thirty seconds.

"Why don't we make a deal?" Brian Senior said, glancing over at my mom and then back at me. "I'll pay you this summer to make sure that you have the time to participate in all of the wedding planning events that your mom is working on."

"So you're offering to pay me to basically just follow my mom around and help her with the wedding?" I asked, raising an eyebrow at him. That was the most blatant attempt I could think of to buy my loyalty. Or he had figured out that getting a job would give me a convenient excuse to not hang out with him, which was the real reason I'd been thinking about it.

"We're paying our wedding planner a lot of money," he said, smiling at my mom as though the cost of their wedding planner was some special inside joke, then turning back towards me. "So think of it like a wedding planning internship if that's better."

That was, if anything, worse. I didn't want an internship that was so clearly made up. And the fact that my soon to be stepfather thought that he could just pay me to make me happy showed me how little he knew about me.

"That's a really generous offer, Brian, and I really appreciate the fact that it means that Kinsey will be able to spend more time with me getting ready for the wedding," my mom said, fixing me with the steeliest stare that she could manage.

I took a deep breath. "I'm not interested. But thanks."

My mom shot me a look, and I swallowed. God, I hated confrontation. Any time Jenna wanted to argue about something, I always ended up just agreeing with her. It wasn't worth the argument.

Brian looked distinctly confused that I was refusing to just take his money. He stared at me for a second, then cleared his throat. "Well. Did I tell you about what Brian is up to?"

That would be Brian Junior, Brian Senior's son. And the man got mad when I had to call him Brian Senior to distinguish between them. "How is his training going?" my mom asked, leaning towards Brian Senior.

"He's doing very well," Brian said, looking over at me. This was clearly supposed to be one of those openings where I was enthralled by what Brian Junior was doing and started asking questions. But as far as I could tell, Brian Junior was a mediocre athlete who thought about his diet too much. Just like his dad.

He and my mom started talking about Brian Junior, and I tuned them out while I looked through the fridge.

"I've got to get back to work, girls," Brian said, loudly clearing his throat to get my attention again. "Emma, I'll see you tonight, love."

My mom smiled up at him. Ew. Save me from this. "I'll come with you, Brian. I've got errands to run."

Wasn't she supposed to be at work too? I shot her a look. "I'm on my lunch break," she said to me. I was going to take that as an apology. "Kinsey, do you want to get coffee later?"

I shook my head. No, because Brian Senior would know about it and crash it. "No thanks. I'm going to hang out with my friends." Just like I'd told her the last time she'd tried to lure me in with coffee.

My mom looked at me. "I thought that Jenna was in Los Angeles."

"I have other friends," I said, it coming out harsher than I meant. "Remember, Ellery?"

"Right, I know," she said, raising her hands. "Well, have fun with Ellery, then."

"I will," I said, my voice still sharp. I glanced down towards the floor.

She stared at me for a second, then waved and turned towards the door. Brian Senior stepped right behind her and put his hand on her back. Ew. So much ew. "Bye, Kinsey," she called, looking over her shoulder as they walked out of the house.

I waved back, sitting down at the counter. I needed a few minutes to recover from that sight before I went and met Ellery. After some therapeutic mindless scrolling, and some excellent videos of baby wombats with fruit, I headed out of the house. It was bright enough that I blinked a few times, wishing I'd found my sunglasses before I left.

"Kinsey!" I heard Ellery's voice from across the street. She came jogging across the street, then threw her arms around me. "Hello! I thought you were going to walk right past me."

"Sorry, I can't see anything," I said, sticking my hand over my eyes to shade them. "What is wrong with the sun today?"

She stared at me, narrowing her eyes. "Are you hungover? What is going on? I feel like I need to immediately hear the news, because you are hinting at something. So? How did the date go?"

Was it bad that I immediately wanted to tell her everything? I took a deep breath. "Ellery, I think it went well. Like, really well."

She pushed her sunglasses up onto the top of her head, then stared at me. "Okay. We're getting something to eat, and you're going to tell me everything."

Forty-five minutes later, we had sat down in the shade along the street, but we were still talking. I wasn't trying to force Ellery to relive almost every detail with me, but she had asked. "I can't believe it," Ellery said for the fiftieth time. "I mean, I knew that he liked you, but he really likes you."

Not that I'd told her he kissed me yet, but I had told her all about the rest of the date. And the burrito mile. And all the jokes he'd made. I couldn't believe it even as I said it.

My phone buzzed, and I glanced down at it. Speak of the devil.

"Who's texting you, and why are you smiling?" Ellery asked, giving me the voice that meant that she knew there was something going on and was just waiting for me to say it.

It was a picture of an ice cream cone from Hunter. *Eating this before it melts in my car.*

I grinned. *Don't worry. You have plenty of time before that happens.*

I think I proved you wrong there last night, he replied immediately.

"You are texting Hunter, aren't you?" Ellery said, narrowing her eyes at me. "You don't even have to answer. I can see it on your face."

I was trying to think up something clever when my phone buzzed again. *Are you coming to Logan's tonight?* Hunter texted.

Hunter was double texting. He was double texting me to ask me about my plans, and he was inviting me to another of the big parties of the summer.

Oh my god. This was real. This was actually happening.

I wasn't going to think about it too much, or I wasn't going to be a functional person. Maybe we'd kiss again. Maybe things with Hunter could be real.

Deep breath. I looked over at Ellery. "Are you going to Logan's tonight?"

"I was going to ask if you wanted to go," she said, looking at me and turning her head to the side. "Are you asking because a certain person on the soccer team has invited you?"

I was apparently that transparent. I nodded. "Want to get ready together?"

"Are you kidding?" she replied, almost jumping off the bench. "Do you know how exciting this is? Hunter Lowen asked you to come to this party."

"Don't say it like that. It makes me feel weird," I said, looking back down at my phone.

"Not to make it weirder, but do you want to walk up and down the street with me?" she asked, glancing over her shoulder.

"Why are we walking up and down the street?" I asked. Not that I minded. I could use a walk, keep myself moving so that my brain didn't get too noisy.

Ellery turned bright red. "I was kind of hoping that – "

"No. Are you saying that you wanted to run into Max?" I said. She wasn't going to tell me that I had news about Hunter and not give me her news in return. "You are not actually telling me that you want to stalk Max and see what he's doing."

"It's not stalking. This is a public street," she said, gesturing. "It's just, I know there's a party tonight, and I feel weird just showing up at the party without having talked to him."

"Can't you text him?" I asked. Not that I had room to talk, really, because I would have absolutely done the same. Stalking was easier than having to actually talk to a boy.

"I don't actually have his number." She tilted her head towards the side. "And I'm guessing it's way too early for me to ask you to get it from Hunter."

"Way too early," I replied. Speaking of. I typed back a quick text to him - *Yeah, Ellery and I were going to stop by*

No exclamation point. Perfect. Seemed nice and casual, like I was just casually thinking about going out to a party and not at all sitting here freaking out about the possibility of going to a party with Hunter there. Because I wouldn't do that. Or at least, I shouldn't.

"So do you want to go for a walk?" Ellery asked again, hitting me with her most ferocious stare.

"Let's go," I said, getting up and following her. We started the walk up and down the sidewalk, Ellery glancing over her shoulder after a few steps as though to make sure that he wasn't in the area.

We stopped and pretended to look in the window of one of the boutiques on the street. "You know that this is a little bit creepy, right?" I asked.

"I wanted to go for a walk, and this is a nice place to do it," she replied. "If we happen to run into Max, great. If not, also great."

I gave her a look. She elbowed me in the side. "You're telling me that you wouldn't do the same for Hunter?"

I would absolutely do the same for Hunter. "Of course not."

"Kinsey, you are a terrible liar," she replied, glancing over her shoulder again. "Okay. We might have to give up on this. I thought the soccer guys were going to be here for lunch after practice."

The soccer boys meant Hunter, and she hadn't told me that. Now we were both being creeps. "Ellery. How dare you not tell me that?"

"You would have thrown up in the public trash can because you were too nervous to talk to Hunter. Come one. Want to go back to my place and go for a run before we get ready?" she asked, pointing over to her car.

She might have been right about that. "I'm down," I said. I didn't want to go for a run, but maybe it would help me get the nerves out before the party.

I followed her and sat down in the car, reaching for my seatbelt. She was about to reach for hers and stopped, her arm across her chest. "Shit! There he is!"

Max was walking out of a cafe in the middle of town, looking down at his phone and then glancing over his shoulder at something. "I knew that we should have waited!" she said, staring at him through the windshield.

Just then, Max turned to look towards the car, and Ellery slunk down in her seat. I stared at her for a second, and then she grabbed me. I tucked myself lower into my seat as well. Oh. We were being sneaky.

"He's coming over here," I said, peering over the dashboard for a second.

"Shit," Ellery muttered, sinking down further in her seat.

Max rapped on the window. "Shit," she mouthed at me, and I grimaced.

Thank god it wasn't Hunter standing outside the car. This was Ellery's problem to deal with.

Ellery pushed herself back up into her seat and rolled down the window. "Max! Good to see you!" she said, a slightly maniacal smile on her face.

"What are you guys doing?" he asked, looking from me to Ellery and back again. "Are you hiding in your car?"

"No, of course not," Ellery said, way too fast for the situation. "I dropped my hair tie and I was leaning down to pick it up."

He glanced at her, then at me, then slowly nodded. "Right."

I was going to die of awkwardness. Seriously, I was going to spontaneously combust right here and now, and that was going to be the end of it all. "Are you going to Logan's party tonight?" I blurted out. Maybe if I started talking, it would make this less awkward.

"How do you know about Logan's?" he asked, looking at me. "It's supposed to be just for the soccer teams."

I couldn't tell him it was because Hunter had asked me. That was way too much information and way too personal. Ellery glanced at me and then sent Max a giant smile. "Our friends invited us."

We weren't fishing for an invitation, I wanted to say, but I wasn't going to tell him that Hunter had invited me.

Max stared at us for a second, then shrugged. "Yeah. Should be fun tonight. See you guys later, then."

"See you later!" Ellery said too brightly.

Max walked away, not looking back. Ellery slowly rolled up her window.

"That was so awkward," I said, looking over at her and grimacing once the window was safely up.

She buried her head in her hands. "I can't believe that I just did that. That was terrible. And what does he mean about how we got invited?"

"I guess he sort of invited us now?" I said. That was probably the most optimistic spin I could put on that conversation.

Ellery thumped her head against the steering wheel. "Let's go. I have to go for a run first to wash off the embarrassment."

I WALKED out of the shower at her house after my run, my hair up in a towel. I tried on one of Ellery's tops, turning in the mirror to check myself out. Cute, but I was going to keep looking.

"If we have too much fun, we're telling my parents that we're staying over at your place," Ellery said, leaning forward towards her mirror and touching her mascara, then glancing back at the YouTube video she was trying to watch. The beauty blogger she was watching seemed to be having an easier time with their makeup than she was having with hers.

"I'm warning you. I'm not kidding about the lack of air conditioning at my house," I replied, going back through Ellery's closet. We were close enough to the same size. Plus, she had a style that I wanted to copy, lots of tops that somehow looked super trendy and also cute.

"You have no air conditioning and no parents, and I have both," she replied. "I'll make that trade with you."

"Fine," I said, sitting back down and reaching for the cheese plate that Ellery's mom had brought up. Her mom was apparently taking an online course in how to arrange cheese plates, and Ellery had been the main beneficiary.

"Max is going to be at this thing tonight," she said, turning towards me and blinking twice, looking like she was trying to dislodge a mascara clump. "I have to look okay."

"You look amazing." That was the only appropriate response. Jenna had a way of looking at me when I said something like that, running her eyes up and down me and then going "Yeah, you kinda do look okay." That managed to destroy my confidence every time.

"Okay, but I have to make sure that Max is interested in talking to me, and I can tell you that telling me that I just look okay is not going to do it," Ellery replied, setting her mascara down.

"You look way more than okay. And I'm not just saying that because I'm your friend," I said, pulling out another top and holding it up in front of myself.

She sighed. "We were flirting all year in study hall. I

don't know why he didn't just ask me if I wanted to hang out then. Now I have to think about it all summer."

Especially after our conversation today, I wasn't sure if I wanted to answer that question. Max was kind of a player. What if he was just playing her?

Yeah, but what if Hunter is just playing you? said the helpful voice in the back of my head.

I wasn't going to think about that. My phone buzzed, and I looked down to see a text message from Hunter. *Logan left the gate closed tonight. The code's 5741.*

Logan's house was fancy enough to have a gate. We literally needed a secret code to get into this party tonight. Maybe that was why Max had been so weird about it earlier.

"Was that Jenna?" Ellery asked, checking her makeup again. "She's mad that she's missing Logan's first party of the summer?"

I shook my head. "I haven't really heard from her since she went to Los Angeles." That was weird. And what was weirder was that I didn't actually miss her. I would have thought that I would be so excited to tell her about Hunter, but I was actually kind of relieved that she wasn't around to ask about it.

If Jenna was so convinced that I was so boring, she didn't need to know the news.

"Makes sense. She's probably having way more fun than we are." Ellery's tone of voice had changed, enough that I noticed it.

"I think we're having more fun," I said. It was true, even if Ellery had forced me to go for a run.

"I think it's time to head out," she said, sticking her mascara onto the side table and grabbing a last piece of cheese. "We've got places to be and people to see."

I followed her downstairs, where she called bye to her parents. I followed her outside and sat down in the car, scrolling through her phone to look for party music. We drove over to Logan's, singing along the whole way there with the windows down.

We pulled up in front of the house, and Ellery leaned her head back against the car seat. "Okay. I am totally brave enough to do this."

"You are totally brave enough to do this." I didn't know if I was hyping her or myself up. I had to go in there and act like I wasn't nervous at all.

"We are totally brave enough to do this," she replied, flexing back her shoulders into the superwoman pose. "I am brave. And you're brave too."

I wasn't sure about the second part. But it couldn't be that awkward, not when Hunter had specifically invited me to this party. He wasn't going to make it awkward, not after our night together. Our *date*.

I took a deep breath and followed her out of the car, heading into the house.

The party didn't seem like a real party. It was just people hanging out at Logan's house. That was so much more intimidating, because I couldn't just vanish into the corner and hope that no one noticed me.

Nope. I was going to be brave. Hunter had invited me, after all. I followed Ellery as she walked through the house and into the backyard.

"Hey," someone called as we walked over, trying to avoid the clumps of dirt around the backyard. It looked like someone had tried to play a sport that had involved hurtling dirt clumps at each other.

"Hey," Ellery said. Behind us, the music from the house was barely audible.

I glanced over at her and raised an eyebrow. All of the people standing around the circle seemed to be the soccer guys and their close friends, not the kind of party that I had expected. I had thought this was going to be another big rager, not a friends party.

"Kinsey!" I heard the voice beside me. My heart started pounding so hard that I thought that I was going to pass out.

Hunter walked up beside me, close enough that I could smell the smell of his soap. I looked up at him and grinned. "Hey."

"I'm glad you made it out, and you didn't get scared away by this being at Logan's," he said, still standing close enough to me that it was slightly hard to breathe.

"I mean, you invited me, so there was no way I wasn't coming," I replied. Maybe that made me sound desperate, but I didn't care. "But I'm really glad you're here."

"Of course I'm here," he replied. He was so much taller than I was that I had to crane my head back to look up at him. "You want to come join my team? We're about to start a round of Jenga."

"Jenga? Seriously?" I asked, but I followed him anyway.

Standing on a table was a giant Jenga set, one of those

that I had only seen online before. "Wow," I said, taking a step back. "That thing is taller than I am."

Hunter grinned. "Kinsey's on my team." He glanced down at me. "We split up into teams of two, and the losing team has to fill a dare we agree with at the beginning."

"Oh god," I said, rolling my shoulders. I had never been on the receiving end of a soccer team dare, but I was going to imagine that it wasn't pleasant.

"Are you doing your stretches to get ready for Jenga?" he asked, the smirk coming back onto his face.

If he was going to make fun of me, I was going to embrace it. "You told me it was competitive, didn't you?"

"And I thought that you told me that you weren't the competitive one," he replied, still grinning at me. My eyes caught his, and I glanced at the ground and then back up at him. Someone would have been able to cut the tension with a knife.

"Okay, you two," Logan shouted from across the table. He and Ethan crossed their arms and leaned against each other like they were at the start of a bad action movie.

"What's the dare?" I asked, looking in between Logan and Hunter.

"Getting thrown in the pool fully clothed. But I don't hate you as much as I hate Lowen, so I'll let you take your phone out of your pocket first," Ethan said, nodding at me.

"McGee," Hunter said, his voice low.

That was not good for me. I had dressed to look cute, not to get thrown into the pool. "Okay," I said, looking over at Hunter. He smiled at me again. "I can do this."

"That's the spirit," Logan called from across the table. "Let's go!"

I hadn't known that Jenga could be so competitive, but it seemed like nothing was off limits in this particular game. When I went to pull the first block of my game, Ethan and Logan started to chant, waving their arms in the air.

"No fair. She's new to the game," Hunter called back towards them.

"We don't go easy on anyone, Lowen. This is serious business," Logan shouted back.

Oh god. I took a deep breath and stared at one of the easy blocks, one in the middle of the tower that looked like it was pretty loose. "No tapping!" Logan called as I started to tap the block to see if it would move easily.

My fingers were slightly trembling from all of the adrenaline, both from the game and from Hunter standing behind me. I pushed on the block and slid it out, reaching up and placing it at the top of the tower. "Nice," Hunter said, clapping me on the shoulder as I took a step back and stared at the tower. "Good move."

Logan reached for his block, adding it to the top, then called over, "Lowen, your turn!"

Hunter grinned at me again, leaning forward and taking another block out. We kept going for another few rounds until the tower started to wobble.

Ethan looked at us from around the tower from the other side of the table. "You guys are going down."

"Stop the shit talking and get to playing, McGee." Hunter nodded across the table, where the Jenga tower was starting to wobble.

Ethan looked back at us and grinned, finding what looked like the last safe block and sliding it out. "Shit," I said under my breath, starting at the tower. It was leaning even more now than before.

"You've got this," Hunter said to me as I stared at the tower. "You've definitely got it."

I stared at the tower, tapping one block down below so that Ethan and Logan wouldn't see. They started a chant.

"She's got the toughest block so far. Shut up, you two," Hunter said, snapping his fingers at the two of them.

"You don't take it easy on us, so we're not taking it easy on you!" Logan yelled back, starting to thrust his hips towards Hunter.

I stared at the tower again. "Okay?" Hunter asked, his fingers brushing my lower back.

Him touching me was not helpful right now. I squinted at the tower again. It was starting to lean dangerously, and there were a few blocks that seemed like they were holding up most of the tower.

I stared at it for a few more seconds. This was totally doable.

Lily and I had been in our elementary school robotics club together. We had spent a lot of weekends building stuff, and this looked exactly like something we'd solved in the past.

There was too much weight on a few of the blocks, and that meant that a couple of the blocks on the left were actually removable. I couldn't remove most of the ones on the right, because that would shift the weight and send the whole thing toppling down.

I took a deep breath and spotted what I thought was the perfect block.

"You're going for that one?" Ethan demanded as I planted my legs in an athletic stance, leaning forward towards the block. I tightened my abs, which was probably unnecessary but felt like it was a good idea anyway.

"Kins, you sure?" Hunter's voice came from behind me. But he didn't touch me again, keeping me from any more distractions.

I nodded without saying a word. I stared at the block for a few more moments, then gently began the process of tapping it out.

The tower wobbled slightly, and I held my breath, as though the tiniest disturbance was going to send the whole thing toppling to the ground. But it held after it shook slightly, and I went back to tapping the block, staring at it and taking a deep breath.

The block was a quarter out, then a half, and then almost entirely. I tapped it one final time and pulled it slowly away from the tower structure. I raised up on my tiptoes, placing it as softly as I could on the top.

I didn't take my eyes away from the tower until my feet were firmly planted back on the ground, but then I turned towards Logan and Ethan. Their mouths were visibly hanging open, staring at me as I took a step back from the tower. "Your turn, boys."

"You are so dead," Hunter said, staring at the tower and then at his friends. "That should not have worked."

"This isn't a naked lap too, is it?" Logan asked, staring at Ethan and then back at Hunter.

"Kinsey's a first time player. It's a naked lap after next practice," Hunter replied, grinning at the two of them. His hand was resting on my back now, and I could feel the heat of it through my top. "Unless you've got a miracle up your sleeve, get ready to get naked."

I stared at the tower for a few moments as Ethan and Logan seemed to confer among themselves. There were a couple of other blocks that you could probably take out if you had perfect execution, but you would have to have perfect execution. And I was willing to bet that Ethan and Logan had had a few drinks before I showed up.

The two of them stared at the tower and then back at me. Ethan finally nodded. "We're going for it."

"Yeah, you go for it," Hunter replied, nodding towards them and taking a step closer to me.

Ethan started to tap out one of the blocks towards the bottom. He wasn't paying attention to any of the physics of the Jenga tower. He couldn't get that one, because the left side of the tower wouldn't have anywhere to rest.

And before he could even get half of the block out, the whole thing came toppling down, cascading over itself, blocks flying everywhere around us.

"Yes!" Hunter screamed, his arms tightening around my back. He picked me up, spinning me around. He kissed my forehead, then stepped back and pumped one arm in the air. "Take that, you two!"

"She has magical powers. Not fair," Ethan called back, giving me the middle finger.

"In the pool!" Hunter called to the two of them, wrapping one arm around my lower back and gesturing towards the pool with the other.

When they didn't move quickly enough, Hunter smiled down at me. "Be back in a second."

Before I realized what was going on, he lifted his arm from behind my back, then placed his phone on the table. He ran towards Logan, grabbing him around the waist and continuing to run.

Both of them flew into the pool together, water splashing everywhere as they hit.

Ethan seemed to know what was coming and charged towards the pool. I started to jog over to see what was going on.

From behind me, Ethan grabbed me. We both went flying, him pulling me into the pool with him. I shouted as I hit the water, closing my eyes against the chlorine.

"No fair," Hunter said, spotting me in the pool. He grabbed Ethan around the shoulders, pushing him under the water for a second. Ethan popped back up to the surface, shaking the water from his eyes.

Hunter swam over to the side of the pool, climbing out. He turned around, holding out his hand towards me.

I grabbed his hand. He pulled me up through the pool steps, pulling me close as I hit the final step. I looked up at him, and his eyes suddenly seemed soft. "My friends are assholes," he said, pushing a piece of wet hair out of my face. "Let's get you a towel."

I followed him to where Logan's family had hidden spare towels. He pulled one out, passing it towards me. I wrapped myself in it. Hunter rumpled his hair with his towel, then threw it over his shoulder like it was no big deal.

I followed him back to where everyone else was sitting. Ellery fixed me with the most ferocious stare that I had ever seen. We were going to dissect all of this later, but for now, I was just going to focus on Hunter.

I sat down, the towel still wrapped around me. "Hey. Do you need a sweatshirt or something?" Hunter asked, holding out something that looked like his soccer sweatshirt.

"Really?" It was cool outside now, and it was going to get uncomfortable fast.

"I figured you wouldn't want to be stuck in wet clothes, and I didn't think you planned for that. There's a bathroom right inside if you want to change," he said, nodding towards the house.

I started to walk towards the bathroom. I was maybe ten steps away from the group when I heard Ellery's voice. "Is that the bathroom? Thank god."

"Okay," she hissed, catching up to me as I pushed open the door into the house. "Are you going to explain what's going on with you and Hunter Lowen?"

"There's only one Hunter here, you don't have to use his full name," I whispered back, walking into the bathroom and closing the door behind us.

She crossed her arms and leaned towards me, her eyes narrowed. "There is something that you are not telling me here, Kinsey."

I swallowed. I had told her everything, but maybe I

hadn't realized what everything was. "Hunter – it seems like Hunter might actually like me. Like a lot, for real."

"Yeah, that's pretty obvious!" She shook her head at me, as though she couldn't believe that anyone could actually be as stupid as I was. I should have warned her that I could be deeply clueless.

"I didn't plan it, I swear," I said, taking off my soaking shirt and pulling Hunter's sweatshirt on over my bra.

"You're literally wearing his clothes, Kinsey." She sat down on the edge of the sink and leaned towards me. "What the hell happened between you and Hunter to make him pack extra clothes for you?"

I didn't totally know, to be honest, but whatever it was, it was awesome. "Ellery. I have absolutely no idea. Can we just talk about it tomorrow?"

She narrowed her eyes at me, then nodded. "I can do that, but you have to promise to tell me all of the details."

"All of the details. I promise." I wasn't getting out of it with partial details this time. She was going to kill me when she realized I'd kissed Hunter and hadn't told her.

"Okay," she said finally, taking a step back and admiring the sweatshirt. "That's actually a great sweatshirt. You should steal it."

"It has Hunter's name on the back. I'm not that creepy. I'm not going to stalk him on the street wearing it." Ellery didn't have moral standing to make fun of me right now.

She rolled her eyes at me. "Let's go."

We arrived back at the circle of people. Someone had lit a fire in the middle, and Hunter looked up as I came back. He patted the seat beside him. "Saved you a spot."

Ellery vanished around the other side of the fire, sitting down close to Max.

"Thanks," I said, sitting down next to Hunter and stretching my legs out towards the fire. Hopefully it would help my clothes dry after everything they'd been through tonight.

Hunter's arm rested on the back of my chair, not quite around me but not far off. "I have shorts, too, if you want them. But I think they're too big for you."

"Are they as comfortable as this sweatshirt?" I had never understood the hype about stealing boys' clothes, but I was going to change my mind now.

He laughed. "No, but if you want them, they're yours. Or I could try to find you one of Logan's pairs of short shorts, but I really don't think you want those."

"No thanks," I said, glancing up towards Hunter.

"Did you hear what happened after practice the other day?" Nova, one of the girls on the girls' soccer team, asked from across the fire circle.

"No," Ethan said, looking at her and then around the group.

Nova launched into her story, something about a stray dog running across the field and the team trying to capture it. I leaned back slightly.

Hunter's arm reached behind my back, and I could feel the weight of it through his sweatshirt. I glanced around the circle again, and one of the girls on the other side was raising her eyebrows, giving me a look. I couldn't read it in the darkness, but I was pretty sure it had something to do with the fact that I was now cuddling with Hunter Lowen.

Across the circle, Ellery had started talking to Max. She was making up for the incident earlier today. He was going to forget that we had been stalking him and he'd caught us.

Maybe this was perfect. We'd both end up with the guys we liked at the end of the summer. It would be a movie summer, just like Lily had told me.

God, I couldn't wait to tell her about tonight. She'd be so excited. I'd need to prepare myself for the sheer theater kid energy.

"Need anything to drink?" Ethan asked, standing up and looking from me to Hunter and back again.

"Kinsey?" Hunter asked, turning towards me. His arm was still resting on my back.

"I'm fine," I said, looking up at him. Then away, because I felt queasy if I looked at him for too long. I had way too many butterflies right now.

His arm tightened around my back. "I think you owe her a hot chocolate for that pool incident. I think that's the rule," Hunter said, looking up at Ethan.

Ethan looked from me to Hunter and back again. "What, do you need one too, Lowen? Your feelings have a bo-bo?"

There seemed to be some kind of wordless communication between the two of them, and then Logan stood up and thumped Ethan on the back. "Fine. We'll go make you a fancy hot drink. Don't be a sore loser, Lowen."

"It's not being a sore loser if I win," he called after them. Ethan gave him the middle finger.

Ellery and Max still looked like they were deep in conversation. Perfect. Max got up, and I tried to give Ellery the most encouragement I could. She looked over at me and sent me another look that clearly meant she saw that I was cuddling with Hunter.

He'd started it, but I definitely wasn't complaining about it. I scooted closer to him and rested my head on his shoulder.

Ethan and Logan returned with two mugs. "Kinsey, we made you whipped milk with chai and cinnamon, and Hunter, you get a cup of sore winner," Logan said, passing us the mugs.

"Says the sore loser," Hunter said to Ethan, who gave him the middle finger again. "Enjoy your naked lap."

I looked up at Hunter. "What is this?"

"Logan's parents have a whole espresso machine set up, and Logan got really drunk one time and tried to teach us all how to make fancy drinks. So now if someone gets knocked in the pool, the rule is that the offender has to make them a drink if they want it," Hunter said, leaning closer to me. "And usually it's slightly less fancy than what they made you."

Despite the fact they'd knocked me in the pool, I was starting to think that Ethan and Logan were okay after all. "Thanks," I said, snuggling tighter into Hunter before I even realized what I was doing. His arm around my back tightened again, pulling me even closer in towards him.

I took a sip. For what it was worth, it was actually a pretty delicious drink. I hadn't been expecting the guys to make anything that tasted good, but Logan had a promising future as a barista. "I like this."

"Good," Hunter said. I was pretty sure I could feel his

finger caressing my side through my sweatshirt. *His* sweatshirt. This was so weird.

"So," Max asked, standing up on the other side of the circle and looking over at me and Hunter, "do the Jenga champions want a rematch?"

SEVERAL HIGH INTENSITY games of Jenga later, I was extremely glad that Hunter was supplying me with seltzer and not with beer.

"It was all a ploy to make sure that we won every game and kept our championship," Hunter said in my ear, bending down towards me.

I nodded. Hunter had created a rule that whoever lost Jenga had to chug a beer, which meant that our opponents had been getting drunker and drunker while I nipped on my seltzer. In retrospect, it had been one of the smartest rules that he could have made.

The party was starting to die down, most people starting to doze off, the music quieter and no one lining up for the next round of Jenga. Ellery was sitting around the fire next to Max, her eyes closing slightly.

"I should probably go," I said, glancing up at Hunter. I always forgot how much taller he was than I was, how he seemed to loom over me when we were standing face to face. It made it so much more intimate feeling to have to tilt my head back to look him in the eyes.

"You sure?" he asked, his hand now resting on my lower back. I could feel the heat of it through the sweatshirt I was still wearing.

Ellery's eyelids were fluttering, and I was sure that the beer she'd had to drink after losing to me at Jenga wasn't helping. "Yeah," I said finally, looking back up at Hunter. "I promised Ellery I'd make sure that she got home."

And I liked hanging out with Hunter. I really liked it. But I couldn't just abandon my friend for him, and on top of that, it felt like it was getting later and later. I didn't want him to get sick of me. This felt like the right moment to go home, even if all I wanted was more Hunter.

"Okay," he said, pulling me into a hug. His arms tightened around my back, and I pressed my head onto his chest. His t-shirt was still damp from when he'd been thrown into the pool. "Text me later, okay?"

I nodded, trying to hide the smile spreading across my face. He leaned back down and kissed me briefly. My heart jumped, and I stared up at him. He smiled at me again, his hand still on my side. "See you later, Kinsey."

"Bye," I said, resisting the urge to wave at him like I was five years old and leaving kindergarten for the day. I turned back over my shoulder to look at him as I walked towards Ellery, and his eyes met mine again.

"Are you ready to go?" Ellery asked me as I walked over to her. "And we're going to your house, right?"

I was kind of hoping she'd forget that, and we'd get to spend the night in her air conditioning. " Are you okay sharing my bed with me? Because I don't have a particularly large bedroom."

"I told my parents that I wasn't coming home tonight," she replied, her voice sleepy. "Let's go."

We walked out to her car. She climbed into the

passenger seat, starting to fall asleep before we'd ever pulled out of Logan's driveway.

In the rearview mirror, as we reached the end of the driveway and started the turn towards the street, I could see Hunter walking towards his car. His hair was rumpled and still wet, and he strode rather than walked.

Part of me wanted to park the car right there and run back to him. I wanted to spend more time with him. I wanted him to pull me in close and make the guys make me drinks and play Jenga with me. I wanted to just be around him.

I glanced back in the mirror again. Yeah, I wanted Hunter Lowen.

But I was committed now. I glanced over at Ellery, who was already starting to doze off in the passenger seat.

I put the car in drive and headed home.

NINE

WHEN I WOKE up the next morning, there were already four texts from Lily on my phone. *Hello, lovely! You didn't text me last night so I assume that you were doing something boring. Coffee? Brunch? Ice cream? Miss you!*

Then another, *Kinsey! Answer me!*

Then another, *I love you and I want to see you and you need to pick up your phone and text me back so that I know you're alive.*

And then finally, *okay we are getting brunch, and I am going to call it brunch because that sounds so much more sophisticated than a bagel, and you are going to text me back with lots of exclamation points and emojis and tell me how excited you are to see me after I've been gone for two whole weeks.*

I rolled my eyes at the phone and tapped back a confirmation, refusing to use any of the suggested exclamation points or emojis.

I glanced over to the other side of my bed, where Ellery

was still fast asleep. This was new. Jenna had never come over to my house, because it was always too hot or too small or something.

I pulled on a t-shirt appropriate for the day and tiptoed out of the room, not wanting to wake her up, heading down towards the kitchen. My mom was still over at Brian Senior's. I reached into the fridge to find one of the iced coffees that was always in there.

It was weird that my mom wasn't here. Not that we had had that much to debrief on over the years, but freshman year, she would always be home when I came back from a sleepover. We'd sit at the kitchen counter and debrief on everything that had happened the night before.

Now it was just me. And Lily soon enough.

I grabbed an apple from the bowl in the middle of the counter and sat down on a stool. I had Hunterr Lowen's sweatshirt upstairs on the floor of my bedroom.

My stomach twisted at the thought, and I closed my eyes for a second. Then my phone buzzed again, this time with a picture of a black lab carrying a lacrosse stick. *I tried to practice this morning and my dog decided to help,* Hunter texted. *The best kind of ball return.*

I wasn't expecting texts from Hunter this early. Oh my god. He was actually texting me. Last night wasn't a fluke. The date before wasn't a fluke.

Hunter Lowen *liked* me.

There was a pounding on the stairs, as though a small herd of elephants was coming towards me. I looked up to see Ellery walking into the kitchen. "I want breakfast."

"Hi, good morning," I replied, looking up at her. She'd

already put on clothes and somehow looked more put together than I managed to look.

"It will be a better morning once I have food," she replied, sticking her head into the fridge. "Why didn't we eat dinner before we went to that thing last night?"

"We had dinner. We had your mom's cheese plate," I replied. My stomach was twisting, something about knowing there was an unanswered text from Hunter on my phone.

"That doesn't count. Those cheese plates are supposed to be works of art, not food. Which is stupid if you ask me, but it's what the instructor always tells my mom." She pulled her head out of the fridge and looked back at me. "You have no carbs here. I need carbs. Brunch?"

"I was getting brunch with a friend from another school," I said, glancing down at my phone. It had started vibrating, but fortunately, or unfortunately, all of the texts were from Lily. Nothing back from Hunter. "Want to join?"

"Absolutely," she said, nodding towards me. "Because I am pretty sure I remember you promising to catch me up on some very important news last night."

Oh god. I had promised to do that. And now that she was literally standing in my house, there didn't seem like there was going to be a way out of this situation.

Forty minutes later, we were both showered and dressed, walking out of the house towards the café where we always got brunch. Technically it was brunch, at least, although Lily and I always ordered their dessert crepe topped with ice cream no matter what time of the day we went.

"Kinsey!" We had barely made it to the entrance to the café before Lily came running up to us, throwing her arms around me as though it had been more like ten months since we'd seen each other. "God, I missed you so much. You have no idea how terrible it was to be stuck in the house with my siblings. Awful. Why didn't you rescue me?"

"Uh, hi, Lily," I said, blinking a few times. She was really channeling her theater kid energy today. I had told her a hundred times that she should really try out for her school play. For some reason, she always refused.

"You're?" Lily asked, turning towards Ellery, who was wearing my clothes at the moment.

"I'm Ellery," she said. "I wasn't planning to crash your brunch, but Kinsey had news that she didn't share with me yesterday, and she promised to tell me, and you know."

"What news?" Lily asked, looking in between Ellery and me. "What's going on?"

I was not going to be ready for this cosmic explosion that this was going to take. The town needed to get its emergency warning sirens ready for the screaming that was about to happen. There were going to be windows in the next five towns that shattered.

"I – " I swallowed.

"Girls, can I get you seated?" the hostess asked, coming up to us with a handful of menus and perfect timing. "We've got a table for three right next to the window."

Even as we walked into the café, Lily started to tug on my arm. "Story. Story. Story."

I was starting to hate my friends a little bit. "Can I have food first?"

"Come on. I know that there was leftover iced coffee in your fridge and you already had it. It's story time," Lily said, shaking her head as she pulled out her seat and sat down.

"How did you know that? That was impressive," Ellery said, nodding at Lily. "And you're right."

"I know everything about Kinsey," Lily said, nodding and crossing her arms over her chest.

"So you know that she's dating Hunter Lowen?" Ellery asked, raising an eyebrow.

I closed my eyes. Lily literally started to bounce up and down in her chair, letting out a scream that was the most dramatic thing that I had ever heard. "Stop! We're in a restaurant!" I said, holding up my hands over my face.

"You're dating Hunter? What?" Lily demanded, slapping her hands on the table and leaning forward into my face. "How dare you have news like this and not tell me!"

"I'm not dating Hunter!" At least, not officially. Not yet.

Ellery leaned forward towards Lily. "She has his sweatshirt on her bedroom floor."

"You're sleeping with Hunter?" Lily's mouth fell completely open.

"No!" I shook my head. I couldn't think about *that* right now. Way, way too much.

"Girls, is everything okay?" the waitress asked, coming over and looking at our table.

"Sorry," Lily said quickly, clapping her hands together. "Can I have the strawberry crepe with extra ice cream and extra whipped cream and extra chocolate sauce?"

"I'll have that, but add Nutella," Ellery said, leaning forward.

Lily's mouth fell open again. "You're a genius, Ellery! Why didn't I think of that!"

"I'll – " I glanced down at the menu again. Maybe it was the fact that we were talking about Hunter that was making my stomach churn, but I didn't feel that hungry all of a sudden. "I'll just have the Caesar salad."

Ellery and Lily both looked at me. "And she'll have the pizza crepe too," Ellery added, looking up at the waitress. "She needs it for our run later. And don't tell me that you're not running with me, Kinsey."

Yeah, I hated my friends sometimes.

"And please don't tell me that you're trying to lose weight now that you're dating Hunter Lowen. Or sleeping with Hunter Lowen," Lily said, leaning towards me across the table. "Are you okay?"

"I'm just not hungry!" It was the butterflies in my stomach. I was too happy to eat, if there was such a thing.

"Lily, you're getting us off track. Kinsey, start from the beginning, please." Ellery laid a hand on Lily's forearm, and they shared a conspiratorial glance.

I wasn't a huge fan of the fact that my two separate friends were now ganging up on me. It would have been easier if they had just stayed in their separate lanes on this one. "I went out with Hunter last week and I think that he might be kind of like me," I said finally.

"He spent all of the party last night with you, Kinsey. He literally gave you his sweatshirt," Ellery said, leaning forward towards me. "You were wearing his clothes."

"I don't want to get ahead of myself, okay?" I said finally, looking in between the two of them. I couldn't ruin things with Hunter. I actually liked him.

"That is valid," Ellery said.

Lily shook her head. "Not valid. I am your best friend, and I demand answers."

I had no more answers for her. I had no idea what was going on with Hunter. Or maybe, I had an idea, but I couldn't quite believe it. "Ellery, why don't you tell us about Max instead," I said, turning towards her and hoping to change the topic.

"Max is nice," Ellery said, staring down at her smoothie and swirling her straw in it. "I mean, I don't know what's going on there. He has so much in his head all the time, and he's one of those guys who seems like he's always off with the team, and he's kind of shy."

"Show me pictures," Lily said, tapping on Ellery's phone. She turned back towards me. "You're only getting out of that because I know that I can find any one of the fan blogs of Hunter Lowen."

The fact that I liked a guy who had fan blogs was getting weirder and weirder.

"It seemed like you and Max were getting along well last night," I volunteered. At least before Max had gotten distracted challenging me and Hunter to giant Jenga again.

"Max wasn't focused on making sure that I didn't get knocked into a pool. And he didn't make sure that he went and got me out of the pool when I did get knocked ina" Ellery replied.

"You got knocked into a pool? What kind of party was this, and why the hell didn't you tell me about it?" Lily demanded.

I glanced in between the two of them. "Hunter and I won a bunch of Jenga games, and after the first one, Logan knocked me into the pool."

"Logan is also very hot," Lily said, nodding. "This is good. Was he doing it to make Hunter jealous?"

"No, he was doing it because he was mad that I beat them in Jenga," I replied. "Would you stop trying to make this into a teenage drama?"

"You know that I watch a lot of Netflix, and it teaches me a lot about the human condition," Lily replied. "One of the things that I have learned is that knocking someone into a pool is usually a reflection of a larger tension in their relationship."

"Hunter helped her out of the pool," Ellery added. "And then he got all romantic with her and pushed hair out of her face and everything."

"Seriously, we can stop talking about this now." It was like hearing it in someone else's voice made it so much more real for me. I knew that Hunter had acted caring and everything when I had been there and trying to get out of the pool, but part of me still wanted to see it as a friendly thing. I had saved him from having to jump into the pool, and so he had been nice to me. Nothing romantic here. No butterflies needed.

But when Ellery and Lily talked about it, it made it sound like I was in the middle of a high school drama soon to be premiering. And then the butterflies started doing loops.

"Can we talk about Max some more? Or running training? Or what classes you're taking next year?" I asked, deciding that it was time to change the subject to literally anything else. "Or Lily, do you have news?"

"Of course I don't have news. I've spent the last months at the beach with my younger siblings, who are too young to do anything interesting. Come on. I'm living through you right now." Lily took a giant bite of her crepe. "Over to you, Ellery."

"I don't know with Max," Ellery said, looking down at her plate. "I think it was good. We talked for a whistle last night."

"You were talking the entire time until he challenged us to Jenga," I said.

"*Us?*" Lily demanded.

"Me and Hunter. Calm down."

"Oh my god, you just referred to you and Hunter Lowen as an us. I can't even get over this," Lily said, pressing her hands together into a prayer position.

"If you are going to keep reacting like this to everything I say, I'm literally putting your name down for the fall play auditions whether you like it or not," I said, reaching for my water.

Fortunately, our food arrived, and the pounds of ice cream and Nutella that arrived for Ellery and Lily were enough to distract them from further questions about Hunter. Maybe that should have been my strategy all along, to supply them with enough sugar that they would forget about me.

"How is it so hot already? They should really turn up the air conditioning more in this place," Ellery said, glancing up at the wall of the café, as though that would magically make the air conditioning turn out.

"Nah. The best part about summer is that you can have ice cream for breakfast, and no one can stop you because it's hot out," Lily replied, sticking her fork into her crepe. "You should ask Kinsey her feelings on air conditioning. She has lots of feelings on air conditioning."

"Your house was actually pretty hot this morning," Ellery said, looking over at me. "Is that why you're always dehydrated? You're sweating all of the weight off because your house is a billion degrees?"

"No, it's because it's an old house and we don't have air conditioning." I shook my head. "And anyway, I'd rather be too warm than too cold. Like, when I got ice cream with Hunter, his car was – "

Lily dropped her forks on her crepe and stared at me. Oh dear. "Sorry, you were complaining about the temperature in Hunter's car?" Lily asked, leaning forward towards me, picking her fork back up and pointing it at me in a rather threatening way. "When were you in Hunter's car?"

I stared at the two of them, a sinking feeling in my stomach. I was going to have to tell the entire story from the beginning. There was no way out of it now. "Okay. You guys might need to order a second round of breakfast, and I'm going to tell this story without any interruptions."

At the end of this story, Lily and Ellery seemed to just stare at each other, having a conversation that was clearly about what a terrible friend I was that I had tried to keep that a secret. "You know, you broke all of the rules of best friend-ness by not immediately texting me these details," Lily said.

"Sorry," I said again. "I just wanted to see where things went before I made a big deal out of it."

"I get that, but he obviously likes you," Ellery said, reaching for her spoon. The waitress brought over the giant bowl of ice cream that they'd ordered mid-story.

"I don't know," I said, but there was a twisting in my stomach that told me I was wrong.

Hunter Lowen liked me. I know that now. Hunter was actually acting like he was my boyfriend.

"You like him, too, right?" Ellery asked, glancing over at Lily.

"Why wouldn't she like him? He's literally the hottest guy to exist in the entire state, and he goes to your school, and he seems like he's not as much of an asshole as most people make him out to be." Lily shook her head. "You cannot mess this thing up, Kinsey."

"Thanks." Not that that was helpful advice, because I obviously knew that.

"No, but I mean, if you date Hunter Lowen, it's not like you can change your mind later and start dating someone else," Lily said, leaning towards me. "There is no guy who is going to cross Hunter Lowen if Hunter decides that he wants to date you. If it gets out that you're dating Hunter, then you're going to be seen as Hunter's girlfriend. Done. The movie is finished."

"She has a point," Ellery said, pointing towards Lily with her fork. "Hunter is making it obvious to everyone that he likes you, and all of the other guys who might like you now have to come out of the woodwork, or they're going to lose their chance."

"I am not some kind of prize that people claim at a party because they can call dibs on it," I said. "And anyway, I don't think Hunter's that kind of guy. He's nice, and he seems to actually care about me."

Which was a weird concept. I knew everything that the rumor mill said about Hunter, and it wasn't nice. He was a guy who most girls stayed away from because they didn't want to have their hearts broken, didn't want to see their reputations at school trampled when Hunter moved on.

But he just seemed kind of normal to me. Normal with a dose of romance in him, at least. He had given me his sweatshirt, and taken me out to pizza, and now –

My phone vibrated, and I pulled it out of my pocket as Lily and Ellery were momentarily distracted by the ice cream in the middle of the table. It was Hunter again, this time with a picture of the same black lab with a lacrosse ball in its mouth. *I literally have spent all morning tossing balls for my dog to catch. I don't know if this counts as practice.*

I smiled down at it, snapping a picture of the ice cream bowl in the middle of the table so that Ellery and Lily couldn't see me do it. *I'm sitting here eating ice cream for breakfast. I don't think this counts as sports practice either.*

What would your stepfather say to that? He texted back. *That's a lot of dairy that's really going to hurt your running performance.*

I bit my tongue to keep from laughing as Lily's eyes narrowed. "What are you laughing at?" she demanded. "Are you texting Hunter Lowen at the table?"

"Maybe," I replied, sticking my phone back in my pocket and trying to keep the smile off my face.

OF ALL THE things that Brian Senior had bought my mom, the car was the most obnoxious.

One of the first times that Brian Senior had taken me out to dinner, he'd insisted on showing off the fact that the car could drive itself. "Look, Kinsey," he'd said, dramatically taking his hands off the steering wheel as my mom watched, beaming at him. "Isn't this so futuristic?"

"I can watch YouTube, thanks," I had replied. Sadly, that had not stopped the comments, and I now heard his voice in the back of my head every time we got into it.

Today, at least, he wasn't in the car with us. "Are you sure that you don't want to drive?" my mom asked. The car was going towards a boutique two towns over, where we were going to go so that my mom and I could try on dresses for the upcoming wedding.

I was not pleased about this. At least Elise hadn't been able to come, because I had no desire to spend any time with my soon to be stepsister. It was going to be tough enough to get through a day of my mom saying nice things about the most boring guy in the world without having to also be nice to Elise. Elise would sniff at my outfits and make comments about how I shouldn't wear a certain color. It was like she was trying to be cutting without actually being funny.

I leaned my head back against the headrest and closed my eyes. "No thanks. I'm good."

"I wish I'd had this car when you were learning to drive. It would have made things so much less stressful for me." She looked over at me, resting her hand on my shoulder. "That was a joke, Kinsey."

"I wasn't a bad driver," I replied. I was definitely better than Lily, who had failed her first driving test because she'd almost run over the instructor. She'd forgotten her car was in reverse.

"But the car drives itself! I would have been able to sign that little piece of paper telling them that you'd done all of your fifty hours or whatever or driving, and I wouldn't have been lying, and I wouldn't have feared for my life every time you got behind the wheel."

"Very funny, Mom." I rolled my eyes.

She smiled back at me. "I'm so happy that you're coming and doing this with me."

I nodded, a lump forming in my throat. It was easy to be an asshole to Brian Senior, because he invited you to be an asshole back to him. Anyone who talked that much about his diet and his training was an asshole.

We pulled off the highway, and my mom parked the car in front of the dress boutique that she'd picked out. My mom had been worried that there would be far too many choices if we tried to go to a normal store and pick out a dress, so she'd picked one store and decided that we were going to get everything there.

It almost reminded me of my old mom, but old mom would have probably had us go first to the thrift store and try everything on. New mom was going to put all of this on Brian Senior's credit card.

My mom pushed open the door to the bridal boutique, and a woman immediately came out to greet us. "It's so lovely to meet you in person after speaking on the phone so many times," she gushed over my mom. Another woman followed her with a literal silver tray with cappuccinos on them. "And we made sure to have coffee ready for you!"

I was not going to look at any prices in this store, that was for sure.

We walked to the back of the store, where there was a whole set up waiting for us. There were two chairs and a giant set of mirrors, a few measuring tapes lying around.

"My daughter is going to be my maid of honor," my mom said, putting her hand on my shoulder and smiling at the women around us.

I smiled and nodded. I was going to smile through it and pretend that I was just so excited about everything. The women brought out the first rack of dresses. "We know that you mentioned that your colors are going to be gray and green, and so we wanted to find some dresses for your daughter that would reflect the theme," the first woman said, looking at my mom.

"Kinsey. My name is Kinsey," I said, leaning towards them and giving a little bit of a wave.

"Kinsey. What a lovely name," the woman replied, ignoring the fact that she clearly hadn't been using my name the entire time we'd been here.

"Why don't we get started trying some things on?" the woman asked, clapping her hands together. Part of me wanted to ask for her name, but the bigger, pettier part of me wasn't going to give her that satisfaction.

My mom looked over at me. "I thought that we could even get the same style for our dresses. We've got the same body shape, so the same things should look good on us. And we're in this together."

We were not in this together. My mom was in this, and I was being dragged kicking and screaming into this. "Sure."

I stepped into the fitting room and tried on the first dress. The green and gray color didn't do wonders for my skin tone, or for my general feeling about the upcoming wedding.

My phone buzzed, and I glanced down at it. *What are you up to?*

It was Hunter. I snapped a picture of me standing in front of the mirror, wearing the extremely ugly dress. *Wedding dress shopping. Save me.*

We've only been going out for a few weeks, don't you think that's a little early?

I snorted in response, but it took a few moments for the message to sink in. Going out. Hunter thought that we were going out. Not that we were just meeting up sometimes to hang out, or seeing each other at parties, or whatever.

Nope. He thought that we were serious enough with each other that he was going to make a joke about me buying a wedding dress.

Okay, I was not going to freak out about this. Maybe only a little bit. Not enough that I was going to scare the store attendants. Deep breath.

I stared at the phone again. Okay, I had to come up with a response. Something funny, something to show him that I could do this banter thing just as well as he could. And I was not going to text him back heart emojis, even though I was pretty sure that mine was on the verge of exploding right now.

It's all a long game to get Chrissy, I texted back. *I want a running buddy.*

He sent back the tongue out emoji, then *You could have just asked about the running buddy thing.*

You'd let me borrow your dog? I typed back.

"Kinsey? Can I see?" my mom asked from outside of the changing cabin.

"It's horrible," I called back. "I'm going to try the next one."

There was a little bit of a sigh, then, "Are you sure that I can't see for myself that it's terrible?"

I was in the middle of making very important decisions about how to send properly flirtatious texts. I didn't know if I could deal with my mom at the same time. I closed my eyes for a second, then pulled open the curtain. "See?"

"That is pretty terrible," my mom agreed, looking up

and down. The dress managed to be too tight in the hips and too big everywhere else, making me look like the Pillsbury Dough Boy in a corset. "You look like a satin sack."

That was a lot nicer than what I would have said about myself. "Thanks, Mom. Always great when I need a self-esteem boost."

She laughed. "You should have seen me in that one. It was worse on me, because I'm older and I'm trying to hide a lot more parts of my body."

I wasn't going to touch that comment. It didn't sound like my mom at all. She was always the one who told me to embrace what I looked like. "Next one?" I asked.

"Next one," my mom agreed.

The next dress was knee length, strapless but with a lace overlay above it. I stepped into it and pulled it up, holding my breath as I scooted the dress over my hips.

Nope. It wasn't going anywhere. "Can I get the size bigger in this one?" I called around the side of the cabin.

"Of course," the attendant said, stepping out at close range and startling me enough that I jumped backwards into the wall. "In just a second. Do you need any help taking that off?"

Nope, this situation was embarrassing enough as it was. "I'm good. I can do this by myself. That means you too, Mom."

"I heard that," my mom called back. "You're never too old to help your daughter pick out clothes."

I rolled my eyes and picked my phone back up. *You can borrow me instead,* Hunter texted.

My stomach flipped again, and the attendant passed

me a dress around the side of the cabin. "Here you go, dear."

"Thanks," I said, resisting the urge to remind her that I was not a small woodland animal. What was it with wedding people calling everyone dear?

Okay, focusing back on the most important things. *Borrow you?* I texted back.

I'll go running with you, and then you don't have to steal my dog for it. And I can help you train to beat the guy who won't eat dairy. Priorities.

"Kinsey? Is your dress on yet?" my mom called from outside. "I have high hopes for this one!"

I had other priorities at the moment, to be honest. I put down my phone and started to unzip the dress. "Give me a second."

I pulled the dress on and looked at myself in the mirror. It actually wasn't all that bad. The dress color, which had looked so awful on the rack, worked well with my hair and my skin, which was starting to tan from the summer sun. And the lace was kind of elegant.

I stepped out of the cabin and looked over towards my mom. "What do you think?" she asked, turning towards me.

She was wearing the same dress, except in white. As much as I didn't want to admit it, it looked absolutely stunning. The dress caught her in all the right places, falling down over her hips, the lace looking delicate but not fusty at the same time. "That's – wow. That's a great dress."

"I think this is the one," she said, turning around to look at her back in the mirror. She stopped and looked at me, nodding. "You look beautiful too, Kinsey. You always do."

I nodded, seeing tears starting to form in the corners of her eyes. The same lump that seemed to be omnipresent for me lately started in my throat again, and I blinked a few times. "Thanks."

She reached out and took both of my hands in hers. "I'm really glad that you came with me. It means a lot. I couldn't do this if you weren't doing it by my side."

I blinked again and nodded. She pulled me in for a hug. "Should we change back into our normal clothes and get lunch?"

I stepped back into the changing cabin, and my phone buzzed again. Hunter. *Okay, so I looked up Brian Senior's times, and he's pretty awful. I can definitely beat him after eating a Chipotle burrito.*

I snorted, blinking back a random tear that had formed in my eye for no reason. It was something about being here with my mom's wedding stuff, with Hunter texting me, with happy and sad and left behind and loved all getting mixed up in my head and spilling over.

I stared down at the phone for a second and then typed a message before I could stop myself. *I don't want to have to go wedding dress shopping with my mom. I hate this whole wedding, and I hate Brian Senior. I just want things to go back to normal.*

"Kinsey?" my mom asked, sticking her head around the corner of the cabin. "All ready?"

I took a deep breath. I wanted to tell her no. But that wasn't me. "Ready."

TEN

"WHAT DO you think about getting lilies in the middle of the table for decoration?" asked the very tall, thin woman who was standing in our kitchen.

It was the wedding planner, who seemed to have materialized out of nowhere. Her hair was bleached and perfectly straightened, and she was tapping intensely on a tablet.

"Is that cliché?" my mom asked.

"It's your wedding, dear," the planner replied, and my mom didn't even seem to blink an eye at the fact that she was being referred to as dear. Normally she would point out that she was in fact not a woodland animal.

Literally, every wedding person I had dealt with so far had called us "dear". They must have had a pact or something.

But she just stayed quiet and nodded. "It is. And I do like lilies."

"I'm heading out," I said, waving to them and pushing

open the door. I had to get out of here before I heard more about flowers. I sat down in Betta, who was faithfully waiting for me in her normal parking spot.

I had to get out of the house. I couldn't just sit there with my mom and a wedding planner talking about things I didn't want to think about. I wanted to get out and think about the normal kinds of things that I'd fill my summer with, not my mom talking about her upcoming wedding,

I stared at my phone. I wanted to text Lily or Ellery, but part of me also didn't want to text them. I'd start ranting about my mom, and it would end up being them asking me about Hunter. I loved them both, but I didn't want to talk about Hunter right now.

Well, there was one person who wouldn't make me talk about Hunter. Hunter himself. *Want to go to the beach?* I texted.

Sounds awesome. I'm bringing my dog, he replied immediately.

Twenty minutes later, I parked Betta at the beach and sat down on the hood, leaning my head back towards the sun. Beach might have been a generous word - it was a town park on Long Island Sound, with a tiny sandy area that was always packed with families. We ran here all the time for cross-country, and I probably should have gone for a run here today.

A car pulled up beside me just as I was debating whether to get my book out of the backseat and wait for Hunter on the beach. He parked his car next to mine. "Hey," he said, walking over and waving towards me. He opened the backseat and grabbed a leash, then reached into the backseat, letting a dog out. "Whoa, buddy," he said as a giant black lab started bounding towards me. "Down!"

I took a step back, tripping slightly and falling back into Betta. The dog leapt up to greet me, placing its paws on my chest. "Down, Chrissy!" Hunter said, yanking the leash back towards him. "Shit. Sorry, Kins."

Was that a nickname? Had Hunter Lowen just given me a nickname, implying that he was going to be using my name so often that he needed a shorter version of it for himself? "Is this your dog that really likes chasing balls?" I asked.

At the mention of the word balls, Chrissy started to run around in circles, and Hunter lifted the leash up so that she wouldn't trip over herself. "We have to call them throw things when she's in earshot. She loves balls too much."

Okay, there was a joke in the back of my head that I wasn't going to make. "Seems like your kind of dog."

He laughed. "Mom always jokes that the reason I'm so good at lacrosse is that I've had to spend so much time throwing and retrieving things for this one. She will never pass up an opportunity to chase after something."

"That's the secret behind all of your athletic skills?" I asked, reaching down and patting Chrissy on the head. She had calmed down a little and was now nuzzling me with her nose.

He nodded, slinging the leash around his wrist. "It's just having a dog who really loves practicing with you. Come on, Chrissy."

We started to walk towards the beach, a bit of a breeze

blowing in off the water. Chrissy ran ahead of us, chasing her tail.

"Apparently she's like seventy in dog years, but you would never know it," Hunter said, nodding towards his dog. "You tell her that you're going for a walk, or that you're going to see one of the small gray animals that run up trees – "

"You mean – "

Before I could say the word, Hunter clapped his hand over my mouth. "Sorry," he said, pulling his hand away almost as fast as he had put it there. "She's very sensitive to some words. She will literally tear my arm off in pursuit."

"She looks way too sweet for that," I said. Not that I'd ever had a dog, because my mom knew too many facts about the communicable diseases in dog poop, but I'd always wanted one.

"Nope," Hunter replied, shaking his head. "Not at all. She is the kind of dog who will stop at nothing if there is a thing to chase after. She is a total menace."

I reached down and scratched her head. She leaned against my legs, rubbing her body against me.

"Hey, she likes you," Hunter said, reaching down and scratching behind her head. His finger grazed my knee as he pulled it back. "She doesn't like most of my friends, so that's cool."

"How does she not like your friends? They all play – the same sport where you throw things that you can catch," I said, hoping that I had avoided all of her trigger words.

Hunter smiled at me, leaning down to give her another head pat. "She's finicky. She has certain people who she likes and certain people who she doesn't like. And if you're on the second list, she just will not interact with you unless you have one of those special round things."

I reached down and scratched Chrissy's head again as we started the walk towards the loop around the beach. Hunter glanced at one of the people biking by us, their feet pumping the pedals of a ridiculously fancy looking bike for just taking around the local park. "I was supposed to bike across the country this summer," he said, nodding towards the bike.

I turned towards him. "Even with all of the stuff that you have to do for soccer and lacrosse?"

Apparently that latter word was interesting enough to Chrissy that she stopped and started to walk back towards me. I reached down and scratched the top of her head again. Hunter nodded. "Yeah. My best friend from when I was a kid and I were supposed to go."

"Who?" I asked, turning towards him. I had assumed that Hunter's friends were all on the soccer team at school, because that's how most things went. Your friends were the people you spend so much time with at school, not people who didn't go to our school.

"Matt. He moved when we were kids, so he's an hour away now," Hunter replied.

"That sucks," I said, looking over at him. "My friend Lily also moved away during elementary school, and she's fifteen minutes away now. But it's enough that I feel like I never see her during the year."

Hunter nodded. "It does suck. We see each other like

once a month, maybe. He gave up soccer, too, so we really never see each other."

"That's better than I do. Lily and I only hang out when she's not gone for the summer and we don't have school. So why aren't you out biking?" I asked, looking back over towards him. Hunter didn't seem like the kind of person to let something stop him if he wanted to do something.

Hunter looked out towards the water. "Matt's mom died last year."

"Oh my god, I'm sorry," I said quickly. I couldn't imagine a world where my mom was gone and there wasn't even the chance that I could get her back at some point.

"Remember when I was gone from school for a week last year?" he asked, looking back towards me.

The rumor mill had had a field day with that one. Hunter had vanished for a week, and as part of that, our lacrosse team had taken the only loss of the entire season. The coach had been furious and made all kinds of ridiculous threats about what he was going to do if Hunter left again.

"Yeah, I do." The explanations I had heard had been that Hunter had gotten some model in New York pregnant, that he'd gotten into a dramatic love triangle, or he'd been scouted by a semi-pro soccer team in Europe.

He pulled Chrissy's leash back towards himself, then patted her head. "I drove out to spend the week with Matt. He was going through some shit, and I couldn't leave him alone."

"That's an understatement." I couldn't even imagine.

My mom was just getting married, and I was still having a hard time dealing with it. "That's a lot to deal with."

He ran his free hand through his hair. "I wanted to bike across the country this summer, but he wanted to stay. And you know, it's his decision. He needs to deal with things however it's going to work for him."

I nodded. There wasn't anything that I could say to that, and words felt too small for something that was that painful. "So," Hunter continued, seeming to be happy to talk about all of this, to say it all out loud, "we canceled that trip, and now I'm just going to lacrosse practice and soccer practice. I was going to go to camp this summer and really work on my skills, but I canceled all that because I thought I'd be with Matt."

"And that's okay with your coach?" My coach would have a heart attack if I told her that I hadn't trained this summer, and I was nowhere near as important to my team as Hunter was to his.

"He can't really do anything," Hunter replied, shrugging. "He needs me on the team more than I need him to want me on the team. We won the state championship last year. I broke the state record for points scored as a sophomore. He can't kick me off the team. There are too many parents who want to have a state championship on their college application."

Of course Hunter was able to just do this. Of course the coach would just let him take off in the middle of the season. I'd be too terrified to even think of asking my coach. That was Hunter privilege. Just do what you want, because you know everyone else needs you more than you need them.

He stopped, then turned towards what I thought was a thicket of trees in the middle of the park. "Want to go back there?" he asked.

"What are you talking about?" I asked. I'd never been back in that section of the park, and I'd run here with the team a lot.

"There's actually an old house ruin back there," he said, starting to walk into the tree thicket on something that was only vaguely a path. I followed him, ducking under a tree branch that snapped back and threatened to hit me in the face.

"I have lived here all my life, and I have never seen an old house back here," I replied.

Then of course, I took another couple of steps and walked into a clearing with a few rocks around the ground. "This is the old house?" I asked, turning towards him.

"See?" Hunter said, pointing down at the rocks on the ground.

I was not seeing, no. "Those are rocks. That is not a house."

He pointed to a different rock, as though that would make it clearer. "That's the foundation of a house from like three hundred years ago. Isn't that cool?"

"I would have thought that it was just a pile of rocks," I replied, looking down at it again. It was somewhat cool that it was a foundation for a house, but it just sort of looked like a rock pile to me.

Hunter took a step closer to me. "You have to use a little imagination, and then it's exactly like a house."

I shook my head, looking up at him, my breath catching in my throat. "Still don't know if I totally believe you."

He looked down at me for a second, then said, "Can I kiss you?"

I stared back up at him. "Did you – did you ask me to walk back here so you could ask me that?"

"Potentially, yeah," he replied, grinning down at me. My entire body seemed to react to his smile, my back starting to arch towards him. "Not that the house ruins aren't cool and all. So is that a yes or a no?"

"That's a yes," I said, and he slipped Chrissy's leash around his arm, taking a step closer towards me and wrapping his arm around my back. He bent down towards me, his lips pressing onto mine and the butterflies taking on my stomach.

Oh god. This was even better than I had remembered from the time in his car.

His hand skimmed up my side. I shivered slightly, pressing closer to him, wanting more and more of Hunter. One hand started to brush my hair back from my face, his lips moving over mine. My knees felt like they were going to buckle from excitement.

I was kissing Hunter Lowen, and it felt amazing.

I pressed closer to him, and his arm around my back tightened. I could feel myself melting into him, my entire body trying to turn to get closer and closer to Hunter.

And then he pulled back from me, his arm around my back loosening, but not in time to keep me from falling slightly forward into him. Chrissy was running towards the side of the thicket, starting to jump up and down. "Damn it, dog," Hunter muttered, pulling her leash back towards him. "I was in the middle of something."

I laughed slightly, the feeling of Hunter's lips still on mine. "Did she get distracted?"

"Or she was jealous," he replied, taking a step back closer towards me, his hand going back to my side.

I might pass out from the amount of adrenaline in my body right now. I could swear that I was barely able to stand up. I was definitely not able to focus on anything except for Hunter. This was the worst and the best at the same time.

"She's a much better lacrosse player than I am. I don't know what she'd have to be jealous of," I said, reaching down and patting her. She'd run back over to me and was sitting at my feet down, looking up.

Hunter laughed, the hand that wasn't holding Chrissy's leash reaching towards me. "Obviously your sense of humor."

"Obviously," I replied, smiling at him. My stomach flipped again.

He reached over and wrapped his fingers around mine for a second, squeezing my hand. "So should we try that again?"

ELEVEN

"I AM SO happy that my mom didn't make me spend the Fourth of July at the beach," Lily said, stretching out across my living room couch. Her mom had a conference, so after a lot of begging, Lily had finagled her way into coming back. It was weird that Lily was more excited about the suburbs than the beach, but she'd told me a hundred times that all the action was here this summer.

My mom had always celebrated the Fourth of July together. We'd go to the parties in the middle of town to celebrate, and then we'd head out to the fireworks, watching the fireworks go off while we toasted the summer. We'd smuggle in a little can of gas so that we could toast marshmallows over a mini fire. We'd almost gotten caught so many times. But this year, Brian Senior had a friend who was hosting a party, so my mom was taken.

To make it worse, Hunter had been busy for the past few days. He still texted me, sent me pictures of Chrissy doing stupid things in the yard and of whatever he was eating. I hadn't been able to see him in person, though. It bothered me more than I wanted to admit. Obviously I was cool about him being busy. It happened. I was able to do the whole delayed gratification thing.

But I wanted to see him again. I really wanted to see him again.

"Do you and Ellery want to go to the town fireworks?" Lily asked, snapping me out of thinking about Hunter.

"You're cool if I invite Ellery? And you know that I'm always down for fireworks," I replied. Maybe my mom wasn't going to make it to the fireworks, but at least I would.

"Of course. I think she's cool," Lily said, flopping back on my bed.

Thank goodness. Last summer, I'd tried to invite Lily out with Jenna, and it had gone horribly. I should have known that they wouldn't get along – Lily wanted to point everything out, and Jenna wanted to act like she didn't notice anything. "Are you seriously friends with *her*?" both of them had asked me afterwards.

I texted Ellery to ask, setting my phone aside as I waited for her to text back. Lily was lying on my bed, staring up at the ceiling, looking lost in thought.

My phone vibrated, and I reached towards it. "What'd Ellery say?" Lily asked.

But the text turned out that it wasn't from Ellery. It was from someone else entirely. Hunter: *I'm having a Fourth of July party at my place while my parents are at – wait for it...*

Don't make me guess. The same party as Brian Senior, I texted back.

Yeah. You want to come to my place?

I absolutely wanted to do that. I glanced over at Lily. *Is it okay if I bring friends?*

Kins, it's a party. What do you think?

I smiled slightly, shaking my head. There was something about the way that everything seemed to be easier around Hunter. Like of course I could bring friends to the party. Of course.

"She hasn't texted back yet, but I'm sure she'll be down," I said. I looked down at my phone and loved the message he'd sent.

"And you want to get ice cream after? Because then we should make sure to park super close to the entrance so that we can actually get out afterwards. I speak from experience here," she said, propping herself up on her elbows.

"I can't," I said, glancing down at my phone again. No more texts yet. "That was Hunter who just texted. He invited us over to his place."

I tried to keep the little bit of pride out of my voice but couldn't. Not that I wanted to be the person who bragged about dating someone, but I had gotten us all an invite to his party. Hunter wanted to hang out with me. Me specifically.

"I thought you'd want to hang out with me because I've been at the beach most of the summer," Lily said, looking up at me.

"I do want to hang out with you. You're invited, too," I said. I glanced down at my phone. No more texts from Hunter.

"Yeah, but you want to go to Hunter's party," she replied, looking at me and tilting her head to the side.

I set my phone down on my dresser. "You like Hunter, though. And he's super cool."

"I've never actually met him, but yes, I am sure that he's cool," she said, pushing her hair back with one hand. "It's just I thought that the two of us could hang out."

"We will hang out. We're literally going to the fireworks together." Obviously, we were hanging out there. It wasn't like I was trying to dump her to hang out with Hunter. But why couldn't I have both?

"I know. It's just – usually we can't hang out because it's Jenna, and you finally have a summer free from her and now it's Hunter," Lily said, pulling a pillow towards herself.

"I don't pick Jenna over you," I said, hearing the sharpness in my voice before I could stop it. It was Lily who'd moved all those years ago. I'd been so lonely at school until Jenna had decided to be my friend.

"Yeah, you do. I know that you like Hunter a lot, and he sounds great, but you've been Jenna's person for the past two years. Now that she's finally not here, you immediately turn into Hunter's person." She pulled my pillow up in front of her, resting it under her chest, and stared at me.

That wasn't fair. If I was really just Hunter's person, I would have just gone over to his house to prepare for the party. I'd be seeing him now, not waiting until after the fireworks. I'd get to spend time with him alone before the whole party started.

"I wanted to hang out with you and Ellery tonight, not get stuck watching you run around at a party," she continued. "It's not like we're going to talk when we're there. It's not worth coming back from the beach for this."

"Are you kidding? Of course it's worth coming back from the beach for this." What was Lily even talking about? This was Hunter's party. It was going to be the biggest party of the summer. "I thought you said that you wanted to have a magic summer and be the cool person who actually goes to parties."

"Yeah, and?" she asked, hugging the pillow closer to herself.

"Lily, this is your chance!" The more excited I sounded, the better this conversation was going to go. "You always tell me that the boys at my school are so much more attractive than the ones at yours, and they're all going to be there tonight."

"I don't know," she said, looking down at my bed and biting her lip.

"I know all the soccer boys now," I said, ignoring that that might be a bit of an extension of the truth. "I can totally introduce you. If you want to fall in love and have a movie summer so badly, why wouldn't you want to go to this party?"

She stared at me for a second, still hugging the pillow to her chest. My phone buzzed, and I looked down. Ellery this time. *Meet you at fireworks in 10?*

"That was Ellery," I said, standing up. "Let's go."

"SO YOU'RE SUGGESTING that we sneak a gas canister into an event where people are exploding colorful bombs in the sky?" Ellery asked, raising her eyebrows. We were standing outside of my car, holding a bag that was full of what I thought were Fourth of July essentials.

I hadn't been expecting this much skepticism when I pitched them on my idea to replicate my mom's traditions with me. I had been assuming that they would agree pretty quickly when I mentioned smores.

"This sounds like a terrible idea on so many fronts," Lily agreed, peering into the bag I was holding.

"Lily, you know my mom and I have done this every year! Why are you agreeing with Ellery now?" I asked.

"Because she's right?" Lily offered, shrugging her shoulders. "I mean, I love you, but you're wrong about this one."

I shook my head, then stuck the bag on my shoulder. "It's a great idea. You get to have smores while watching fireworks."

"And then you also might die in a fiery explosion, at which point you become a smore," Ellery replied. "Not a good plan."

"A great plan," I object. The two of them exchanged glances. "And we need snacks, therefore smores."

"We do absolutely need snacks," Ellery said, looking in between us. "I agree with that. It turns out that my mom is really good at snacks." She pulled Tupperware out of a bag and set it dramatically down in front of us on the car hood.

"Is that a cheese plate in a Tupperware?" Lily asked, picking up the container and opening the lid.

Ellery shook her head. "Nope. This is a Tupperware cheese array. Because you actually need different cheese and different arrangements when it's in a square container than when it's laid out on a board. My mom is really into this."

"Almost scarily," Lily agreed, poking a piece of cheese.

"Don't ever let me become an adult. I'll get really into things like cheese boards and lose my will to live," Ellery said, pulling out a wad of napkins from her bag.

"Is that worse than fanfiction? Because that was Lily's big thing last year," I asked, locking the car and starting the walk towards the fireworks. We were going to sit out with the rest of the town for a while watching bombs in the sky, as Ellery called them, then go over to Hunter's party.

"There is nothing embarrassing about fanfiction. Most of Western literature is really just fanfic of old Greek stuff," Lily said, reaching for the cheese. "It gets dismissed by art people because it's done by teenagers on the internet instead of by angsty white dudes in their twenties. Don't give into the stereotypes."

"Even if you are dating one," Ellery interrupted, and Lily gave her a high five.

"No one should have let the two of you hang out. You are a menace together," I replied, walking through the gates and spotting a place where there was still room to spread out a blanket. I beelined over there and spread out my blanket, making sure to claim it before someone else could. Lily and Ellery were not hustling enough for the good spots.

"Do you not have friends? This is what friends do," Lily said, sitting down on the blanket and cracking up the first container full of cheese. "Come on."

My phone vibrated with a text from Hunter, a picture of his backyard decked out for the party to come. He'd strung up lights all around the pool, and it actually looked good. Something that I never thought I'd say about his decorating prowess. He'd definitely made the team help. It seemed like a rite of passage for people on the junior varsity team to have to do the party prep.

I stretched my legs out on the blanket and stared up at the sky. It was a beautiful night, one of those early summer nights that I absolutely loved. Not that I wanted to read too much into the weather, but it felt like the kind of night where anything could happen, in a good way.

"Try this," Elley said, passing me a piece of cheese across the blanket. "It's the best cheese that I have with me right now."

My phone buzzed again, and I sent a picture of the cheese to Hunter. *My snacks are better,* I sent back.

After the fireworks show, when the families around us started to gather up their bags and head out, Ellery nodded towards me. "Time for part two?"

I nodded, my stomach flipping. This was going to be the first time that I had gone to a party with Lily and Hunter in the same place. And it was going to be the first time that I was going over to Hunter's, even if it was just a party.

Hunter apparently knew how to throw a party. Last year, he co-hosted with most of the soccer team, and it had been legendary, in Jenna's words. I hadn't gone, because I'd had my Fourth of July plans with my mom. And to me, that was far more important than going to some high school party.

This year, everything was different. I was going to show up to Hunter Lowen's party with a personal invitation.

We climbed into Betta, and I started the drive towards Hunter's, my stomach flipping more and more as we drove. I was actually going to do this. I was going to go to a party at Hunter Lowen's – well, maybe not girlfriend exactly, but his person.

"Where are we going to park?" Lily asked, staring out the window as we drove up. Hunter's house was off the road, set back on a long driveway. "How does anyone wear cute shoes to this?"

Just as if on cue, my phone vibrated. *You can park up at the house. I saved you a spot.*

I glanced over at Lily, grinning. "I think I might have that taken care of."

We pulled up to the house. We stepped out of the car, and I locked it behind me. I glanced back at them, and we headed over towards the front door, me a step ahead of Lily and Ellery.

I took a deep breath as we stood in front of the door, staying up at the giant entrance. "Ready?" I asked, looking in between Lily and Ellery. Ellery raised an eyebrow, as though she was telling me that I was already being extra.

I was being a little extra. But this was basically the biggest party of the summer, and my boyfriend was throwing it. My *boyfriend.*

We pushed open the door and walked into Hunter's house. There were already plenty of people here, all standing around with their drinks. Someone glanced towards me for a second, their eyes staying on me, before they looked away.

"Do you want to go find a drink?" Ellery asked, looking at me and Lily.

Lily glanced around the room, as though she was checking for anyone she knew. "Yeah."

I wanted to find Hunter. I didn't want to text him again and tell him that I was here, because I'd already been texting him all night. I wouldn't be desperate. I'd get a drink with Lily and Ellery first, and maybe I could even find the soccer guys to introduce Lily first.

We walked into the kitchen. Ellery reached in the fridge and passed us both spiked seltzers, clinking them as we popped them open. "Which one of us isn't going to be drinking tonight?" I asked, looking in between the two of them. "Because someone has to drive Betta home."

Ellery rolled her eyes. "We can call an Uber or something. Betta is basically parked in Hunter's garage."

"I know you love your car, but I also don't think anyone is going to pick the twenty year old Honda Civic if they're going to commit grand theft auto," Lily said, looking over at me over the top of her seltzer.

That was a valid point. "Let's go see if there's anything going on," Ellery said, starting to walk into one of the other rooms. I didn't see the soccer guys in there, but I wasn't going to be that person. Ellery would want to find Max anyway, so we'd find them sooner or later.

"Want to see if we can get in on one of these games?" Lily asked, nodding towards a couple of games that were starting on the other side of the room.

"I – " I paused.

Ellery shot me a look. "Come on. You know that Hunter's around here somewhere, and you can find him any time. He'll probably come find you first. Just text him, and come play a game with us first."

She was right, technically. I just wanted to see Hunter now. "Sure," I said, following her towards the other side of the room.

We pushed through the crowd, and I heard Logan's voice before I saw him. "Yo, Kinsey! Ellery! And other person! Come join us!"

In case I could have missed his voice, he was also waving both arms above his head like an air traffic controller. "Hey, Logan," I said, coming over and punching him lightly on the shoulder.

"Kinsey Greenwood, everyone," he announced, reaching over and holding up my hand like a wrestling announcer. He leaned towards me, raising an eyebrow. "It's truth or dare. Are you guys up for it?"

"Sure," I said, sitting down next to him. I hated truth or dare as much as it was possible to hate a game, but Ellery and Lily already probably thought I was a spoilsport. Logan grinned.

Max was on my other side. "Hey!" he said, grinning at me. Hopefully that excited tone of voice was for Ellery, who glanced at me and then took Max's other side.

Lily got settled on the other side of the circle, meeting my eyes for a second. She was sitting over by Parker and Chase, two of the other guys on the soccer team who were home for the weekend. They were both quite cute. Maybe truth or dare would be her romantic meeting in the subway.

"What's the punishment if I don't take a dare?" I asked Logan, looking over at him.

"You have to take a shot from the bottle in the middle," he said, nodding towards it. "And I can tell you that that stuff is nasty."

"What bet did you lose in the past?" I asked, resisting the urge to check my phone.

"Streaking the girls' soccer team," he replied, shrugging. "I think the dare person thought that it was going to go to another one of the girls on the team, and I wanted to keep my pants on."

I snorted. "What, were you wearing your Superman boxers and scared to show them?"

Max reached over and high fived me. "Kinsey, you're finally learning how to give him shit. Nice work."

Across the circle, Nova, one of the girls on the girls' soccer team, grinned at one of her teammates before tapping something on her phone. "Kiss the person to your right."

Lily glanced at the person to her right. That would be Parker, who was the goalie and objectively quite cute. Maybe this wasn't the worst thing that we could have gotten pulled into.

Nova dramatically placed her phone down in the middle. "It's a random number generator," Max explained. "We were using a bottle for a while, but that felt stupid, and so we moved over to the phone thing."

"And," Logan said, leaning towards me on my other side, "you get to see who's texting whom."

"Are you going to put your phone down? Because I'd love to see who's desperate enough to text you tonight," I said, grinning at Logan again.

"Kinsey, when did you get this sassy?" Max asked, looking at me. His eyes were right on mine for a second, and I looked away. I couldn't let Ellery think there was anything.

"I think I've been hanging out with you guys for too long," I replied. Logan snorted.

The phone number kept running through, then stopped. "And that is," Nova said, snatching her phone from the middle of the circle before anyone could see her texts, "it's Max."

Who was sitting to my left.

Shit. I wasn't going to kiss him. It was just a game, but I couldn't do that to Hunter. I actually had feelings for Hunter. I wasn't going to kiss his friends.

Max glanced over at me and then around the circle. "Can't do it. Spin again."

Thank god.

"What do you mean, you can't do it?" Alessia asked across the circle. "Come on. Kiss Kinsey. You know it's just truth and dare."

My stomach pulled together. This was so awkward. "It doesn't matter if it's in truth or dare. I can't do it," he said again, looking over at me.

Ellery's face pulled together. "That's good, because I don't want you to either," I said, trying to meet Ellery's eyes. She met them for a second and then looked away. She couldn't be mad about me because of the game. I definitely wasn't trying to flirt with Max.

Obviously not, because I was with Hunter.

"You two are so lame," Alessia said, tossing her ponytail over her shoulder. "It's just a game."

"You can say that, but I don't have a death wish," Max said, reaching for the bottle in the middle and unscrewing the cap.

Wait, I thought he wasn't kissing me because he had feelings for Ellery. "Death wish?" I asked, looking over towards him. "What do you mean?"

Max didn't answer, lifting the bottle of vodka to his mouth and taking a long drink. He set the bottle down and then glanced back over at me. "Maybe you shouldn't play."

I stared at him for a second. Was he implying that I was too lame to play the game? But he was the one who hadn't taken the dare.

"Yeah," Logan said, punching me gently on the shoulder. "We love you, Kinsey, but this feels like not your game."

Not that I disagreed with him, but I wanted to be the one to decide that, not him. I cleared my throat and stood up. I glanced back at them, then stood up. This was one of those situations where I could demand answers and seem paranoid, or I could just back out of this politely enough. "I'm going to get another seltzer. Be back later."

I glanced back towards the game as I walked out of the room. Lily was watching me, then looked away and towards Nova. Maybe this would be the chance she needed to actually talk to the boys. I headed back towards the kitchen, glancing around at all of the people who had started streaming in.

I didn't know half of them, and I didn't know if Hunter did either. It was kind of weird how many people just showed up to his house.

"Hey," Ethan said, nodding towards me as I walked into the kitchen. "Kinsey."

"Hey," I said, opening the fridge and looking around for something to bring back to the circle. "Didn't know you were going to be here."

"Of course I was going to be here. It's one of Hunter's parties, and Hutner's parties are always legendary," he replied, leaning back against the counter. "Are you looking for a drink?"

I sighed, shutting the fridge and turning towards him. "I was playing truth or dare over in the living room, but it got awkward."

Ethan grinned at me. "Did they challenge you to run naked across the soccer field after practice? That's my favorite one."

"I thought that's what you had to do because I beat you in Jenga during my first time playing," I said.

He snorted. "I'm never going to let Hunter off the hook for that one. I should have known that you were a ringer."

"I was in the robotics club for a while," I replied. "We learned how to build stuff, and my mom is really into science. I think she's bummed that I didn't become one of those kids who just love dinosaurs."

"What do you love then?" he replied.

I leaned against the fridge. "I like science. I took biology last year, and I actually really like it. It's so interesting, how all of the parts of your body just know how to work together. Like, it's incredible that all of this," I gestured to us, the house, everything around us, "it all came from these little single celled organisms."

"Right," he replied, leaning back against the counter. "I dropped AP Bio for this year. I made too many jokes about asexual reproduction in biology last year, and the teacher wouldn't let me in."

Of course that would be the reason that Ethan got kicked out of class. I rolled my eyes at him. "You are literally the worst. You are even worse than Logan."

"Ouch. So what happened with truth and dare?" he asked. "Did you try to give Hunter a lap dance? Because I did that once, and then I got kicked out. Mostly because I farted in the middle of the lap dance, right in his face."

Ethan might be the most chaotic person I'd ever met. "Nothing like that. Max got challenged to kiss me, and then everyone got super weird about it."

"I understand," Ethan said, nodding. "That makes sense."

"Not that I wanted him to kiss me, obviously, but everyone got so weird about it," I said. I didn't want the reputation of being the spoilsport, and that was definitely the reputation I was getting.

Ethan glanced around the kitchen, then beckoned me closer with one hand. I took a step closer to him and leaned against the counter next to him, then turned and raised my eyebrows at him. "I don't think I'm supposed to tell you this," he said.

"You sound like Jenna. Spit it out."

He snorted. "Ouch. I'm offended. But just so you know, Hunter sort of threatened us today to stay away from you."

"What?" I asked. Hunter didn't threaten people. That wasn't his style. He didn't need to.

Ethan glanced away from me. "Don't hate me when I tell you this."

"Don't hate you or don't hate Hunter?" I asked.

"Yeah, both. So – " He paused and glanced away. "And maybe don't tell the rest of the girls this either?"

"If you're going to tell me something super problematic, I am probably going to tell the girls," I replied, narrowing my eyes at him.

"Okay, okay!" He held up his hands in protest and shook his head. "So there may have been a thing for a while on the team that we referred to as sloppy seconds."

I closed my eyes. "If you were trying to think of something problematic, you are on the right track."

"Look, Hunter has a lot of luck with girls. It's one of the things that we all know about him, right? And the rest of the team doesn't. So sometimes, if there's a girl who likes Hunter, the rest of us swoop in instead. You know. Because Hunter isn't going to actually date anyone," he said, taking a sip of his beer.

My heart was starting to race uncomfortably. This was just proof that the boys were really as gross and awful as I expected all along.

"But the point is, Hunter told us today that you were

totally off-limits. That he really likes you, and that if anyone tries to mess with you, he's going to mess them up." Ethan shook his head. "And none of us have a death wish, so obviously we all listened."

"Hunter told you guys to leave me alone?" I asked, wrinkling my eyebrows. My heart was still beating too fast, and now my stomach was joining it in feeling weird.

"Yep," Ethan replied, nodding. "So you know, after that, it's not like Max is going to be jumping over himself to try to kiss you. Even if he does think you're hot. Hunter would kill him."

"That's – wow," I said, looking down at the floor, then back up at Ethan. "He's really that jealous?"

Ethan stared at me for a second. "Hunter doesn't get jealous. He wins everything. Why would he get jealous?"

I swallowed. I didn't know how to say that I was flattered but also a little bit overwhelmed. I'd suddenly acquired a whole soccer team looking out for me.

"We're his friends. You're the girl he likes," Ethan said, finishing off his beer. "And he knows that we can be a lot. Like, I did throw you in the pool the first time we hung out."

"Right. I think I'm still mad at you about that," I said, looking over at him. "You're lucky that my phone survived, or I might have killed you."

"See?" he said, pointing at me again. "This was Hunter's point. No homicides. Don't mention that I told you this to him, though."

"I won't get you in trouble, don't worry," I replied. "I owe you one. I'm not going to throw you under the bus."

"Thank god," he replied, finishing off his beer and dropping it back onto the counter. "Telling you would probably count as screwing with you. Lowen would kill me. You need another drink?" he asked, nodding towards my now empty can of spiked seltzer.

"Yeah," I replied. "I should probably get one and then go say hi to the people I left playing truth or dare."

"You got kicked out of the game, and you're just going to go back and say hi?" Ethan asked, raising an eyebrow.

"Maybe bring them another round of drinks?" It felt weird to just leave and not do anything after that. I probably should check on Ellery and Lily.

"You don't have to be nice to people who aren't being nice to you," he replied. "You in fact don't have to be nice to people at all."

"Yeah, I don't think I work that way," I said, leaning back against the counter.

He bent down and opened one of the cabinets to reveal a second miniature fridge. "Well, since you're in the circle of trust, this is our stash."

"Your stash?" I asked, bending down to check out the fridge, which was absolutely stuffed with cans of seltzer and beer.

"This is the good stuff, which we always hide away," Ethan explained, passing me a much nicer can of spiked seltzer. "Can't let everyone have it."

"Not as impressive as Max's parents' wine collection," I replied, cracking open the can of seltzer, and clinking it with Ethan. "Cheers."

"Cheers," he replied back, clinking his beer against my seltzer.

"I see Ethan showed you where to get the good stuff," a voice behind me said. I turned to see Hunter standing there, smiling towards me.

It had only been a few days, but it felt like so much longer. It felt like I hadn't seen him in weeks, like I had been on some great journey and I had finally reached the end.

"Hey," I said, my face flushing slightly as I just kept grinning like an idiot. He smiled at me again, reaching his arm around my waist and pulling me towards him. He clicked his beer against mine and then against Ethan's.

"I couldn't let her get stuck with terrible seltzer flavors," Ethan replied. "You'd have been pissed if you came out and saw her drinking, I don't know, pomegranate."

"I don't mind pomegranate," I replied. All of the seltzer was better than beer.

"Low maintenance," Ethan said. Out of the corner of my eye, I could see Hunter grinning down at me again. I looked up at him, my stomach flipping. He reached down and kissed me on the forehead.

Ethan groaned, rolling his eyes. "You guys can skip it with the public displays of affection. We get it."

Hunter responded by resting his chin on the top of my head, tightening his arm around my waist. "Ethan, they're looking for you downstairs. You're up next on the table."

"Sweet," Ethan said, reaching over and giving me a gentle punch on the shoulder. "Kinsey, you're welcome to come join my team if Hunter lets you escape his."

"Not a chance," Hunter said, pulling me even closer to him. "Kinsey's mine."

My heart felt like it was squeezing together at that comment. "Maybe some other time," I said to Ethan. He saluted and walked off.

"Hey again," Hunter said, turning me around to face him. He reached down and kissed me again.

"Hi," I said, my face flushing again.

"I was going to head outside," he said, nodding his head towards the deck in the back of the house. "Want to come with?"

"Of course," I said automatically. He could have asked me to go to Mars with him, and I would have said yes. I just wanted to be where he was.

He grabbed my hand and pulled me towards the door. He opened the door and held it open for me as we slipped out onto the back patio.

"Somehow I thought that you would be dying to get outside into the nice night air," he said, grinning at me again, his eyes seeming to sparkle in the reflection of the lights from the house.

"You make it sound like I only come to these things so that I can escape them and go outside," I replied. "Just so you know, I just spent the whole evening at the town fireworks so that I could get my outside time in before I came to the party."

"Really," he said, his arm sneaking behind my back and pulling me closer. "You prepared to come to a party by going to a town party with a bunch of little kids and their parents."

"Don't you like fireworks?" I asked, looking up at him. "You can't tell me that you didn't want to also go to the fireworks show."

"I don't think I've been to the town fireworks in several years," he replied. "Since like elementary school."

"You're missing out." I leaned into him for a second, smelling the same soap that he always used. I could just stand here with him all night. "Fireworks are so cool. They look spectacular, and I love thinking about how you have to make them. You have to figure out how to get all the different colors and the timing of the explosion just right."

Hunter's hand started to cup my chin. I swallowed and looked back up at him, the adrenaline starting to rush through me. As though I knew why he'd be looking at me like that. "Do you mind if I interrupt you?" he asked, his other hand still on my waist.

"Depends," I replied, looking back up at him. "Is it going to be interesting?"

His eyes looked like there was a fire burning in them. "I'm going to kiss you for real now."

"Yes please," I said back. He bent his head down, pressing his lips onto mine. I closed my eyes and stepped closer to him, pressing as close to him as I could.

I could get lost in this, kissing Hunter, standing outside with his arms around me.

From inside, music had started pounding. Hunter took a step back, picking up a piece of hair from my face and tucking it behind my ear. "Should we go inside and be good hosts now?"

"In five minutes?" I offered in reply. He grinned back

down at me, moving back in for a kiss. I closed my eyes again and wrapped my arms around his waist.

From somewhere behind us, there was a wolf whistle. That was enough to finally get me to step back and step away from him. He looked over at the people in the house, a flash of annoyance across his face. "Are there seriously people watching us right now?"

Us. It was something about that word that made my stomach flip over. The fact that I was out here with Hunter, and he was talking about it like it was a totally normal thing that we were hanging out. That there was an us, not just a Hunter and a Kinsey. "I think that's the downside of a party. People can actually see us."

He grinned at me, the annoyance vanishing from his face. "So we should find a more private place later?"

Okay, I was going to throw up from all of the acrobatics that my stomach was doing right now. The thought of finding someplace private with Hunter was more than I had reckoned for, terrifying and thrilling all at the same time.

Sort of like Hunter himself, if I thought about it.

"That – yeah," I said, grinning up at him again. He reached down and squeezed my waist again, moving in for a final kiss.

"Let's go," he said, nodding back towards the house, and I followed him. Logan had taken over the sound system and was attempting to DJ, and there were people making their way to the dance floor that had started in the living room.

We walked back into the party. Hunter's hand stayed

on my back, guiding me through the crowd. "Hey," Logan said, coming over and nodding towards Hunter. "What's the password for the stereo system again?"

"Five six seven eight," Hunter replied. He leaned down towards me. "My parents decided that we were going to protect the stereo system so that my sister couldn't play obnoxious stuff all day long when she wanted to get back at them. But it turns out that it's a pretty easy code to guess."

"It wasn't your taste in music they were defending against?" I asked. Hunter laughed, pulling me in again.

"Hey," a guy said, walking straight up towards us. He looked vaguely familiar, but I couldn't place him. "Hunter!"

"Hey, Matt," Hunter said, reaching towards him and giving him a fist bump, then turning back towards me. "Matt's my best friend from elementary school. He's the one who moved away and left me. Matt, this is Kinsey."

"Oh, the girlfriend you won't stop talking about," Matt said, turning towards me and giving me a hug. I hugged him back, standing on my tiptoes. "Finally getting to meet you."

Wait. The girlfriend. Hunter and I hadn't had a conversation about any of this. Hunter seemed to pause for a second, then nodded towards Matt. "Yeah. Kinsey. She's awesome."

"Nice to meet you, Kinsey," Matt said, giving me what looked like a real smile. I blushed a little. "Make sure this guy stays in line, okay?"

"Hey, no fair, man," Hunter said, clapping him on the shoulder. "I didn't tell your boyfriend that when you started going out."

"Because I'm not you," Matt replied, punching him on the shoulder. "I'm not the one who's always in trouble."

"Hunter gets in trouble?" I asked. Hunter never seemed to actually be in trouble. He had some sort of magic protection around him.

"See, I told you. Kinsey knows," Hunter said, looping an arm around my waist again.

Matt laughed. "Kinsey, this guy once convinced me to build a slip and slide in his yard with a tarp and dish soap. We killed the grass, and his parents were pissed."

"Whatever. We were eight," Hunter said, shrugging. "It was a great time."

"I'm excited to hear all of the embarrassing Hunter stories," I said to Matt. Hunter sometimes felt too perfect, and I needed to know that inside, he was just like me.

"Let me tell you about his dinosaur phase sometime," Matt said, grinning at me. "Or the time that he convinced his sister's friend to eat deer poop, and I had to stop him. Or -"

"You come to my party in my house and you have to bring up that story?" Hunter asked, reaching over and punching him gently on the shoulder. "Bro. I thought we were cooler than that."

"I'll stop then. But seriously, Kinsey, we should all go out sometimes. Jeremy would love to meet you too. He's out with his family this weekend, or I would have dragged him here to meet you," he said, giving me another smile.

"I'd like that," I said, looking at Matt and then back at Hunter. Hunter leaned now and ruffled my hair.

"I'm going to go see some other people. Hunter, I'll text you. Let's go for a ride this week," he said, nodding at me.

Hunter clapped Matt on the shoulder. "Good to see you, man."

Matt nodded. He turned towards me, giving me a last smile. "And really great to meet you, Kinsey. I mean it."

"Thanks," I said, glancing in between Matt and then back up at Hunter. Matt headed off into the party, turning and giving Hunter a look over his shoulder as he walked away.

"Want to go join people over there?" Hunter asked, nodding towards a group of people starting to play some kind of drinking game. "Go hang out and sit on the couch a bit?"

No. I wanted to be alone with Hunter again, kissing him on the back porch, off in our own little world. But this was Hunter's party, and I couldn't drag him away like that. "Sounds great," I replied, following him over towards the couch.

We spent the next couple hours sitting on the couch. It was like everyone at the party had to come by and say hello to Hunter. He'd dismiss half of them with a bit of a head nod, and in the times that people weren't coming over, he'd turn back to me and start telling me stories about the past parties at his place.

"You didn't come to this party last year, did you?" he asked, resting a hand on my knee.

I shook my head. "I normally go out with my mom on the Fourth of July. That wasn't even an option this year."

"That sucks," Hunter said, his hand tightening on my

knee. "I mean, obviously I'm happy that you're here and not there, but that she didn't even ask you what you wanted to do."

I shrugged. "There's no point in trying to argue with her about it."

Hunter looked at me for a second, his eyes traveling over my face, then finished off his beer. "Can I get you another drink?"

I glanced down at my can. "Yeah, I guess. I'm going to go to the bathroom."

"Use the one in my room," he said, glancing around the room. "Up the stairs and to the right. The other ones will be trashed."

I nodded, and he walked off. I started to walk towards the stairs, then paused. Going into his room without him felt way too personal. I couldn't do it. I'd just brave the downstairs bathrooms and hope they weren't gross.

"Hi, Kinsey," someone I didn't know said as I walked by them, pushing through the crowd. "Great party."

"Thanks," I said, giving them a nod. They vanished into the crowd.

Another group of people nodded to me as I walked by. Was this what it was like to be Hunter? Everyone seemed to know me all of a sudden.

I ducked into the bathroom, not carrying my drink this time, and then back out to the party. Maybe I was being ridiculous, but it even felt like people were letting me pass by them. Or maybe I was just so happy to be here that nothing could annoy me today.

"Back again?" Hunter asked when I finally reached

him again. He passed me another drink. "In case yours got warm."

"Thanks," I said, snuggling back into him.

A few hours later, the party was finally starting to wind down. Hunter and I had gotten pulled into an intense game of Mario Kart, which I realized that I was nowhere near as good at as I was a giant Jenga.

I glanced around the room. I hadn't heard from Lily or Ellery. Not surprising, because Ellery was terrible at texting when she was drinking, and she was probably with Max anyway. Hopefully Lily had found her soccer boy too. "I should probably get a car home," I said finally, leaning into Hunter slightly.

"What?" he asked, glancing down at me. "Why?"

"Because," I said, gesturing around to the party. "People are leaving. The party is over, and you just told people that it was time to head out."

He looked down at me and shook his head. "Kinsey. You're welcome to stay."

"It's okay," I said, glancing around the living room. "I don't want to crash on the floor or something."

"Are you serious?" He took a step back and stared me directly in the eyes. "Kinsey. Seriously. This is my house. You don't have to leave. In fact, I would like you not to leave."

Oh. I swallowed and looked up with him, my stomach flipping again. He reached down and pushed a piece of hair out of my face, and I swallowed again. "Okay. I can stay. I can definitely stay."

We walked through the living room, and Hunter

glanced down at the few cans of beer that were still lying around. "Cleaning up is always such a pain," he said, staring down at one of the cans on the floor and nudging it with his foot.

"The real reason that you want me to stay over is so that I can help you clean up tomorrow morning?" I asked, reaching for his hand.

He burst out laughing and pulled me close. "Yeah, Kinsey. That is totally it."

I didn't see Lily or Ellery as we walked back through the party. They must have already left and gone home. The party had been dying down for a while, and I didn't see Max either.

I didn't blame them. If Hunter hadn't been here, I would have left a long time before. I looked down at my phone, which was dead. Of course.

"Want to go upstairs?" Hunter asked. I nodded, then I followed him up the stairs and then down a long hallway. He pushed open the door to his room and I walked in, heading towards the bed and immediately collapsing into it. "God, I'm tired."

Hunter flopped down on the bed next to me, then looped his arms around me, pulling me in. I sighed and relaxed into him, closing my eyes.

"Sleepy?" he asked. I could feel his voice on my forehead.

"Yeah," I said. His arms tightened around me again, and I could feel his heartbeat through his chest.

His chin rested on top of my head. "I can get you a shirt to sleep in if you want," he said.

I forced myself to sit up. "Thanks," I said. He passed me a shirt, and I ducked into his bathroom to change. I stared at myself in the mirror for a second.

I was at a party at Hunter's house. And I was about to climb into bed with Hunter, and I just felt happy.

I pulled off my shirt and put on his instead. It hung almost to my knees, and I stared at myself for a few more seconds before I went back out.

Hunter was sitting on the edge of his bed, and he held out his arms towards me. I walked over to him and cuddled into him, closing my eyes again.

He kissed me again, his arms tightening around me. "I'm really glad you're here with me, Kins."

TWELVE

WHEN I WOKE up the next morning, it took me a few blinks to remember where I was.

Next to me in bed, Hunter rolled over and looked at me. "Hey."

"Hey," I replied, trying not to stare at Hunter's chest. I was wearing his t-shirt in his bed, and he was only wearing boxers. I didn't think that I was superficial enough to only care about what Hunter looked like, but he was hot.

"We should probably start cleaning stuff up," he said, pulling me towards him. I rolled over towards him and closed my eyes, very much enjoying the fact that I was in bed with Hunter Lowen.

This was not normal. But this was great.

"Five minutes?" I asked, resting my head on his chest.

He laughed and ran his hand through my hair. "Sure, five more minutes."

After what was definitely longer than five minutes, I rolled out of bed, pulling on my shorts from the night before. He also got dressed, grabbing a t-shirt and tugging it on over his head. "Ready?" he asked.

I did not want to have to leave this very comfortable room and go downstairs and deal with the remnants of the party. I didn't want to leave my little Hunter bubble. But it was clearly time to go and clean up.

I followed Hunter downstairs, checking out the scene. The house was a total disaster. There were beer cans every-where, and I lifted my foot out of a puddle of something sticky. "Is it always this bad?" I asked Hunter, nudging a beer can with my toe.

"No one slept in my parents' room last night, and that's all I can ask for," he replied. "That happened last year, and my parents were furious for months."

"And they still thought it was a good idea to let you throw this party?" I thought that my mom and I were cool with each other, but Hunter and his parents took it to another level.

He snorted, turning towards the kitchen. "I don't ask them before I throw parties."

Hunter walked straight over to the fridge and pulled out bagels and cream cheese. I wandered towards the living room, where it looked like there were a few people sleeping on couches. I spotted Logan sprawled out on an ottoman, and then –

"You're up." Oh god, that was not a happy voice. I turned to my left to see Lily, her arms tightly crossed over her chest. "I'm ready to go home, Kinsey."

"Lily!" I stared at her for a second. "I thought you had gone home last night."

"Well, considering that I told my parents that I was staying over at your place, and that you had the car keys to Betta, it was going to be a little hard for me to leave. Although it would have been helpful if you had maybe answered your texts last night," she said, staring straight at me.

"I – " I hadn't even checked my phone, because the only person who I wanted to text was Hunter, and he was with me.

"Let's go," Lily said, narrowing her eyes. "I had to sleep on a floor last night while you were off doing whatever you were doing, and I'm not happy."

"It wasn't that bad," I said quickly.

She spun around to face me, her feet still pointing towards the door. "It was. And you knew that I wasn't going to know anyone here, and you just left me anyway!"

"Don't speak to her that way," Hunter said, coming up and standing beside me, his hand landing on my back. "You could have taken a car home if it really bugged you so much that she was here."

"You're being an asshole, Kinsey," Lily said, looking from me to Hunter. There was something about the fact that Hunter was standing next to me that seemed to make the situation worse.

"Get out of my house," Hunter said, staring straight at Lily.

I glanced in between him and Lily, my heart starting to pound. "I – "

"Kinsey, you can give her the keys, and I can drop you by your house later," Hunter said, glancing down at me, his voice softer. He turned back towards Lily, squaring his shoulders. "But if you're going to come into my house and call my girlfriend an asshole, I'm going to tell you to leave."

Ellery had wandered in as well, her eyes widening as she saw the scene. Lily was never mad at me. We were supposed to be the inseparable people who took on things together and made them work out in the end. We didn't fight. That wasn't us.

"Kinsey, give me the car keys, and we can go back," Ellery said, nodding towards Hunter and then towards me. She seemed to read the situation faster than I could, make the decision that I didn't know how to make.

Hunter looked down at me, and I swallowed. Part of me wanted to go over to Lily and tell her that I was wrong, but that didn't seem like it would do anything. Because she was just standing there looking furious at me, like anything that I did was just going to make things even worse.

"Kins?" Hunter asked, his voice softer, his hand resting on my back. "I can handle cleaning up by myself."

"No, it's fine," Lily snapped, turning away from me and towards the door. "You better stay and make sure that Hunter's house looks all nice for his parents. And I can go home alone, because the best friend that I came back to hang out with doesn't care about me."

"Give me the keys," Ellery mouthed towards me. I fished them out of my pocket and passed them to her. I didn't even know what else to do. "I'll park Betta in her normal spot."

"Thanks," I said, staring down at the ground. Hunter put his arm around my shoulder and pulled me in. Ellery and Lily started to walk towards the front door and then out of the house, Ellery glancing back to wave by and Lily refusing to turn around.

I heard the door slam behind them and took a deep breath. "That was an asshole move," Hunter said, nodding towards the door.

"No, I should have texted her last night." I should have known that she was going to be at a party where she didn't know anyone. If Ellery started talking to Max, Lily wouldn't interrupt, but she wouldn't have anyone to talk to. I knew how that felt. Jenna had done it to me enough times.

"Don't be so hard on yourself," Hunter replied, looking down at me and pulling me into a side hug. "And seriously, Kinsey, you can't just let people trample on you."

"Lily's my friend. She's not trampling over me," I said as Hunter released me from the hug. I walked back into the kitchen, heading towards the bagels.

"Kinsey, you let people trample over you all the time. You don't stand up for yourself." He opened the fridge and grabbed a drink.

"That's not true," I protested. That wasn't true at all. I stood up for myself.

"My friends would never have talked to me like that," he said, his voice dropping.

That was because he was Hunter. "My friends are different than your friends." Lily wasn't scared of me the way Hunter's friends were apparently scared of him.

"And you told me last night that you haven't told your mom anything," he said, shutting the fridge.

"That's different." That was my mom. You couldn't just tell your mom what to do.

Hunter stared at me for a second, narrowing his eyes. "Seriously."

Could we just go back upstairs and forget this conversation had ever happened? I swallowed and turned towards Hunter. "Do you want to wake the guys up and get this house cleaned up?"

Hunter stared at me for another second, something clearly running through his mind. I looked up at him for a second. The best thing was that I started moving, so that Hunter wasn't going to force me to talk about things more.

I went over to Logan and shook his shoulder gently. "I think it's time to wake up."

Hunter glanced over at me, shaking his head. He beckoned me back towards him. "That's not the way to do it. You might want to go into the kitchen."

I raised my eyebrows. He motioned me towards the kitchen again.

Well then. I walked back into the kitchen, leaning against the counter. Maybe Hunter was going to pull off Logan's pants or something.

A giant noise boomed through the house, loud enough that the windows started shaking.

Hunter had turned on the stereo system and was blaring Taylor Swift. The windows in the living room were actually rattling.

"Time to get up and get cleaning, boys!" he shouted. I could barely hear him over the noise.

I peered around the corner. Logan had pulled the

couch cushions off the couch and was covering his head. Hunter walked over and ripped them off, throwing them onto the floor. "Get your ass up!"

"Make it stop," Max yelled from the other side of the living room.

I could barely hear them over the music. Hunter picked up his phone and turned down the music. "You losers should just be glad it wasn't kid's music this time."

Ethan wandered into the kitchen, only wearing a pair of boxers. He stared up at me, then stuck his hands over his crotch. "Morning, Kinsey. Don't look."

"Morning," I said, looking anywhere but at Ethan. "What is going on here?"

"Ethan, put some pants on," Hunter yelled from the other room.

"We're cleaning. And I'm putting pants on," Ethan said blearily. He blinked a few times. "This is how Lowen gets the house clean after parties."

"It's too early for this much Taylor Swift," Logan said from the couch, where he was still lying with a pillow over his head.

Hunter punched him in the shoulder. "Get up and get cleaning. We've got two hours."

This might have been the most effective cleaning strategy I'd ever seen. Max had already rubbed his eyes and was in the process of starting to fill up a trash bag. "Can you at least change the music?" he asked.

"My house, my music," Hunter replied.

Logan finally left the couch and staggered into the kitchen. He opened the fridge and pulled out a Gatorade, looking at me. "My parents have people who do the cleaning. This is why parties at my house are better."

I had heard the rumors that Logan's parents were extremely wealthy and also extremely hands off. "And Hunter forces you all to do it?" I asked.

"Yeah. If you try to sleep any longer, Hunter will just turn up the music until you get up," Logan said, slowly drinking his Gatorade. "We all clean. And then anyone who's stupid enough to stay over without permission really gets it."

"Right," I said, nodding. I glanced around. Hunter had walked back into the kitchen and put his arm over my shoulders.

Alessia came walking down the hall. She glanced up at me and then turned towards Max, who was dragging a trash bag into the kitchen. "Is the party starting again?"

"Clean up time," he said, looking at her. "This is what happens when you spend the night at Hunter's."

I wasn't going to look at them too much, but was there something going on there?

It couldn't be. Max was supposed to like Ellery. And Ellery liked Max. I wanted the two of them to get together like me and Hunter.

This had to just be a fluke. I wasn't seeing right. And I couldn't assume the worst.

"Incoming!" Ethan shouted, and a ball of paper towels came flying over my head.

"Don't be a jerk," I yelled back at him. He launched another ball of paper towels at me, and Hunter swatted it out of the air before it got close.

Alessia had started to wipe down the counters next to me. She looked over at me and rolled her eyes slightly. "How do we all get dragged into this?"

It was weird that I was hanging out with Alessia and the soccer guys right now. I was hanging out with the most popular people at school at the afterparty to the party, and they were all acting like it was totally normal that I was there.

Usually, I would have been back at my house with Lily right now, sitting around the kitchen and dissecting everything that had happened. We'd get crepes with ice cream for breakfast, then sit in the park and spy on people. But instead I was over at Hunter's, and Lily might not be speaking to me.

I reached under the counter and picked up a spray bottle. It was clearly labeled *Water Only (for vegetables!!)*. I turned it over in my hands. Hmmm.

I snuck around the corner and positioned myself. When Ethan turned the corner, I unleashed an attack.

"What the hell?" he shouted, waving his hands in front of his face. "Hunter!"

"Got you back," I said, giving him another squirt for good measure.

"Kinsey!" He stared at me, his mouth dropping open. "Such betrayal! I would have never thought!"

"You threw the paper towels at me. You started it," I said, putting down the spray bottle.

He reached over and gave me a high five. "Nice work, Greenwood. And just so you know, those towels were supposed to hit Lowen, not you. I've got no problem with you."

I rolled my eyes at him. "So nice of you."

"But if you ever want to gang up on - " he started.

"Don't say it, McGee," Hunter said, striding up next to me. "If you're trying to pull Kins over to the dark side, don't even start."

"Incoming!" another voice yelled. Logan sent another giant wad of paper towels flying back towards us.

We somehow managed to finish the cleaning within an hour, even with the guys managing to find some way to attack each other with cleaning supplies every few minutes. I was pretty sure the other people who had slept over had done most of the cleaning and then snuck away.

Once we'd finished, Hunter glanced over at me. "I have to go to practice in a couple minutes with these idiots. Want me to drive you home first?"

I didn't want to leave here. I wanted to stay with the guys and hang out and have fun. But they were heading to practice, so I had no other option. "Yeah."

We drove back towards my house. Hunter pulled his car up in front of my house and paused so that I could climb out of the car. "Do you want to come by tomorrow?" he asked, leaning back in his seat to look at me.

I shook my head. "I wish, but it's the start of Mandatory Two."

"The what?" he asked, his eyes on my face.

"I have to spend two weeks a year with my dad. I'm doing one of the weeks this summer because it's easier than doing it during the school year." Most summers, I didn't mind that much, but I really minded this summer.

"So you're just going to be trapped with your dad? Like, everything's okay there, right?" Hunter asked, completely turning in his seat to face me.

"Nothing really bad. It's just boring, and I don't know anyone there," I said.

"That sucks," Hunter said finally, leaning back and looking at me. "And there's no way that you can get out of it?"

I shook my head. "I wish. But it's literally in the paperwork."

"I'll miss you," Hunter said finally, leaning across the car seat and giving me a kiss.

"Ew, I'm gross," I said. "I haven't showered, and I'm wearing the shirt I was cleaning in."

He grinned. "I don't mind. And it's cute seeing you in my old shirts. I think you should wear them more often."

I looked at him again, my heart doing the leap in my chest that I always associated with Hunter. "I'm going to miss you a lot this week."

THIRTEEN

I FINISHED PUTTING my clothes for my week of the Mandatory Two into my bag and zipped it up. This wasn't a good week for me to go. But it was never a good week to go away, and at least I'd get out of hearing about wedding planning for a few more days. I was going to lose it if I had to hear about Brian Senior's buffet choices or venue choices or flower choices. It was amazing how a man with so little personality could have so many opinions about random things.

"Do you want me to walk you to the train?" my mom asked, standing in the living room as I came out with my bag.

"It's fine." *Maybe she's secretly relieved that you're going away for the week and she can hang out with Brian Senior more*, said a voice in the back of my head.

"Are you sure?" my mom asked. Her car keys were already in her hand, the sign that she was about to run out. "I don't mind!"

The tone of voice was a giveaway. Yeah, it would have been great if she'd walked me to the train station, like she had every other year before. But that wasn't happening now, when it was clear that it would have just been keeping her from something else. "No. I'm good."

"Well, have a fun time! I hope your stepsister is there at least," she said, leaning forward and giving me a kiss on my forehead.

I nodded and started the walk down to the train. I got my ticket and waited on the platform until it finally came, trying to find a shady spot to stand in.

When I was younger, my dad had had a car service pick me up from the house, but that had gone away at some point. Too much coordination for him, probably.

I stepped onto the train and reached for my phone. There were a few text messages.

From Hunter, a selfie of him after practice. There were tiny flecks of glitter in his hair. *Ethan tried to glitter bomb me during practice. What do you suggest to get him back?*

My heart did a little squeezing thing, as though I didn't see pictures of Hunter all the time. *More glitter?* I texted back.

There was a message from my dad telling me that the doorman would let me into the apartment, and I gave it a thumbs up. I wasn't expecting my dad to bed at the apartment anyway, because he was probably out with the Evil Stepmother doing something.

The last text was from Ellery, something about going for a run.

I hadn't texted Ellery since the blow up after Hunter's party. It had been complete silence from Lily. It was only a day, but Lily was one of those people who sent a dozen memes a day. But instead, she'd gone back to the beach without a word.

She could have just gone home, said the voice in the back of my head. *You don't owe her anything. She's your friend, yeah, but she has to take some responsibility here.*

But you know how you feel if Jenna leaves you at a party? Imagine that, but it's before you knew Hunter and it's super awkward, said the other side of my brain.

I slumped down in my seat. The conductor came by and took my ticket, and I stared at my phone again.

Another text from Hunter. *He wanted a ride home after practice. I made him sit in the back so he didn't get glitter on your seat.*

My seat? *Honestly he's lucky you didn't make him sit in the trunk,* I texted back.

Hunter sent back a bunch of laughing faces. *Kinsey with the best ideas.*

I smiled at my phone then slipped it back into my bag, staring out the window at the land flying by.

I got into the city and immediately had to close my eyes for a second against the noise. It was always so much busier than I remembered here. I eventually found a taxi and gave them my dad's address, trying to block out the noise as I drove uptown. I arrived, and the doorman gave me a spare set of keys.

"Hello?" I called as I unlocked the apartment. As I had

suspected, the apartment was completely quiet. I dragged my bag into the guest room and flopped down, staring up at the ceiling.

My dad would probably make plans for tonight, mostly because he had to do something to prove that we did things together during the Mandatory Two. Until then, I was on my own with just my thoughts to keep me company. What a day for it.

My phone buzzed again. I picked it up. Not Lily, but Ellery double texting me. *Run? Are you avoiding the question because it's a bajillion degrees out?*

I'm in New York visiting my dad, I replied.

The phone rang, and I answered it. Ellery's face popped up on the screen. "Did you tell me that you weren't going to be here?" she asked.

I shook my head. "No." There had been enough after that party that it had somewhat slipped my mind. And since I was in the middle of a fight with Lily, it wasn't terrible that I was gone for a little bit.

"Are you okay?" she asked, tilting her head to the side.

I took a deep breath. It felt selfish to complain about Lily to Ellery. "I'm just annoyed because I fought with Lily, and she's not talking to me, and Hunter was mad at me afterwards."

"Hunter is mad at you?" Ellery asked, her eyebrows raising. "Hunter can get mad at you?"

That wasn't quite the right word. The conversation bothered me, though. I didn't want Hunter to be disappointed in me. "He's not actually mad. It's just – "

"Okay, I have a proposal," Ellery said, leaning back on

her bed. "You get your dad to agree that I can come visit you tomorrow. I'll spend the night with you, and we can go running and talk."

"Seriously?" I had never had a friend who had visited me on the Mandatory Two before. Lily's mom wouldn't let her take the train by herself, and Jenna had never made the effort. Hunter had intensive practice this week, so as much as I had hoped he'd be able to come, no luck there.

"Yeah," she said. "You seem like you're having a moment, no offense."

"I think if you can tell over the phone, I probably am," I said.

"Ask your dad, and fingers crossed, see you tomorrow," she said, waving on the other end before she hung up. "And you better find me some good pizza if we do it."

Thanks, I texted her. *I really appreciate it. I mean it.*

I HEARD noise in the kitchen around six, and I stood up to check out what it was. Surprisingly, it was my dad, searching through the cabinets for something. "Hey," I said, sitting down at one of the counter stools.

"Hi, Kinsey," my dad said, walking over and giving me a hug. He was usually a handshake and nod kind of guy, so that was unusual. "It's great to see you. You got in okay this afternoon?"

"Yeah. The train is really easy," I said. My dad was a big fan of the questions that he already knew the answer to. It kept there from being any surprises.

He placed two glasses on the counter. "The doormen

messaged me that you had picked up your key. What do you want for dinner tonight? We can order anything."

"Is Evalina not here?" I had accidentally called her Evil Stepmother directly to my dad before, and he didn't think that it was quite as funny as I did.

"We were invited to a gallery opening. She decided to go by herself so that you and I could have dinner together," he replied, shutting the cabinet door.

That was unusually nice of her. Evalina was kind of a grown up Jenna. You had to be okay with her being the center of attention if you wanted to hang out with her.

Not that she would ever describe it as hanging out, because she was the kind of person who socialized. She didn't hang out. Her life could only be properly described with multisyllable words.

"I'll order salads," my dad said, looking down at his phone and starting to tap something. "Does that work for you?"

"Yeah, sounds good," I replied. It was lame to come to New York City and eat salad of all the things that I could get, but if that was what my dad wanted, fine. It was probably healthier anyway after I'd spent the day basically sitting on my bed.

He opened the fridge and pulled out two water jugs. "Do you want still or sparkling? I just got a sparkling water machine, and it's pretty good."

"I'll take still, thanks," I said.

"Are you sure?" he asked, holding up one of the jugs. They both just looked like water to me. I nodded, and he poured the water into the glasses, sliding one over to me.

"This is kind of awkward, but can I have a friend stay over tomorrow?" I asked, taking a sip of my water.

"Of course you can," he said, then paused, putting his water glass back on the counter. "What friend? Are they cool?"

What a weird question to ask. "It's my friend Ellery. She's on the cross-country team with me, and she was going to come for a training run with me. It's easier if she can stay over, and her parents are okay with it if you are," I said.

"I have a work dinner tomorrow, so I can stay out of your way if you want," my dad replied, leaning on the counter. "I'll leave my credit card here, and you and Ellery can get whatever you want."

"Thanks," I said. I was going to order all of the Nutella and all of the carbs. It was going to be delicious.

My dad's phone rang, and he looked down. "I'm really sorry, Kinsey, but this is a live deal. I need to just answer this, and then I'll be right back, okay?"

"Sure," I said, reaching for my phone. Hunter had texted me again, sending me a picture of his dog chasing after a ball in his yard.

I sent back a heart emoji, then stared at the kitchen counter. My dad came back out of the room much sooner than I expected. "I'm sorry about that. My team is having some trouble with this one, and – " He shook his head. "How's school?"

Was this actually a question he didn't already know the answer to? "Well, it's fine. But it's summer now, so I haven't been thinking about it. It's junior year next year, and that's the one that the guidance counselors are always stressing out about."

He nodded again. "What are you thinking about for college? You still really like biology, right?"

Before I had a chance to answer, the doorbell rang. My dad walked to the door and then returned with our dinner. I opened mine up and took a bite. It wasn't bad, actually. My dad's, I was happy to note, had a fair amount of cheese on it.

"You're not vegetarian, right?" my dad asked, taking another bite of his salad.

I shook my head. "No. I mean, I feel terrible about factory farming and all that, but I'm not vegetarian."

My dad reached for his water. "I think I'm going to try it soon. My cardiologist yelled at me last week about my diet, so I think it's time. I was hoping that you had some advice for me."

Oh boy, did I have advice for him. I knew all about the carb-free, dairy-free diet from Brian Senior. But I wouldn't subject him to that. "Nope, unfortunately. I love junk food too much."

He laughed, mixing his salad. "Me too. My weakness was always cinnamon rolls and anything espresso flavored."

"So that's where the cinnamon roll thing comes from," I blurted out, then took a drink of my water. "I love them too. Mom doesn't really like cinnamon, but there's this place near us that makes the best cinnamon buns. I go there with my friend Lily all the time."

"So I passed on the cinnamon gene. What about the espresso one?" he asked, leaning forward.

I shook my head. "No. It's too bitter."

He smiled, looking down at his salad. "That's what you think now. Just wait. I guarantee you're going to hit college and become a coffee snob."

I snorted, then took the last bite of my salad. "I don't think so. But now that we're talking about it, is there any chance that you have dessert here?" I asked.

He looked at me for a second, then shook his head. "But I do know a good ice cream spot nearby. Maybe we could take a walk?"

ELLERY DROPPED her bag in the guest room next to mine. "So are you ready to go for this run or not?"

I reached for my running shoes, which I'd stuck under the bed. It felt too weird to leave them in the entryway, and I didn't want to deal with Evalina's look about it. She was not a fan of me leaving things around the apartment. *Children should be not seen and not heard,* I could imagine her sniffing.

Maybe I wasn't being fair to her. Maybe she was actually okay. But given that she'd sent my stepsister off to camp for most of the summer, maybe I was being totally fair.

My dad was being pretty cool, though. We'd walked to get ice cream last night, and he'd asked me a bunch of questions about school and cross-country. He'd apparently run the New York marathon the year before, on the advice of his same cardiologist, and so he had plenty of questions about my training.

And, I was happy to note, he did not mention anything about avoiding dairy once.

I tied my shoes and looked up at Ellery. "Not really, but you're not going to let me out of it."

"The season is starting soon, Kinsey. We've got to get in shape again. And thanks for getting your dad to say I could come," she said, flexing one foot. "My parents would have been a little bit skeptical if he hadn't said he'd be here."

"Thanks for coming all the way here," I said. It felt like a different world here.

"Now you have to pay me back by going for a run with me. Let's go," she said, nodding towards the door.

I followed her out of the apartment and then down the elevator, out onto the street. It was busy outside, and I blinked in the sudden sunshine. Dick and the Evil Stepmother had a nice apartment, but it was still way darker than outside.

Ellery turned on her watch, and I started to run with her. We jogged towards Central Park, which my dad had recommended as the best run that we could do. I'd texted him this morning to ask for a route for a six mile run, and I'd immediately gotten a reply.

"So what's wrong?" Ellery asked me as we reached Central Park and started to run.

"Do you think I'm a terrible friend?" I asked.

She looked over at me for a second, her ponytail blowing behind her. "Do you want the truth?"

That was not the greatest opening to a conversation. "If you have to put it that way."

"I don't think you're a bad friend at all. That's why I'm

here. I would have dumped you if you were terrible. But you were a jerk to Lily," she said, looking away from me back at the road. "You just went off with Hunter. We could literally see you on the porch making out for half the night. Lily's sitting there trying to make small talk with people she's never met before, and you and Hunter are just all over each other in the corner."

My face turned red. I could feel it. I hadn't been trying to leave everyone and just hang out with Hunter, but it was what had happened. Lily had been standing there in the corner by herself, not knowing anyone but me or Ellery.

"It's hard," I said finally. "Lily was all excited about me getting together with Hunter, and now she's getting mad at me because I hang out with him too much. I don't know how to win."

Ellery shook her head. "You're changing. You're different when you're with Hunter."

"No, I'm not," I said, turning the corner and narrowly avoiding running into a trash can.

"Yeah, you are," she said. "We never hung out before this summer. You basically never talked to anyone during cross-country, and you were super shy. And now you're at all these parties. It's different."

"It's not a bad thing!" I protested. I had always been shy before, but that was almost because I didn't know how to not be. I wanted to be louder and more fun and out doing things with people, but I didn't know how to do it. I didn't know how to get from quiet Kinsey to this person I was now.

"I'm not saying it's a bad thing," she replied. I sped up

slightly to keep pace with her. She was pushing the pace today. "And it's weird for the people on the outside to see it, I think. Like when you and Lily went to parties before, what did you do?"

"I never went to parties with Lily before. I only went anywhere with Jenna." And when I went somewhere with Jenna, I had always been the person who stood back and let Jenna be the center of attention. Now I was in the middle, and Lily was on the outside.

Ellery looked over at me. "Jenna. Right."

"I need to apologize to Lily, don't I?" I said, glancing over at Ellery.

She nodded. "Yeah. You definitely need to apologize. It wasn't a great thing to do to your friend. And I think you already know this, but the way Hunter reacted made it worse."

I stared down at the ground for a second. I did know that. I knew that Hunter wanted to defend me, but I didn't want to be defended against Lily.

And I hated apologizing. This was going to be so awkward. But I could do it. "Thanks, Ell. It means a lot that you came out here to talk to me."

"That's what friends are for," she said, bumping me with her shoulder.

We turned onto the path around the reservoir. My dad had recommended it as the spot with the best views of the skyline, and I wasn't going to turn that down. "So did I miss anything else at that party?" I asked, looking over at her.

"Max and I talked again," she said, picking up the pace again.

"And?" I asked. I definitely hadn't seen him with Alessia. I had thought I might have for a second because she had also slept over at Hunter's, but that didn't mean anything. I wasn't going to say it. I couldn't say that to Ellery unless I knew the truth.

"I think he might like me." She looked over at me. "I mean, I really think he might like me. But I can't tell."

There was no way that he couldn't like her. Ellery was so much fun, and pretty, and just a great person. "You should just ask him," I said, looking over at her. "Just straight up tell him at the next party."

"I don't know if I'm that brave," she said, jumping over a puddle.

"You are totally that brave!" I nudged her shoulder again. "And come on. He'd be stupid not to like you. You're awesome."

She took a deep breath. "I know. I should do it. Just get it over with, because we've been flirting all summer and I don't even know."

I hoped this would work. Ellery would be with Max, and I'd be with Hunter. I'd have my best friend and my boyfriend in the same group of friends. Ellery and I could go to soccer games together, and Max and Hunter could come to cross-country meets.

Well, maybe on that second part. I wasn't sure that I was ready for the soccer boys' cheering.

"Do it. You can totally do it," I said again.

She looked over at me, then shook her head. "You are really trying to hype me up, arne't you?"

"Of course," I said. We stopped, and I grabbed my phone. "Selfie?"

She glanced back at the skyline, then nodded. "To friends forever. Even when I make you run."

FOURTEEN

I WAS VERY ready to go back to the suburbs at the end of the Mandatory Two, even if it had been better than I expected.

My dad had actually been somewhat talkative this time. He'd gone on runs with me when he got back from work. He'd taken a half day on Thursday so that he could take me to his favorite bakery, a place way out in Brooklyn that he claimed made the world's best cinnamon buns. He'd gotten me an espresso to try, too, and it was okay once I dumped a whole cup of sugar into it.

But even if things with my dad had been a lot better than the low bar that I was expecting, I was so ready to get back.

My phone buzzed again. I picked it up, turning away from the train window. Hunter. *When are you getting back?*

On the train now, I texted.

He gave the message a heart, then texted. *I have practice all afternoon but you're coming tonight?*

Of course, I texted back. It had been an entire week since I'd seen Hunter. He'd thought about coming into the city, but there was no way that we could make it work. My dad had been really chill about Ellery, but he might feel differently about my boyfriend spending the night.

Boyfriend. It was still so weird to get to use that word to describe Hunter. He wasn't just some guy I met up with at parties. Hunter Lowen was my boyfriend.

The train pulled into my stop, and I grabbed my suitcase and started the walk back towards my house. We lived so close to the train station that it was more complicated to try to drive there than to walk, even if I did hate dragging my suitcase up the hill.

Hunter sent me a picture of Chrissy chasing her tail, and I sent back heart eyes. She was a very cute dog, even if she didn't seem like she was the smartest.

Okay, I had forgotten how hot it was. My dad had air conditioning, so I had become a total wimp in the past week. I was going to be melting when I got home. I pulled my bag up the street, stopping and wiping my face halfway there.

Didn't matter. I would survive. I was going to shower and then get ready to go to see Hunter tonight.

I reached the house and pushed the front door open, dropping my bag on the kitchen floor and heading for the fridge. I needed water after that walk.

"Welcome back," my mom said, walking out from the living room.

"Thanks," I said, filling up my glass in the sink. I leaned

back against the counter and took a first sip. "How was it?" she asked, leaning against the counter.

I shrugged. "It was fine. Dad asked me more questions than normal. And Evil Stepmother was gone all week at some art thing, so it was better than I thought, honestly."

My mom nodded. "I'm glad that he's trying to build a relationship with you."

I gave her a look. That did not sound like my mom. My mom was normally one of those people who was super cutting about my dad. "He's gotten into running so we talked about that a bunch," I said.

What was it with middle aged men and running? First Brian Senior and now my dad. Thankfully, my dad hadn't batted an eye when I'd used his credit card to order two dozen bagels for me and Ellery.

My mom nodded, not quite meeting my eyes. I reached into the fridge, looking for something else to snack on. I should have had something to eat before I left the city, but I hadn't. I had to get ready to go over to the party at Logan's, and I needed sustenance before that.

Plus, I hadn't seen Hunter in a week, and I wanted to look cute. I had a green sundress that I hadn't worn in a while that I could dig out of my closet.

"Kinsey?" my mom said behind me, her voice sounding serious.

"What?" I asked, digging through the fridge. There was even less than usual in it. "We're out of yogurt?"

"Do you have a minute to talk about something?"

No, I had a minute to try to find something to eat. I had a party to get ready for, and I needed food and a shower. I pulled my head out of the fridge and turned to look at her. "What?"

My mom visibly swallowed. I raised my eyebrows at her. She could go ahead and say whatever she was thinking, so that I could get back to finding something to eat. Maybe I'd run out and get a sandwich or something.

"Yeah?" I asked again after she didn't say anything. I shut the fridge and straightened up. "You were saying?"

"Brian and I have been talking – "

Oh god. No good conversation ever started with the mention of that name. "What?" Were we banning all carbs from this house too?

"We're going to be moving in together next week," my mom said, leaning forward on the counter.

That wasn't that surprising. She was basically over there all the time. If she wanted to spend all of her time at his stupid apartment, she could. "Cool, I guess?"

My mom looked at me for a second, her eyes right on mine. "We closed on a house yesterday. I didn't tell you earlier because we weren't sure if the deal would go through."

A *house?* That was a lot of space for two people, even if one of them was Brian Senior and needed space for his bike and his rowing machine and everything else. "And?"

"We're moving," she said, looking right at me. "We. The three of us."

There was buzzing in my ears. I had to have heard her wrong. "The *three* of us? You think I'm moving?"

My mom visibly swallowed. "This house is too small for the three of us. Brian can afford more house than I can, obviously, so we bought something much nicer further out from town. It's got a pool and everything."

I wasn't going to be bribed with a pool. "You just bought a house and decided that I'm going to move without even talking to me?" I asked. "Are you serious?"

"Kinsey, Brian and I are getting married. The three of us are a family now," my mom said. I stared at her again. She looked back at me, and I could see her swallow again. "You'll really love this house. It's so much more space than you have now. You'll have your own bathroom."

This was such bullshit. She couldn't make a decision like this without asking. Without even thinking about me. "You think that I want to move in with Brian Senior just so that I can have a bathroom of my own?" I had lived here all my life. I didn't need my own bathroom. I needed my house. "Did you even think about asking me?"

"Kinsey, you've been so opposed to anything that Brian does that our conversations haven't been productive," my mom said, crossing her arms over her chest. "I've tried so many times to find things for us to do together or time for the two of us, and you've turned down every single one."

"Just because I don't want to play wedding planner for the summer doesn't mean that you can buy a house and not tell me!"

"Brian's old house wasn't in your school district, so we decided that doing this would actually be the best," my mom said. All I could hear was the buzzing in my ears. "It would have been even more of a transition if you'd had to switch schools in the middle of high school."

"You can't just do this!" I'd lived in this house my

whole life. Brian Senior showed up last year. This was where I'd always lived. This was my house.

I wasn't moving. I just wasn't.

"It's done, Kinsey. There are movers coming this week. Brian and I thought it would be easiest to do now so you have time to settle at the new house before school starts."

"Time to settle?" My mom wasn't even speaking English any more. That had to be the only explanation.

"The movers will be starting to come by the day after tomorrow. If you want to pack anything up in advance, please do, or they'll take everything in your room and set it up in the new house," my mom continued.

My ears were buzzing. I had no idea what she was saying.

I couldn't listen to this. "I - "

My mom took another deep breath. Oh no. She was going to use one of Lily's mom's techniques on me, pretend to give me space so that I could say something, then ignore everything that I had said. I couldn't do this. I wasn't putting up with that.

"Kinsey, I'm your mom, and legally, yes, I can make you move," my mom replied, taking another obvious deep breath. "And it's not a good idea for you to essentially be living by yourself in a house when I'm not here. And I want us to be a family, and that means that you have to spend more time with Brian."

"I've spent enough time with Brian to know that I don't like him and don't want to spend any more time with him," I replied. "And we've lived here for my entire life! I don't want to move to some random house with people I don't like because you have a crush on some guy."

"Kinsey, that's not a fair statement."

"It is!" I stood up. "This is my house. I've lived here for my entire life. And just because you don't seem to want to be my mom any more, that you'd rather run around being Brian's wife, that doesn't mean that you can just rip my life away and demand that I move!"

"Kinsey – "

"I'm not moving. I'm not!" I said, turning towards the front door.

"Kinsey," my mom called after me. No point in that. I wouldn't stay here and listen to her tell me why this was actually a good thing.

I had to get out of here and get somewhere where I could think. I needed the buzzing in my head to stop so I could figure out what to do.

My mom couldn't just sell the house. She couldn't do that. We'd always lived here. This was our house.

I had grown up here. I had literally been in this house as long as I could remember. I couldn't just leave to go to some generic house in the fancy part of town.

I pushed open the door. I walked up the street, turning onto the main street and then down towards the water. Where my mom and I used to go when we wanted to sit out at night and talk.

It wasn't like my mom had asked me in the beginning. She'd been all about Brian Senior and how wonderful he was. I'd always assumed that it was temporary, so it never really bothered me. And now I had to leave the house that I'd always been living in to move in with him?

I ran, darting in front of traffic on the street. I couldn't stop. I had to be alone. I reached the benches along the water and sat down, staring out.

This couldn't be happening. I had just come home, and it wasn't going to be home for long. I could have just stayed with my dad.

I knew my mom. If she and Brian had already closed on the place, she'd decided. She wasn't going to let me out of it.

I buried my head in my hands, then took a deep breath. I sat on the bench, staring out at the water. I didn't know how long I'd been sitting there until I finally started to feel calm. It had started to get dark around me, and I could hear the cicadas.

I took a deep breath and started the walk back up to my house. *My house.* Not that I was going to say that for much longer.

I couldn't think about that right now. I was going to just go home and get something to eat.

I grabbed my phone and dialed my dad's number. The phone rang, going to voicemail, and I closed my eyes for a second. I literally never talked to him about anything, and then one time that I wanted to actually talk to him about something, he wasn't there.

Maybe I could do the mandatory fifty-two there. I could just move in with him to the city and take the train to school every day or something. There had to be a solution that wasn't me moving into Brian's house.

But none of that seemed to matter, because my dad

wasn't answering his phone. I never called him, and he should have known that it was important. He was probably out with Evalina doing whatever they did. God, both of my parents were useless.

I got back to the house, pushing open the door.

My mom was still sitting in the kitchen. She had to pick the worst times to be in the way. I just wanted to eat something and leave.

"Kinsey, I want to continue our conversation," she said, looking up at me and trying to meet my eyes. "You can't just leave in the middle of a conversation."

"You can't just make me move without asking me!" If I thought I'd been okay before, it was all gone now.

My mom looked at me. "I can. I'm the parent and you're the kid."

"Seriously?" That line? That line was bullshit. She didn't get to use that one and pretend that she was somehow so morally superior to me.

"Kinsey, if you don't want to talk about this like an adult – "

"If you want me to act like an adult, you have to treat me like one. And that means asking me about these things!"

My mom's mouth tightened again, and she blinked. "I know that you and Brian – "

"I'm done with this," I said, turning the corner and heading into my room. "I'm going to go see my friends."

"Kinsey," my mom said, taking a step towards me.

I wasn't turning around. I wasn't going to let her suck me back in and act like she was here for me. "No. We're done. I'm going to go see my friends, and I don't want to talk to you any more."

I slammed the door to my room shut behind me.

Shit, the party. How was I supposed to go and hang out with Hunter and act like everything was fine when it was all falling apart?

Hopefully my mom was leaving now. She could go and get out of here and go hang out with Brian, since he was so much more important to her than I was. She could spend all of her time with him. I didn't care. I didn't care at all.

My phone started ringing. "What?" I asked, answering the call.

"Kinsey?" It was Hunter's voice, surprisingly deep. I could hear the music behind him, the bass thudding at the party. "Where are you?"

"Home." Not that this was going to be my home for that much longer. I was at the place that had been my home that I wanted to keep as my house, but that was getting ripped away.

"Aren't you coming?" Behind him, I could hear Ethan shouting for him. "I thought you were coming."

"I can't." I couldn't see Hunter. I couldn't pretend to be happy.

I wanted to see him. That wasn't it. It was just that I couldn't force myself to be happy when I was there. What was Hunter going to do about it anyway? Stand in the corner and try to tell me that everything was okay?

"Why?" He was starting to sound annoyed. Oh god. I had one good thing left for me and I was screwing it up. "I haven't seen you in a week."

"I just can't right now." It had nothing to do with Hunter. It was because of my mom.

"Kinsey, what do you mean? I want to see you. You told me you were coming!" He was starting to sound pissed. I could visualize it. He was starting to pace around the room, running his hand through his hair. My stomach turned.

"I can't, okay?" I was shouting back at him. I didn't want to be shouting, because it wasn't fair to Hunter. It wasn't his fault, but I needed to shout at someone, and he was here.

"Seriously?" he demanded. "You're going to ghost me and not even tell me why?"

"Yes, I am!" I screamed back. I couldn't deal with this. I just needed to be alone.

He was quiet for a few seconds. "Kinsey, is everything okay?"

No. Nothing was okay. "It's fine. I need to go."

And I hung up the phone before I could say anything else. I wasn't going to take this out on Hunter. I couldn't talk to him right now. I'd lose it.

My phone started ringing again. I couldn't handle it if it was Hunter again.

But it wasn't. It was Ellery.

I didn't want to answer. But I had just had a fight with Lily, and now Hunter too. I couldn't lose my last friend standing. "Ellery?"

I could hear the sob she choked back. "Max just told me he didn't like me."

It was silent on the other end. Shit. I took a deep breath. "Where are you?"

"Sitting on the grass outside the party," she said, sniffling again. "Where the hell are you? Hunter was looking for you."

Don't make it worse for me, I wanted to say. "I'm at my house." Not that it would be that for much longer. "I need you too. I'll come get you."

I grabbed my bag from New York and headed into Betta. At least my mom had left my car keys where I could grab them, not hidden somewhere so that I was forced to talk to her. I turned the car on and started the drive to Logan's.

I drove over the speed limit the whole way, the music in the car as loud as I could make it. I needed the music, all the bass that I could get out of my old Honda. I punched in the gate code and pulled up towards Logan's. I couldn't stop the car, couldn't let Hunter see me like this.

Ellery was standing in front of the house, the light from the house lit behind her. I could see the tears on her face, the strap of her romper slightly ajar.

"Get in the car," I said, reaching over and unlocking the child locks.

Behind her, Ethan started to come out onto the porch. He peered into the dark, right towards my car. I thought I could see his mouth open, *Kinsey?* come out.

I wasn't ready for that. "Get in!" I yelled to Ellery. She threw herself into the car, and I peeled out of Logan's driveway.

"Your house?" Ellery asked, looking over at me.

I shook my head. I didn't have a house any more. I

couldn't go home and deal with my mom. "Can I stay with you for a bit?"

"I don't know. I'm a mess and Max doesn't even like me, and you want to hang out with me?" she asked, reaching for one of the tissues in the console between us.

"My mom literally already has movers packing up my stuff. She wants to move in with Brian Senior," I replied.

"What the hell?" Ellery asked, turning towards me. "Are you kidding? The two of us really got screwed today, didn't we?"

"Ice cream is still open. There first?" I asked, checking the time on the dashboard.

"Good idea." She reached for my phone and turned the music up as loud as it could go. We started screaming along, loud enough that I couldn't hear anything else.

We arrived at the ice cream place, and I parked right in front, ignoring the No Parking sign. My mom would deal with it if I got a ticket. Brian Senior could deal with it.

We got our cones seconds before they closed. I walked outside and sat down on the bench outside, looking over at Ellery. "So what happened?"

She took a deep breath, looking down at her ice cream. "I finally took your advice and decided to just ask him if he was into me. I was so tired of running around and flirting with him."

"And?" I asked, looking over at her. Her mascara had run, and she rubbed her eyes.

"He laughed, Kinsey. He literally laughed. He thought Ethan had put me up to it," she said, biting her lip.

I stared at her. Max couldn't have been that mean. He

couldn't have been stupid enough to say that to her face. "I'm so sorry," I said. That wasn't enough for how cruel Max had been, but it was the best that I could come up with.

"I know." She ran a hand through her hair. "Maybe I'm the stupid one. It's obvious he didn't like me. It's not like he ever went out of his way to talk to me at the parties. It was always me trying. It was always me putting in all the work with him. But he could have at least said it in a nicer way."

We sat there for a second. I reached my arm around her shoulder and pulled her into a side hug.

"I'll be fine," she said, her voice soft. "I know I'll be fine. I'll get over it. He's not worth it. But did it have to be this way?"

Maybe it was my fault. I'd been the one who had been telling her all summer that I thought there was something. I wanted there to be something between her and Max, because there was something between me and Hunter. I wanted Ellery to be happy the same way I was.

Ellery tilted her head back towards the sky, blinking a few times. I took a bite of my ice cream and scooted closer to her. "I just didn't want it to end this way," she said.

I knew that feeling. I felt that so deeply.

Just that moment, my phone buzzed. Hunter: *Ethan said he just saw you outside with Ellery?*

Hunter: *What the fuck, Kinsey? You can't just ghost me like this*

I closed my eyes and rested my head on Ellery's shoulder. "I know. But I think we're going to be okay."

· · ·

I WOKE up the next morning at Ellery's house.

I'd fallen asleep in her bed last night. We'd talked when we got back from ice cream, but not for that long before we'd just decided to go to sleep. We ran out of things to say, honestly. My mom was being an asshole and insisting that I move with her and Brian Senior. Max was an asshole to Ellery. There wasn't anything left.

Ellery rolled out of bed. "I'm going to shower," she said, standing up and stretching her arms over her head.

"I need to find food." I had totally not eaten last night other than the ice cream, and now I was starving. At least we'd had ice cream.

"Me too. Everything sucks right now. At least I'll go be clean, and then we get food," she said, walking out the door.

I sat back down on the bed. I was ready for a snack now, but it was too weird to walk downstairs without her. I didn't want to run into her parents and have to make small talk or something.

The phone kept ringing, and I sighed and picked it up. Oh god. Jenna.

I didn't have to answer, did I? But if I didn't, she'd just call again. I could handle talking to Jenna right now, because all I had to do was make some sympathetic noises when she complained about Emberleigh.

It had to be early in Los Angeles. Maybe it was an actual emergency. I should be a good friend. I had barely talked to her all summer.

"Hey, girl," I said, tuning on the phone and setting it on speaker.

"I'm on my way to a sunrise photo shoot, but I heard

some news that I had to tell you about," Jenna said, her voice breathless. "You won't believe this."

'What?" I asked. My heart was sinking, as though it knew that there was no way that Jenna was going to call me if it was good.

"I heard that you were dating Hunter Lowen," Jenna said, her voice on the verge of laughter.

Well. Yeah.

"I – " My voice stopped, and I swallowed. Where did I even start with this? "I mean – "

She snorted. "God, I knew that you wouldn't believe it. Ridiculous, right?"

Okay, I didn't appreciate the idea that I was so unattractive that there was no way that Hunter would be interested in me. I opened my mouth, about to start to correct her when she kept going. "And anyway, you know Hunter. He's such a player. That's why I kept turning him down last year."

That wasn't quite what I remembered happening. "I mean, Jenna – "

Jenna sighed dramatically. "He's one of those guys who just goes around hooking up with people who don't know to say no to him. And then he just moves onto the next one, no harm, no foul, right?"

That wasn't the Hunter I knew. "Yeah," I said finally.

"So catch me up on everything." Jenna said, sighing on the other end of the line. "I thought you'd think the Hunter rumor was hilarious. Like you'd be hooking up with him and not telling me."

"Of course not," I said quickly before I could stop myself.

"So, news?" she asked again.

I swallowed. "My mom is going to move in with Brian Senior."

"And?" Jenna asked.

"And I would have to move," I said, the words sounding fake to me. I still couldn't quite believe them. "I don't want to move in with Brian."

"I bet his house is so much better than yours, though," Jenna said, and I heard honking in the background.

I bit my lower lip. "Yeah, but I've always lived in my house."

"Come on. Your house was always kind of a dump."

I knew that Jenna had sort of thought that for a while, but it was awful to hear her say it. "That's not nice," I said, so softly I wasn't sure if the phone had picked it up.

It didn't matter anyway. Jenna cleared her throat. "You wouldn't believe it." She launched into a story about how Emberleigh had stolen her sunglasses for a photoshoot, and it had meant that Emberleigh had ended up getting a ton of likes on something that Jenna had originally bought. I made supportive noises through the whole thing, hoping that she'd get the message and hang up.

"Okay, well, keep me posted on all the drama," she said on the other end of the phone line at the end of her rant. "Bye."

"Bye," I said, hanging up the phone and then staring at it for a few seconds.

It was like there was nothing to talk about for us outside

of what was going on in her life. Like making fun of Ember-leigh was the only thing that we had left.

Maybe our friendship had actually run its course. Maybe this was the end.

I heard the shower turn off, and I put on clothes. Ellery came out, and we walked down to the kitchen. The house was quiet this morning. "Are your parents ever here?"

She shook her head. "They're on call because there aren't enough doctors in this town. They used to be around a whole lot more, but then they got promoted and now they're always off being doctors. It's actually kind of great."

It wasn't all that different from my past year, where my mom had started seeing Brian Senior and going out on weeknight dates. Ew.

"The greatest bit is that my mom tells me that they see the worst of humanity in the emergency room, so as long as I'm better than most of the people they have to treat, they are okay with it," Ellery said, turning into the kitchen.

She opened the bread drawer and passed me a jar of Nutella. She slathered her piece of bread with it. It was amazing how much more junk food her family had than Brian Senior, despite being doctors. It was really a testa-ment to the fact that not all junk food was that bad for you, or so I was going to believe. "Lily's mom has the same thing. She's a therapist and writes all these books about how it's okay if your kid is mediocre. I'm pretty sure she lumps Lily right in there," I said.

"Speaking of, have you called her yet?" Ellery asked, taking a giant bite of her Nutella bread. "Hm. Needs peanut butter."

Another thing that I was supposed to have done. I hadn't talked to Lily in a week, which was so weird to think about. We hadn't even texted. I shook my head. "Not yet."

"Kinsey." Ellery put her bread down on the counter and stared right at me. "You have to talk to her and apologize."

I knew that Ellery was right. She was at least not entirely wrong. "I know. I'm not trying to avoid her."

"Come on. You're trying to avoid her." Ellery stuck the bread into her mouth again.

Maybe. It was just easier to avoid her than to apologize to all of the people I needed to apologize to. It wasn't just Lily. It was everyone. And all I wanted to do was sit on the couch and not talk to anyone.

There was a knock on the door, and Ellery and I looked at each other. "I can get it," I said, as Ellery's entire mouth was stuffed full of Nutella toast.

I walked to the front door and pulled it open, expecting to see one of Ellery's brother's friends standing there. Instead, it was my mom, wearing a t-shirt and athletic shorts, her hair back in a ponytail. "Hi, Kinsey. Can we talk?"

I stared at her for a second. I didn't want to talk. And how did she even know where I was? "What about?"

"I know that things didn't end well last night, and I wanted to come check on you," she said, looking around the yard and then around the house.

"Why? I'm just staying with my friend," I replied, nodding towards the neatly landscaped garden. That had been Ellery's mom's project last summer, apparently, and it was now maintained by actual gardeners who didn't kill every plant they saw.

"True," my mom said, clearly trying to choose her words carefully and not insult the people whose food I was currently eating, "but I'm really concerned that you responded to the situation by running away."

I looked at her again and then shrugged. "What was I supposed to do?"

My mom closed her eyes for a second, and I felt bad for maybe a millisecond. Maybe. But then she opened her eyes again. "I'd like a chance to talk it out. To make sure that I understand what you're feeling and how we can move forward."

"How I'm feeling?" Seriously? That was a question that she needed me to answer? "Right this instant? I love it here. It's great. Ellery's family is super cool. They don't lecture me about eating carbs. I'm having Nutella toast for breakfast this morning."

My mom looked at me. "Kinsey, that wasn't what I meant."

I knew that, but I wasn't going to admit it. "It's fine. I'll go stay with Dad in the city. I mean, he told me that I should feel free to go stay with him whenever I want, because he understands that it's really hard on the family when someone decides to get remarried without asking their kid."

My mom stared at me for a second. "You'd rather move in with your dad than stay with Brian?"

The honest answer was no, because my dad had Eva around, and I found Eva just as annoying as Brian Senior.

For every comment that Brian Senior made about his diet and how he was so healthy and training for all of these races, Eva made a comment about how she was making sure to work on her art. And that would mean moving away from all of my friends and from Hunter, which was a no go.

But I obviously couldn't tell my mom that, because that would be admitting defeat. "Yeah," I replied.

"Your dad actually told you that? That you were welcome to stay with him for as long as you wanted?" my mom asked, crossing her arms over her chest.

This was the problem with my parents knowing each other. My mom was able to tell that that explanation was clearly bullshit. She ran her hand through her hair. "I don't think this is productive," she said. "But – "

I stared at her for a second. "But what?" I asked.

"But it's really hard for me knowing that you're this upset about everything and feeling that we can't talk it out. I want to go to family therapy with you and talk about things, or at least have you start therapy to make sure that you're getting the support that you need," my mom said, nodding towards me slowly. "And it feels like right now you won't give me that."

I couldn't give her that, because going to therapy to deal with something meant that you first had to admit that the thing was happening. "No thanks."

My mom closed her eyes for a second and then nodded. "Look, Kinsey, I'm not going to pressure you into doing anything that you don't want to do. But things aren't going to go back to the way that they were."

"Okay," I said, looking at her and then away towards

the dead garden, blinking a few times to make sure that there weren't any tears forming in my eyes. I wasn't going to show weakness. Not now. "Are we done so I can go back to eating my breakfast?"

My mom closed her eyes and then nodded. "Okay. We'll talk more soon, Kinsey."

"Great," I replied, turning around and heading back in towards the house. "Bye."

"Was that your mom?" Ellery asked as I walked back into the kitchen, heading straight towards the jar of Nutella. I knew that stress eating was a bad coping mechanism. I should go running or find a therapist or something, but right now, a jar of Nutella felt like a better solution.

"Unfortunately," I replied, taking a piece of bread out of the bread box, which was apparently another thing that Ellery's family actually had.

Ellery raised her eyebrows at me. I took a deep breath. "I told her that I was staying over with friends, and I guess maybe she went and visited all my friends until she found me?"

Not that I would have expected my mom to know that Ellery was my go to friend now. I assumed she'd been tuning that out all summer, like she'd done with everything else.

Ellery looked at me as she finished chewing her Nutella bread. "Okay. We need an intervention here. You want to go run a workout before it gets too hot out?"

"No." I could not think of anything that sounded less appealing than going to run a workout right now. I wasn't Ellery, who was really good at running and practiced so that she could be the best on the team. I was mediocre, and I was totally okay with that.

"I'm going to give you options. You can either come run a workout with me or get the conversation with Lily over with," she said, licking the last bit of Nutella off her knife.

Had I mentioned that I was pretty sure Ellery was evil? "Seriously? I don't want to do either of those things."

"I know. That's why I'm forcing you to do them," she replied. "You need some way to work out your feelings, and I hate running workouts by myself. Come on."

I was going to take back all of the nice things that I had thought about Ellery. "Fine," I said, pushing myself up from the counter. "I'll go put on a sports bra and get out of my cute clothes."

"Come on. Those weren't cute clothes. Those were the random clothes you had on the floor," she replied. "I know what cute clothes are. You're just complaining now."

Yeah, I might have just been complaining because I really didn't want to go run a workout. I'd had a very bad night.

I very slowly put on my shoes and my workout clothes, then walked back downstairs. Ellery was already bouncing from foot to foot. "Legit, running a workout is the best way to get the anger out if you're dealing with stuff," she said. "My mom used to tell me to do sprints when I was feeling upset about something, and it really works."

I was not sure that any amount of running could fix my life right now. "That sounds so wrong. My life is awful. Workouts are awful. Why are you telling me that this will be better than Netflix and more Nutella on the couch?"

"Because then you will feel gross," she replied, picking up her car keys and walking out to the car, too confidently. I followed her slowly. Maybe if I walked really slowly, she'd change her mind. "And we can watch all the trashy TV we want after we finish this."

I hated knowing that Ellery was absolutely right. We drove to the track at the high school, and I shot her a look as we parked. "I actually do hate you right now. If you were wondering."

"I know. But you'll stop hating me soon," she replied, getting out of the car and checking her shoelaces.

"In forty-five minutes when the workout is over," I said, closing my car door.

"An hour. Don't forget the warm up. We have like a month of training left before our first meet, and I want to do well," she said, closing the car door and starting to walk over towards the track.

"You know that I picked cross country because it was the chillest sport," I said, following her towards the track. Cross country even had shorter practices than the rest of our school's sports. It was designed for people like me.

"Come on. You are complaining too much." She clapped her hands. "Are we moving here?"

She was using that word just to make me angry and get me to run with her. It worked. "Let's go. I hate you right now."

Forty-seven minutes later, I was ready to lie down on the track and never move again. "Another one?" I asked, my voice sounding like a pant.

"What, you don't want to run another one?" she asked, looking over at me.

How was she able to say these things in a normal voice? Ellery was a robot. "You go."

"I'm not leaving you," she said, giving me a pat on the back. "Come on. Two last ones."

"Then after those two I'm done," I said. "You are not making me do more of these. My legs cannot do more of these."

"Then you're done after two more. I'll run a few more, but you can be done," she said, looking down at her watch. "Let's go."

I hobbled through the last interval. My legs were on fire. My lungs were on fire. Why did anyone do this stupid sport anyway?

This track was so long. It had to be more than a standard track. It was not possible.

I reached the end, sticking my hands on my thighs and bending over for air. Ellery grinned at me. "Thirty seconds. Then we're going again."

She seemed to genuinely enjoy this. She was not normal. I tried to suck down as much air as I could. "And go!" Ellery said, flying past me.

I would have hated her if I'd had the strength left for it. I pushed my legs forward, forcing them to move. I could do this. I could totally do this. I reached the end of the track, staggered to the middle, and flopped down on the grass. "Ellery. I hate you."

"Come on, let's jog it out," she said, leaning down and offering me her hand. "We can jog a bit, and then I'll do a few more. The season is coming up, so we should get practicing anyway."

I got to my feet and started slowly jogging with her around the track again. I knew that I was supposed to do a cool down, but I was done with this. Ellery had made me work out harder than I had worked out in weeks.

That was probably not a good sign for my overall fitness going into the year, but still. I could deal with that when the season actually started.

"Are you not even out of breath?" I asked, looking over at her.

"I mean, I am when we sprint, but it's back now," she said, even managing to sound cheerful. "And I feel way better, you know?"

"I feel like I'm going to pass out on the track," I replied.

She shook her head at me. "This is why you should have been practicing more all summer. I'm not just saying this to be a jerk, but Coach is going to annihilate you."

I would have stuck my tongue out at her, but that would take too much energy.

We rounded the track again, and I rolled my shoulders. We slowed down to a walk. "That felt good," Ellery said, swinging her arms.

Now that I was almost breathing normally again, she had a point. The physical pain of running had nicely blocked out all of my thoughts about Hunter and Lily and my mom. All I had to do was keep going in the circle, and I'd be okay.

I stopped and put my hands on my knees, leaning down. I was finally going to catch my breath.

"Oh." Ellery's voice was not happy.

I looked up to see the soccer guys walking across the field toward us. "I thought they had afternoon practice," I choked out.

"Oh no," she said, staring at the guys.

Max was walking in the front, looping his arm around Logan's shoulder. "I'm running more," she said, turning away from me.

"Ellery!" I couldn't run any more. She was just leaving me here, flying around the track.

But she was taking off around the track before I could stop her. My legs weren't going to keep up with her.

I looked back at the guys again. In the back of the group was Hunter, striding forward.

He wasn't going to notice me. I wasn't ready for that conversation. I was going to stretch, and –

"Kinsey!" It was Logan, waving towards me.

Goddamn it. I looked up. Hunter had clearly spotted me now.

There was nothing I could do now. Hunter jogged over, his soccer bag over his shoulder. I couldn't read his face, couldn't tell what he was thinking. "Kinsey."

I forced a smile. "Hi," I said. My voice sounded obnoxiously high and wispy. Which wasn't my fault, because Ellery had been making me run intervals with her and I was out of breath.

"What the hell happened last night?" Hunter asked, stepping directly in front of me.

I swallowed. "I – "

"Seriously, Kins. You told me you were going to be

there, then didn't show up. And when I called you, you sounded like you were having a breakdown. What the hell?" He ran his hand through his hair. It stuck up with sweat.

I glanced back over at Ellery, who was still running around the track like she didn't notice us. She was going even faster than we had been going before. It must have been the pure rage of seeing the guys fueling her. "Are you mad at me?" I blurted out, in the stupidest thing I could have said.

He stared at me, his lips narrowing into a thin line. "Of course I'm mad at you! I'm furious. You can't just ghost me. You literally hung up on me."

That wasn't fair. It wasn't like I had blocked out Hunter because I didn't like him or didn't want to tell him. I just hadn't known how. There were too many things that were still in my head that I hadn't figured out.

"Bro, are you coming?" Logan called, looking over his shoulder back towards Hunter.

Hunter waved his hand, and Logan nodded and kept walking. I swallowed and turned to face Hunter. "I'm sorry," I said finally. "I get why you're mad."

"I'm mad because I'm worried. And because you just left me at the party even after you said you'd come," he said again, rolling his shoulder back. "You ghosted me, Kinsey."

"I know," I said, staring down at the ground.

"You cannot tell me that you're going to be somewhere and just not show up, Kins!" He squared his shoulders and stood in front of me, the same position he'd used when Lily had yelled at me.

At least he's using your nickname, said a voice in the back of my head. *So maybe he won't just dump you right now.*

Deep breath. "I had a super rough night last night."

Hunter crossed his arms over his chest. "Really." He spat out the word.

Shit. He probably thought I meant that I had gone out without him. I'd been out partying and had gotten drunk without him and ignored him. I swallowed again. "Not like that. My mom told me I had to move in with Brian Senior."

Hunter's eyes widened for a second. He took a step towards me, his hand reaching towards my side. "What?"

I nodded, swallowing. I wasn't going to cry now, even though the tears were bubbling up. "She didn't even ask. She decided all of it while I was on the Mandatory Two, so I didn't get a chance to say anything. And she just started moving my stuff."

"She didn't tell you at all?" He took another step towards me.

I stared down at the ground and blinked a few times, trying to stop the tears. "I found out right before your party, and I was just not in a good place."

"Why didn't you text me and tell me?" he asked, his hand resting on my arm. I glanced down, and he pulled it away.

Wasn't it obvious? "Because you were out at a party. I wasn't going to text you and be like, my mom just told me that I have to move in with Brian Senior."

"Yeah, but," he said, running his hand through his hair

again, "I want to be there for you on stuff like this. I would have left the party."

"You would have left the party? But I wouldn't want you to leave the party." I wasn't going to be the downer who told him that he couldn't have fun with his friends, because I needed him more.

"Of course I would have left the party to be with you!" Something flashed across his face, almost disbelief. "I can't believe you think I wouldn't have. Kinsey, we're together. I want to be there when you are having a bad day. That's more important than partying with my friends."

It was hard to imagine that. It was hard to think that Hunter would actually leave a party for me. Especially in the world where Max would just tell Ellery to her face that he didn't like her.

"Thanks," I said finally, looking down at the ground again.

"And I'm sorry. That really sucks," he said, his voice deep and final.

That was what I had been waiting to hear. An acknowledgement that this was terrible and shitty. That I didn't want to move in with Brian Senior, that I didn't want to leave behind the house that I had grown up in to live with him.

I glanced up at him. He reached his arms around me and pulled me into a tight hug. I buried my head in his chest, letting the tears out for a second.

It was okay. It was going to be okay.

One of the soccer guys yelled something, and Hunter released me from the hug. "My offer to eat a burrito and a pint of ice cream and beat him in a half marathon still stands."

"Imagine me having to live with him and having to listen to all of that every day," I said. I couldn't think about it right now. I rested my head back on Hunter's chest, and he wrapped an arm around me.

"You can always stay at Ellery's, I guess," Hunter replied. "Or you can let me beat Brian Senior in the burrito mile, and then he will have to move out in shame and you can keep his house."

"That's a generous offer," I said. "But I just want my own house back. The house where my mom and I lived for so many years, you know?"

He laughed. "I get that. But I'm going to plug the burrito mile again."

I snorted. "I don't think that's the real answer to my problems, but thank you."

"I'm just saying, I bet if he ate a burrito and then ran a mile, he'd have to puke. Even if I let him have one without any dairy."

I shook my head, catching myself starting to smile. Hunter made everything seem easier. "I don't know how I'm supposed to get through the next few weeks. My mom has all this wedding stuff that she's insisting on, and I have to look happy and excited for her. Or enough that it won't all backfire on me."

"You need a wedding date?" he asked.

"A what?" I asked, looking up at him. I always forgot how much taller he was than I was, how I had to look up at him when we were standing next to each other.

"A date to the wedding. Because I'm great at making parties more fun," he said, grinning down at me.

My heart picked up a few beats. It would be so much easier if Hunter was there. I'd have someone who could tell me that it would be okay, someone who could tell me that I wasn't being unreasonable, someone who could distract me.

"Not Ethan?" I asked finally. I didn't know how to tell him that it meant a lot, and it was easier to be funny than to try to say that.

Hunter snorted. "Ethan would bring the party, but your mom might disown you."

Ethan would have way too good of a time at a wedding. There might be glitter bombs. "I would really like it if you came."

Hunter grinned at me and pulled me into a hug. We were both so sweaty from practice that it was a little bit gross, but I didn't care. I leaned into him and closed my eyes for a second. Everything was going to be okay.

Hunter released me from the hug, and I took a step back, glancing over my shoulder. Ellery had finished the workout and was in the middle of her cool down now. "You weren't running with her?" Hunter asked, looking over towards Ellery.

"I couldn't keep up. I'm going to not be able to walk for weeks." My legs were already hurting.

"She's really fast, you know?" Hunter said, nodding towards her.

"Yeah, I know. I'm on the team with her, and trust me, she's impossible to keep up with during practice," I said. It was going to be a rough start to the season.

Ellery slowed to a walk and then came towards us. "Hey, Hunter," she said, wiping the sweat off her forehead with her shirt.

"Hey, Ellery. Nice run," Hunter said, nodding towards the track.

She pushed a piece of sweaty hair out of her face. "I needed it. Had to get out and run it out."

Hunter glanced at me for a second. I wouldn't tell him about Max right now. That felt like Ellery's thing to tell him.

"Lowen!" someone shouted from the parking lot. "You're supposed to give me a ride home!"

Hunter glanced at us and then back over at the parking lot. "I should probably go. Text me later, okay?"

I nodded. "I mean it," he said, his hand sitting on my side. He made direct eye contact and held it. "Kinsey. Tell me if things are okay."

I nodded again, swallowing. I would. I would trust him this time. "And tell me when for the wedding stuff," he said, starting to walk backwards towards the parking lot.

I watched him go, my heart doing a little flutter. Ellery nudged my shoulder, snapping me out of it. "You guys are all good again?" she asked, starting to stretch next to me.

I nodded. "He was just upset that I didn't tell him what was going on."

"You didn't tell him about Max, did you?" she asked, looking up at me from where she was hanging her head in the middle of her stretch.

I shook my head. "Good," she said. "I don't think I

could look him in the eyes again if he knew the whole story."

"Want to get egg sandwiches?" Ellery asked. "We could go to the Nest."

"That is my absolute favorite breakfast spot!" I said, turning towards her.

She grinned at me. "You've mentioned it. And I've never tried it. So it seemed like a good moment for it."

And I deserved it after that workout. Keeping up with Ellery was no joke. "Perfect."

I WAS DRIVING HOME from Ellery's when it occurred to me that I should probably do another apology.

I hadn't talked to Lily at all. I hadn't even texted her. We were having a straight up silent fight, and that was something that I would have thought it was impossible to do.

I still wasn't convinced that I'd been wrong. But at the same time, I didn't want to be right but lose my best friend.

I paused where I was going to turn off towards my house and hopped on the highway instead.

Twenty minutes later, I pulled up in front of Lily's house and rang the doorbell. Her mom came to the front door and saw me standing there. "Kinsey! What a nice surprise!"

"Is Lily home?" I asked, trying to avoid too obviously glancing through the doorway to see if I could spot her.

"She is," her mom said, nodding towards me. "She's upstairs."

"Do you mind if I come in?" I asked.

I was waiting for Lily's mom to tell me that she knew about the fight, that I was no longer welcome at their house. But my imagination was being overly dramatic as usual. Her mom stepped aside and let me in. "Of course."

I glanced to the side as I started to walk up the stairs, seeing the enormous pile of toilet paper that was sitting next to the bottom of the stairs. I took the stairs two at a time, reaching Lily's door and knocking. "Hey. It's Kinsey."

Lily pulled open the door and stared at me. "What?"

I swallowed, shifting my weight from one foot to the other. "I came to apologize."

She stared at me for a second, then waved me in. "You can come in."

I walked around the doorway and sat down on the edge of her bed. "Hi."

She raised her eyebrows at me. "That's all I get? You dump me for your fancy new boyfriend and all I get is a hi?"

I stared at the wall for a second, then took a deep breath. "I didn't mean to dump you for Hunter."

"But you did," she said, picking up a pillow and clutching it to her chest. "Literally, I went to a party because I wanted to hang out with you, and then you started making out with your boyfriend on the back porch."

I wanted to argue with her and tell her that that wasn't fair, but I knew that it was. I had left her so that I could hang out with Hunter. Even if I hadn't meant to hurt her, I still had.

"I'm sorry," I said, taking a deep breath again. "Like I

am really sorry about that. I get how it's awkward for me to leave you at a party when you don't know anyone."

"I know that Ellery is one of your friends, but I barely know her," Lily said, clutching the pillow even tighter. "She's super nice, but I can't just steal her away from the guy she's talking to."

"Yeah." I knew the feeling. I knew what it was like to stand on the outside of the party, when Jenna was in the middle talking to everyone because she knew everyone. Before this summer, I was always the person who got left out.

Deep breath. Before I could say anything, Lily kept talking. "It just feels like you've changed so much this summer. Like you were my friend Kinsey last year, and now you're Hunter Lowen's girlfriend and popular and always in the middle of everything."

"I'm not popular." Just because I was dating Hunter didn't make me any different.

"Yeah, you are," she said, leveling me with a stare. "I feel like I can't tell you anything about my life right now, because anything that happens in your life is automatically a bigger deal."

"That's not true!" I would never have pushed Lily to the side just because I had Hunter. I cared about Lily, and I would never leave my friends for a guy.

"I know you don't think that it's true, but any guy I like is going to be less of a big deal than you being with Hunter Lowen. He's Hunter Lowen. Every time we've talked this summer, you've always had so much news about Hunter," she said, still keeping her arms wrapped around her pillow.

"But that's because I spend a lot of time with Hunter!" It wasn't that I was trying to ignore Lily or that I thought I was somehow better than she was because I was with Hunter. It was just what had happened because Hunter was in my life.

"I know." She shook her head. "And I'm not saying that you shouldn't. But it makes me feel like I'm nothing, you know? You're the person with a boyfriend now."

I stared at her. It was true. Lily had been the one of the two of us who had always believed in true love. She was always going on about how she wanted to meet someone. She wanted her Netflix relationship, and I had been the one who'd stumbled into it instead.

"I know," I said finally. "I guess I can see how it's really exciting for me but not for you."

She nodded. "That's kind of it. Like you're off having this big adventure this summer because it's your first boyfriend, and it's stupid Hunter Lowen on top of that, and I'm still here. I'm still the same person."

"I don't think it's Hunter that changed me. I think I changed. Like I like being the Kinsey who goes to parties and knows people and hangs out with people. It doesn't mean that I'm Hunter's person or something. I like who I am," I said, turning back towards her.

She took a deep breath and looked at me. "Do you think that's true? You're not just playing it all up because all of a sudden, you're dating Hunter?"

"I don't think so at all. I like going out to parties. I like who I am," I said, swinging my feet in the air for a second.

"You've changed a lot," she said, leveling her eyes at me.

"You're nothing like the Kinsey I knew at the start of the summer. No offense, but it's true."

It was hard not to take offense at that. I took a deep breath. "I know that I'm changing, but it feels right to me. At the same time, though, I know that I shouldn't have made you feel like you were second to him."

Lily released the pillow from in front of her slightly. "You think?"

I nodded. "No, I mean, I know. I shouldn't have done that, because of course it was going to make you feel like you weren't important to me. And you are important to me. I just don't always do a good job of showing it, and I need to work on making it more obvious. And I'm sorry. Again."

She looked at me and then nodded. "Okay."

"Forgive me?" I asked, my heart racing.

"Dude, of course," she said, leaning forward and giving me a hug. "You're an idiot, but you're my idiot, and I'm always going to forgive you for being a little idiot."

I rested my head on her shoulder, wrapping an arm around her. "Oh, thank god. I don't know what I'd do without you."

"You owe me, though," she said, pointing her finger at me. "I get to hold this over your head for a long time."

"Of course," I replied, giving her a tighter hug. "You're the best, Lily."

FIFTEEN

"HOW LONG DO you want to wait to get out of the car?" Hunter asked, turning towards me.

"Maybe forever," I said, glancing out my window. I could see my mom and Brian Senior's cars sitting in the parking lot.

There were a lot of things that you could say about my mom and Brian Senior, but you couldn't say that they didn't move fast. Somehow, they'd managed to pull off organizing an entire wedding and buying a house in literally two months.

I was starting to think that they'd been planning this all along and just wanted to surprise me, so things were already in motion before I could say no. *They were probably hoping to go on a honeymoon while you were on the Mandatory Two,* said a voice in the back of my head.

It was the rehearsal dinner tonight. It was going to be a small wedding, which I was pretty sure was because all of Brian Senior's friends had decided to be friends with his ex rather than with him. I too would have made that choice, so I understood.

"I don't think that we can avoid it forever," Hunter said. He was wearing a button down shirt, a blazer hanging up in the back of the car. I'd told my mom that Hunter was going to be coming with me to all of the wedding festivities, and probably because we were still fighting, she'd said yes.

I leaned my head on his shoulder and sighed. "I just want to stop this," I said finally. "I just want the world to go on pause for a minute so that I can enjoy having a summer with my mom and not be thinking about all of the stuff that's coming."

I wanted to go back two weeks, when it was just me and Hunter, and me and my mom in our house. I wasn't ready for everything to change all at once.

Hunter reached his arm around me. "I'm always here to run the burrito mile when you need me. But I don't think you can undo all the stuff with your mom."

He was right, but that didn't make it any better. "What if we just didn't go?" I asked, turning towards him. "I could say that you threw up in the car and had to go home."

"They would definitely know that you were making that up," he replied.

"But then I'd get to skip one of the most awkward things of all time." We were sharing the space for our rehearsal dinner with the restaurant's weekly jazz night, because my mom and Brian Senior had booked late enough that they could only get a Thursday.

"Let's get it over with," Hunter said, reaching over and

squeezing my knee. "Come on. An hour and then we can get ice cream."

"Fine," I said, opening the car door. Hunter waited for me as I walked around towards the front door. He squeezed my hand.

The valet took the car, and I followed Hunter through the hotel doors. Here it went.

We hadn't even made it all the way to the restaurant before Brian Senior spotted us. "Kinsey! Your mother was getting worried about you!" he announced to literally everyone within earshot.

Hunter squeezed my hand again, tighter this time. "I told her that I was going to be here at this time. There was no reason that she'd be worried," I said, forcing a smile.

"Brian and Elise are already sitting at the table," he said, crossing his arms and looking at me. "They weren't late because they were hanging out with their friends. This is a family dinner, Kinsey."

Oh, Brian was big mad because I had brought Hunter. I was upstaging Brian Junior. "Okay," I said, turning towards the room where everyone was gathering. Hunter put his hand on my lower back.

My mom was already in the room when we walked in. "Kinsey!" she said, rushing over to me and giving me a hug. "Isn't this just so exciting?"

I could feel Hunter's hand on my back. I could do this. I could pretend this was actually exciting and not the worst thing to happen to me. I forced a smile. "Yeah."

"You and Hunter can sit next to Elise and Brian," my

mom said, giving me a smile that definitely looked a little bit plastic to me, or maybe I just hoped that.

With the worst timing, my future stepsister looked up at Hunter, then me, then right back at Hunter. "You can totally sit with us," she said, flipping her hair over her shoulder.

I made temporary eye contact with Brian Junior, who rolled his eyes. Brian Senior sat down at the front of the room and looked around at us. "Before we begin, I'd like to give a speech."

Oh god. Hunter grabbed my hand under the table.

Brian Senior stood up and clinked his glass, the patio around us falling quiet. "I'd like to make a toast to my lovely bride to be and to my new family," he said, looking around the room at everyone looking back at him.

Sure. His new family. Totally.

"Emma," he said, lowering his glass and then staring at my mom with puppy dog eyes, "you are the most wonderful woman I have ever met."

Kill me now. I pressed my lips together, forcing myself to keep them in something that looked like a smile. In the room all around me, people were beaming up towards our table, as though this was just the best thing they'd ever sat through.

"You enchant me every day," he continued. My mom seemed to actually be enjoying this, "and I cannot be prouder to soon be able to call you my wife."

Okay, this is where my mom would normally have looked at him and reminded him that she had a rich identity outside of being his wife, and that there were many more appropriate descriptors that he could have used. But instead, she just smiled at him like this was the greatest thing that she'd ever had happen to her.

Which before this event, she'd usually said was the day that I was born.

"Thank you, Brian," my mom said, looking up at him.

Brian Senior sat down, and I turned away to look towards the wall. Hunter's hand rested on my knee, letting me know he was still here. I took a deep breath, forcing myself to look back towards the party.

"Well, let's all eat!" Brian Senior said, sticking his arm around my mom's back. The wait staff started to come out, carrying out plates.

"Please tell me this isn't sugar free and no dairy," Hunter whispered to me, nodding towards the plates.

Elise looked over at the two of us. "And who are you?" she asked, leaning towards Hunter.

From what I had gathered about Elise, she was just a mean girl who liked to be mean. Maybe I was judging her too hard. But given that she was only smiling at Hunter, I was going to be snarky to her.

"I'm Hunter Lowen," he said. Brian Junior snorted. Hunter didn't look over at him. "I'm Kisney's boyfriend."

Elise looked at me, then back at Hunter, then back at me. "I didn't know that you were dating anyone, Kinsey," Elise said in the sweetest voice that she could manage. "Dad made it sound like you were – you know."

I didn't actually know, but I didn't want to know. "He was wrong, then," I said, forcing myself to keep the nicest tone of voice that I could manage.

Hunter's hand reached back for my knee under the table. "It's all good," he mouthed to me. He turned back towards Elise. "Kinsey and I have been going out all summer. She's awesome."

A waiter dropped the plates on our table. They did not seem like they had quite enough food to count as a dinner. "Is this what we're getting?" Brian Junior asked under his breath.

It was fish without sauce and some boiled vegetables next to it. "At least you should run your fastest ever mile without dairy tonight," Hunter whispered to me.

I snickered. "I should tell Ellery. Think I can outrun her tomorrow?"

Hunter snorted, his hand resting on my thigh for a second. "I bet you could out sprint me tomorrow. There's not a single bit of dairy on your plate."

I finished picking at the piece of fish and looked over at Hunter. He'd finished inhaling his and was looking at mine. "Are you going to finish that?" he asked.

"Was a single piece of overcooked fish not enough food for you?" I slid my plate over towards him, and he placed it on top of his.

He rolled his eyes at me. "Do you think Brian Senior specifically asked them not to bring out bread before dinner?"

"We can go to Chipotle after," I whispered back.

My mom sent me a look from where she was sitting. She was probably salty that I was talking to Hunter and not Brian Junior and Elise, but that was her problem.

Brian Junior pushed his plate towards the front of the

table and looked at Hunter. "So you go to school with Kinsey?"

Hunter nodded. "Yeah, I do. I'm on the soccer and lacrosse teams. We're pretty good." He caught my eye for a second and smirked before I had a chance to roll my eyes at him.

"I think I've seen you play before. Dad made me join the soccer team this year," Brian Junior said, looking at Hunter and picking at his fish again.

Elise cleared her throat and leaned towards us. "You're the state record holder, aren't you?" she asked, her voice breathless.

"Yeah," Hunter said, looking over towards me and not towards Elise. "I set the record for goals scored in soccer last fall. Almost broke it in lacrosse, too."

"So are you going to set another record this year?" Elise asked, leaning towards him again. She honest to god fluttered her eyelashes. I was really starting to hate her almost as much as Brian Senior.

"Hopefully. Our team is really good again," Hunter replied. He looked over at me and put his arm around my shoulder. "Want to go look at the water?"

"We have dessert coming in a little bit. Your mom insisted on it," Elise said, finally acknowledging my presence.

"I think we can come back for that," I said, standing up and shoving in my chair.

Hunter followed me out of the room and towards the outdoor porch. It was so beautiful here, and I wasn't going to be sitting inside listening to Brian Senior drone on or pretending to be nice to Elise and Brian Junior.

"I thought you were going to lose it at your stepsister in there," Hunter said as I leaned against the railing, staring out at the water.

Did it make me petty that I loved that he just called her my stepsister? Absolutely, but I was going with it. "Maybe I'd be less mad at everything if I'd had enough to eat." I turned towards the water and closed my eyes for a second, letting the breeze hit my face.

Hunter snorted, his hand resting on my back. "I feel that. I am starving. This dessert better be fantastic."

"I hope it's ice cream. Dairy and sugar. Topped with whipped cream for extra sugar and dairy." Brian Senior didn't have dietary restrictions. He just didn't have a soul.

"I would eat a gallon of ice cream right now," Hunter replied. "Good job not getting mad at him during dinner."

That was not funny. Hunter might have thought that he was funny, but he was not. I tried to give him a look, but then I saw that he was already laughing. "You're just screwing with me," I said, shaking my head at him. "You know that I'm going to be hungry and already dealing with Brian Senior."

"And someone should have told Brian Senior that that was a bad combination," he said, looping his arm around me.

One of my mom's friends wandered outside and saw the two of us. She smiled at me, then at Hunter. "Kinsey, you look so pretty! Let me get a picture of the two of you!"

Hunter passed her his and pulled me towards him. I

leaned my head towards him, looking up at him for as second as he pushed his hair back. "So cute!" she trilled, passing Hunter back his phone and then starting to stagger back towards the bar.

"She's definitely drunk," Hunter said, nodding towards her as she slipped back into the party. "Do you think that she was in love with your mom or with Brian Senior?"

"What do you mean?" I asked. There was no way that anyone was in love with Brian Senior.

"I learned from my cousins that when people get drunk at a pre-wedding event, it's usually because they're upset about the thing and looking for a way out," he replied. "In my cousin's case that meant that the ex still wanted to get back with the person who was getting married."

"And that's why they got drunk?" That didn't seem like it would solve the problem.

"I didn't say it was the smartest. Just that my cousins have had super amusing weddings," he replied, pulling me into a side hug again.

There was a noise inside, and I looked up to see the cake being rolled out. "Is that actually cake?" Hunter asked, his fingers drumming on my back. "Like, with sugar and eggs and milk in it?"

"Don't get me excited. We're going to get up there and be cheated. It will be a sad compromise cake. And the worst part is that if he'd thought about it, we could have a relatively healthy cake and still have it be delicious." There were so many good options for cake in the world, and of course Brian Senior was going to be one of those people who didn't want us to have nice things.

"I don't think Brian Senior would agree with you that you have healthy cake. Cake has dairy," Hunter said.

"I am going to have to ask you to run the burrito mile," I said. "I'm going to get guilt tripped about my upcoming cross country season if I go have a piece of that cake, and you know that then I will absolutely lose it."

"I'll get your piece of cake," he said, squeezing my waist. "I am not going to let Brian Senior guilt you out of your cake."

Had I mentioned that Hunter might be the world's greatest boyfriend? "I'm going to run to the bathroom and then meet you in there."

"I'll make sure to grab as many pieces as I can," he said, nodding towards me. "I bet there's going to be a run on the cake. Nobody had enough to eat at that dinner."

"I'll be right back," I promised, squeezing his hand before I turned towards the bathroom. I walked down the hall and then found it. It was one of those fancy bathrooms with a whole sitting area and cloth towels. I would have expected better food from how fancy this bathroom was.

"Kinsey?" my mom's voice asked behind me.

I turned around to see her. She was standing there, staring at me, with her hair pushed off to the side. "Is everything okay?"

"What do you mean?" Nothing had been okay between me and her all summer. Nothing had been okay for months.

"You seemed really out of it at dinner," she said, looking at me, one corner of her mouth bending down. "You weren't talking to Brian and Elise at all."

"I don't know Brian and Elise. I don't have anything in

common with them." I pulled my hair back over my shoulder.

My mom took a deep breath. "But they're part of our family now."

I stared at her for a second. She didn't get it. She still didn't get it. "You and Brian Senior signing a piece of paper doesn't make them my family, Mom. My family was you. And now I've gotten traded in for some random guy with a dad bod and kids who hate me."

"Kinsey – " my mom said, reaching towards me.

I took a step back, away from her. "I guess I thought that you and I were inseparable. And then Brian Senior showed up."

My mom stopped and started to say something, but I took a deep breath. I had to say this before I talked myself out of it.

"Please let me keep going." I swallowed, reaching my hand down onto the counter and bracing myself. "It's like, I was always happy with you. I thought it was the two of us against the world. And then you started dating Brian Senior, and telling everyone that he was the person who made you happier than ever before. You didn't need me any more, that I'd failed, that you didn't want me around any more."

"Oh, Kinsey," my mom said, reaching out towards me. I looked down at her hand and refused to grab it. "That's not it."

"Maybe, but that's not what it feels like," I said.

My mom looked me directly in the eyes. "You have to understand that I love you like you're my child, because you are. What I feel about Brian is something different, and it doesn't change how I feel about you."

"You left me behind because all you care about now is Brian Senior. Literally, the only thing that you ever talk is Brian Senior! Every decision you've made this summer has been for Brian Senior, not me." I could hear my voice getting louder. I swallowed.

"And I'm sorry that that's how it came off, because I never want to leave you behind. You are the person I care the most about, Kinsey. You're my kid. And you know that for a parent, there is nothing more important than making sure that your kid is happy. Parents will do anything for their kids," she said, giving me a smile.

Sure, but then she'd just spent the entire summer with Brian. We were moving into a new house because of stupid Brian. She couldn't stand here and tell me that after everything that had happened this summer. "Oh, right. That's why you decided that we should move without even asking me. And why you skipped every single thing we used to do together this summer. Nothing's more important than making sure I'm happy. Sure."

My mom swallowed, not quite meeting my eyes. "I wanted to make sure that you never felt like I was leaving you behind for Brian. I'm really sorry about that, and that you felt like I could ever abandon you for anyone else."

I swallowed and looked away. Even if she hadn't meant it that way, that was how it had felt. "Did you even know that I'm dating someone before I asked to bring Hunter?" I asked.

My mom stared back at me for a second and then took a

deep breath. "My answer is no. And I know that that answer means that I need to be paying more attention to you and what's going on in your life."

"He's amazing." I took a deep breath. He was even more than that word could capture. "But I didn't abandon my friends for him, Mom. I made a point to actually still spend time with my friends and didn't throw them away just because I met Hunter. And that's what you did to me with Brian Senior."

"Oh, Kinsey," she said again. She swallowed, looking over at me. "I thought that we were close enough that you would tell me these things. I asked you about Brian, and you said you liked him, and I never heard you say anything else. I thought you'd trust me enough to tell me."

"The first time I met him, I said he was okay. What was I supposed to say, that I think he's the most boring person in the world? I never thought you'd be serious about him." I hadn't thought that much of it the first time I met him, because I hadn't thought that my mom would actually go for him.

We stood in silence for a few seconds. I couldn't look directly at her. My mom took another deep breath. "I'm really sad that we're only now having this conversation, Kinsey. We've had a lot of time to talk about things, and I do feel a little hurt that we're in a situation where I can't change things any more."

If there was even a little bit of hope that my mom was going to call off the wedding, it was gone. But I think I had known that all along. My mom wasn't going to call off the wedding, because she didn't want to stop what she had with Brian Senior.

And even if I didn't understand it, I got it. I wouldn't give up my friendships, but I wasn't going to let Hunter go. I was too happy with him to let it go.

I looked away towards the mirror. I couldn't take it back. I couldn't change how I felt about the situation. And even if it made my mom sad, I had to say my part.

"Maybe once this is all over, we could try family therapy?" my mom offered, looking at me. "I don't know how to fix this, Kinsey. I think it's going to take time. But things are going to keep changing. But I want you to know that I want to get through them together. I want to make sure that going forward we're still Kinsey and Emma against the world, and that we make room in that circle for Brian and Elise and Brian."

"I'm not making room in the circle for Brian Senior and Elise and Brian Junior, Mom." That was way too much for her to ask after everything.

But things were changing, and what I had to decide now was whether I wanted to hold onto the pieces that I cared about or throw everything away. And in the moment, it felt like throwing everything away was the wrong choice.

It was the choice that I could make in the moment, and it would feel good. I wanted to push away Brian Senior and my mom right now. But that wouldn't buy me happiness in the long term, that I would be fighting the same battles over and over again, and that at the end of the day, I'd just be sad. I couldn't stop it, no matter how much I tried.

I took a deep breath. "I can do therapy with you, Mom.

But I'm not treating Brian Junior and Elise as my new brother and sister. I'm not accepting Brian Senior as my dad. I have one of those already."

My mom looked at me for a second, then nodded. "Okay. If that's where you are, then I can meet you there. We can go from there."

I looked down at the ground. "That's it."

My mom pulled me into a hug, burying her face in my hair. "I love you to the moon and back, Kinsey. More than anything."

I forced myself to smile, then nodded.

My mom dabbed at the sides of her eye with one of the many fancy towels, then smiled again. "I should get back out there. We'll talk more later, okay?"

I nodded, then sat down for a second as I watched her leave. I took a deep breath. I would never turn into Brian Senior's biggest fan. I might never like him. But I could deal with this. I could start here, and then I could figure it out.

I wiped my face, then headed back out to the party.

Hunter was standing in the corner holding three plates of cake. "I saved you as much as I could," he said, nodding towards the plates. "Brian Junior helped."

I looked over to see Brian Junior standing nearby. He lifted up a stack of plates towards me in acknowledgement. Maybe he wasn't the worst after all.

"All good? Or just a line for the bathroom?" he asked as I picked up the first plate of cake.

I took a deep breath, looking up towards him. "I talked to my mom," I said, blinking twice.

"Kinsey," he said, taking my piece of cake and wrapping me in a hug. "Is everything okay? Do you want to go outside?"

The worry in his voice was overwhelming. I buried my head into his shoulder and took another deep breath. "No, I'm really okay."

"Are you sure?" he asked, tightening his arms around me.

I nodded, and he released me from the hug. Beside us, Brian Junior held up the cake plates again, raising an eyebrow at me.

I started to laugh, looking back up at Hunter. "Did you seriously save me six pieces of cake?"

"Seven, but I ate one," he said, grinning down at me. "I figured six was still enough."

"You know how to make everything okay," I said, leaning against him again and closing my eyes. "I'm going to be okay, Hunter. I really am."

SIXTEEN

I WOKE up the next morning at my house. The movers had gotten delayed moving my bed, so I had one last day with the house that had always been my house.

I had a billion notifications on my phone. I stared at it for a second, not quite sure what was going on.

The first was a text from Jenna, *Did you lie to me?*

Oh god. This was not good.

I pulled open my phone, and way back in the list of notifications, I saw why.

Late last night, Hunter had posted a picture. It was the one that the drunk friend of my mom's had taken, the two of us standing by the water. I was staring directly up into his eyes, laughing about something, our arms around each other.

A girl worth running the burrito mile for was the caption.

Underneath, the guys had already started commenting.

I don't care if you're dating, she's my partner for Jenga next time, Ethan had written.

Burrito mile? Kinsey, I want in on this, Logan wrote.

There were a lot of comments that were just heart faces. I stared at them.

You are on the fan blog this morning!!!! came a text from Lily, then a second text. *It's not the greatest angle of your face. Super cute photo, but you need to get on Hunter about those angles.*

It was a good thing that my fame couldn't go to my head with my friends around or anything. *Thanks, you're the best,* I texted back, my stomach heaving.

Look, now that you're famous too, someone has to keep you honest, she texted back. *But omg you're famous!*

Not helpful, Lily, I texted back.

My phone rang, and I stared down at it. Jenna. How was she even awake? Wasn't she three hours behind me?

"So," she said as soon as I picked up the phone. "You and Hunter Lowen?"

I knew this discussion was coming, but that didn't make it any more comfortable. "Yes," I said, taking a deep breath. "Hunter and I are sort of a thing now."

"Sort of a thing? What does that mean?"

I thought it would be obvious from the comments on the photo. "Hunter and I are going out. We met at a party this summer and have started dating."

"Oh, so it's just one of those things," Jenna said, her tone of voice immediately changing. "You're just Hunter's flavor of the week."

Ouch. "No. I don't think that's the case," I said, sitting up in bed.

"I mean, if all you and Hunter did was kiss a few times," she said, her voice dropping into what I thought of as her pity voice, "I hate to tell you, but you are just who he was hooking up for the summer. It's not going to be a long term thing."

How dare she? She hadn't been here all summer. She had no idea. "I know," I said finally, trying to choose my words carefully. "It wasn't just kissing, though."

"Oh my god, tell me you didn't sleep with Hunter Lowen because you thought that it was going to make him start dating you!" Her voice sounded like she was about to burst into hysterical laughter. "God, Kinsey, you are so naïve. I feel so bad for you, honestly."

Nope. The last thing that I was going to get out of this situation was pity. "No, Jenna. It's really not your business, what Hunter and I have or haven't done. But we are dating."

There was silence on the other end of the phone line, and I swallowed. "What?" she said finally, her voice low.

"Hunter and I are actually dating. You can ask him if you want." I stood up out of bed, throwing the blankets to the end of the bed.

"Seriously? You're telling me that Hunter Lowen is your boyfriend?" she asked, her voice getting higher. "Yours? And you're actually exclusive and everything?"

Okay, I wasn't appreciating that tone of voice. "We're exclusive. I really like him, and he likes me. He posted that picture without telling me, to be clear."

"Okay," Jenna said finally, her voice tense. "So how long have you been dating?"

Oh god. Maybe that's what all of this was about. It was that she was furious that I hadn't told her when she'd mentioned it, and had thought that I was lying to her.

Jenna thought that she had the right to be in the known at all times, to be the person with all of the gossip and all of the latest intel. She might just be mad that I hadn't told her about this.

Somehow, part of me knew that that wasn't the real story, that this wasn't about Jenna not having intel. I'd changed our relationship too much. She'd always been the cool friend, and I was the dorky sidekick. But I'd moved out of that role, and our friendship couldn't take it.

"I don't know, exactly," I replied. There was never a time where Hunter and I had officially decided that we were dating. It was more like it had happened naturally, that over time I'd gotten closer and closer to Hunter, and now we were a couple.

It felt so uncomplicated in some ways. Like it was supposed to be this way, and Jenna had been making it harder than it needed to be. Hunter and I could just decide that we liked each other and start dating without thinking too much about it.

"And why didn't you tell me?" she asked, the question that was floating around my mind. I opened my mouth to try to say something, but before I could come up with any words, I heard her snort. "Never mind. Don't try to answer that. I know it."

I knew it too. Because I didn't want to be friends with Jenna any more, and I had to say it and be true to myself.

We'd been friends for the past few years because we'd been stuck together by school. But I'd never trusted Jenna or felt the way about her that I did about Lily or Ellery. I hadn't missed her this summer when she'd been gone. She clearly hadn't missed me.

"I don't really like how you're talking to me. I don't think it's very nice, frankly, and I don't want to talk to you any more right now," I said, swallowing. "I'm going to go."

She snorted on the other end. "Right." And before I could say anything else, she just hung up the phone. Of course she was going to have to get the last word.

I guess you couldn't always get the closure that you wanted, but that would be good enough for me.

My phone buzzed with a text. *I hope you're stocking up on your carbs today*, Hunter wrote.

I snorted. *Please bring me a bagel later.*

He sent back a picture, a bag of bagels sitting on the floor of his car. *Don't worry. I've got you. I went before practice just to make sure they had the good ones.*

I smiled at the photo, my stomach flipping again. It was actually time for me to go, though. I looked around at the walls of my bedroom for the last time.

So much of my life had been in this house. This was the room where I'd lost my first tooth and cried about a friend for the first time and screamed into my pillow when I realized Hunter liked me. This was my whole history.

But I couldn't stay here. I had to keep going and leave it behind.

I blinked a few times, then walked downstairs and picked up the keys to Betta.

My mom was already standing in the parking lot when I arrived and parked. "Kinsey!" she said, waving towards me. "Brian and Brian are getting ready together, and I was just going to start hair and makeup."

The fact that there were two men here named Brian necessitated calling them Brian Senior and Brian Junior, clearly. Not that I was going to have that argument today. That was for tomorrow.

"I see," I said, blinking a couple of times. I stuck Betta's keys into my bag.

"So glad to see you," she said, smiling at me. We started the walk into the country club. Elise was standing at the doorway, her hair already partially done into an updo.

She looked at me up and down, clearing her throat. "Good morning."

That didn't sound like a friendly good morning. That sounded like the kind of good morning that actually translated to "I would prefer to kick you out of my life and never see you again, but social norms and all that."

But she was polite enough to not actually say that, at least. "Morning," I said back to her.

"Emma, can you come with me for a hair wash?" one of the hair people said, looking at us.

My mom nodded, turning towards me. "I'll be back in a couple of minutes, girls."

Elise didn't seem to acknowledge her. I took a deep breath and sat down next to her on a giant couch, fishing my phone out of my pocket.

Another message from a random person at school about the photo with Hunter. I opened up my phone and stared at the picture again.

I looked so happy. I had no idea that the woman was still taking the pictures when I'd turned towards Hunter, but I looked so happy. I was in the middle of laughing about something, looking like Hunter was the funniest person in the world. I'd never believed that people could glow before, but I was glowing.

I just hoped that Brian Senior made my mom feel like this too. Because if that was the case, maybe we could work something out. Maybe I'd learn to tolerate him.

I heard a sniff next to me. I ignored it and stared at my phone. Elise was probably allergic to the incredible amount of hairspray that was currently being used to hold her updo into place. The hair people here really seemed to have decided that they could defy gravity.

There was another sniff beside me, and I turned my head slightly. Elise was sitting there, dabbing her eyes with a tissue.

That didn't look like allergies. "Are you okay?" I asked. Not that I liked Elise, but it was mean to let someone just cry next to you when they were clearly going through something.

"I just don't want to be here, but thanks for asking," she said, wiping at her eyes again.

"Me either, if it makes you feel better." Well. I probably shouldn't say that out loud, because I was trying to be supportive of my mom, but it was true.

She shot me a look. Her eyes were red rimmed, and she

blinked again a few times. "What do you know about it? It's not like it's your parents who got divorced."

"That's true," I said, looking at her for another second. She blinked again, fast enough that I couldn't tell if she was trying to blink back tears.

"Until last year, I had a normal family. And then all of a sudden, my mom sits me down and tells me that they're splitting up. And my dad packs up his stuff and leaves for an apartment immediately. And then three weeks later, he's coming home and telling me that he's met the woman of his dreams." She shook her head, then blinked a few more times. "You know who was supposed to be the woman of his dreams? My mom."

"I didn't ask for him to fall for my mom, if that makes it any better," I said, even though I knew that it didn't.

"I have zero interest in calling you my sister." She crossed her arms and sunk down in her chair, narrowing her eyes at me.

"Same. Really, I would be happier if I had never met you," I said, then swallowed. "Sorry. That was a little bit mean."

She glared at me for a second longer, then made a noise that could have been a laugh. "Well, it's true."

Just because it's true doesn't make it not mean, I wanted to say, but that was what I should have said to Jenna this morning. It was the wrong moment to say that to Elise. "Anyway," she continued, "a year ago I had a regular family, and now I'm sharing my dad with your mom, who I don't like. I don't want things to change. I don't want to have to deal with having your mom around at the holidays. I don't like it. I don't want to be here."

"Me either," I said, taking a deep breath.

As bad as I felt for myself, there was a little part of me that actually felt worse for Elise. Neither one of us had expected this, and it had to be worse when you were standing in the existing family watching things fall apart around you. Her entire life had shattered.

"And I swear, if I have to hear one more word about how fantastic your mom is and how much my dad never knew what love was before he met her, I am going to hurl. I will throw up all over all of them. And I will walk out," she said, crossing her arms over her chest. She was already in her dress for the afternoon, a terrible lace and satin mixture that had definitely been picked out for someone with my body type, not hers.

"Can we just agree that we don't like each other for the day, but that we both hate this more?" I asked, turning all the way towards her. "And then we can go back to hating each other tomorrow."

She snorted. "Deal. Nobody wants this."

Nobody except my mom. Maybe this was what my mom wanted, and she just hadn't told me before because she'd assumed that this was what I had wanted too.

I thought my mom wanted to run off with some doctor from Doctors without Borders, who she was going to meet when I was in college and she was traveling around helping the world. But maybe that was what I had always assumed, and my mom actually wanted to marry someone like Brian

Senior. She wanted to be with someone who was boring and stable.

Well, I couldn't get past the tight workout shorts and the obsession with carbs. But other than that. Maybe I could see it.

I gave that comment a few more seconds. Nope. Still not seeing it.

My mom walked out of the hair room, her hair already in its updo. She looked better with it than Elise. Elise's hair was naturally curly, and they must have straightened it before doing it updo. There was so much hairspray in it that it looked crinkly.

Okay, I was going to give it to her. She was really getting the short end of the stick.

"Can you get into these robes for the pictures?" the wedding planner said, sticking out fuzzy robes towards me and Elise. "We're going to do a set of pictures of the three of you getting ready on your mom's special day."

Elise stared at me and then back at the robe, then back at me. "And we have these too," the wedding planner said, pulling out a pair of giant slippers with honest to god bunny ears on them.

This was not real. This could not be real. We could not actually be expected to wear bunny ears.

There was nothing that was less me or my mom than the giant fuzzy pink robes that I was supposed to put on. "Are you for real?" I asked, looking at the robe and the slippers. "I am not going to wear this like I'm in second grade."

"Kinsey," my mom said, giving me a look. She was already wearing her giant fuzzy robe, which was white. "I think it'd be fun for us to take matching photos together. The three of us."

Choose your battles, I reminded myself. "Fine, I'll get changed," I said, picking up the robe and heading towards the bathroom. "I'll be back in just a second."

I locked myself into a stall and took a deep breath. Today was going to be tough. I was making it through, but it was going to be tough.

I unwrapped the robe and put it on. The wedding planner must have gotten the rejects, because the sleeves managed to be tight and too short while the rest of the robe ballooned out. The pink fabric was all frizzy, sticking straight out to the sides.

My phone buzzed, and I looked down at it. *See you soon. Do you think your mom will kill me if I come before I've showered?*

He had a selfie of himself after practice, his hair totally stuck up from sweat. It was amazing how he could look so good right after working out. I sent back a picture of the robe and the slippers. *Kill me now. I have to wear these.*

He sent back a series of laughing faces. *You better make sure I get to see these pictures.*

Don't even think about it. I'm going to delete all of them.

Don't you dare. I need to see these for history, he texted again. I smiled and stuck my phone in the pocket of the ridiculous overstuffed robe.

I walked back out to the room where my mom was, almost tripping over the end of my robe. This thing was a hazard to human health. "Are we ready for this?" my mom asked, turning towards us.

Elise shot me a look that meant that she would never be ready for this. I plastered a smile onto my face, taking the glass of fake champagne that the photographer passed me. We couldn't at least get real champagne? My mom definitely knew that we drank. I would guess that Elise also went out to parties.

I wasn't going to hate her for it today, because we were both going through it today. But I was going back to being snarky about her tomorrow. This was only a temporary truce.

"What a lovely bride!" the photographer, coming over towards my mom. "Let's take some more photos with your daughters. Maybe the three of you can do a group hug?"

Plural. Ugh. Elise and I didn't even look related. Elise shot me a look, rolling her eyes. I rolled mine back in agreement.

"Let's do it," my mom said, holding out her arms towards us.

This was going to be a story to tell Hunter later. I snapped a selfie of me in my robe again, holding it up to capture just how tiny the arms were.

"Are you trying to take a picture with me?" Elise asked.

I shook my head. "No you were just in the way," I replied. "But we can if you want."

"Why not," she said, giving me a bit of an eye roll. I snapped another picture, which somehow perfectly captured how tiny the arms were on these stupid robes.

Help me, I texted Hunter, sending him the picture of the robe. *The circulation in my arms is getting cut off.*

He sent me back a long string of laughing emojis. Not the response that I was exactly looking for. *I can cut you out of it later,* he wrote back eventually.

Nope, not going to let my stomach do a flip on that.

My phone buzzed again, this time Hunter sending a picture of himself getting ready at his house. *My mom had to run out and borrow a suit jacket for me. My old one didn't fit.*

God, he was really attractive. *Finally building arm muscles?* I texted back.

He sent me a kissy face and *only for you. I'll be there soon.*

"What are you doing?" Elise asked, snapping me out of staring at my phone.

"Just texting," I said, sticking my phone back into my pocket. "My boyfriend is coming to meet me here when we're done getting ready."

"Hunter Lowen," she said, raising an eyebrow.

It was a little bit weird how many people knew Hunter, even the people who didn't go to our school. "Yeah. Hunter Lowen," I said, taking a deep breath. I forgot how every school we played in sports knew about him.

Elise nodded again. "He seems really nice," she said finally, glancing over at me.

I was going to take this as an apology for the night before, where she had so clearly been trying to flirt with him in front of me. She had tried to get his attention, failed, and now we were going to be friends. Okay.

But I didn't have to worry about Hunter trying to get with her. Jenna might have tried to tell me that Hunter was a player, but I knew better.

Or at least, I believed better. I believed in Hunter. I believed that our relationship was strong, and that he was someone I could always rely on. I believed in us.

I heard the clicking of the camera again and again. I shifted my weight, forcing myself to keep a smile on my face. "He is," I said, keeping the smile on my face and turning back towards Elise. "I'm really serious about him."

She shrugged, then tried to shake out her arm in her robe. "I would be too."

My mom threw an arm around each of us, staring straight at the camera. "I'm so glad that we all get to be together today. We're going to have such a lovely wedding today, aren't we?"

We would not be having a lovely wedding. I nodded, which was the nicest answer that I could give. "I hate this robe," Elise muttered to me through clenched teeth. "I swear I can't feel my fingers."

"It makes your biceps look pretty good," I muttered back. It wasn't a lie, but that was because this robe was basically a muscle shirt.

The photographer forced us to pose again with our fake champagne, lifting up our glasses towards my mom. She beamed at the two of us.

"We should finish my hair," my mom said, releasing me and Elise from the hug. "You girls should finish getting ready without me."

The wedding planner beamed at me and Elise. She

seemed very friendly when my mom was around. "But the girls are welcome to stay here! We want to make sure you are all comfortable. Why don't we bring some breakfast up?"

I was not interested in what she was going to call breakfast. Brian Senior was paying for this wedding, which meant that it was probably some variation of tofu and lentils with no seasoning. "We have wheatgrass smoothies and some juices that won't bloat you at all before the big day," she continued.

Yep. I had totally called it.

"I wouldn't mind another cup of coffee," my mom said, looking up at the wedding planner.

"I can get it," I said, jumping up. It would be a good reason to get out of this room for a little bit.

"Thank you, Kinsey," my mom said, giving me a giant smile. I stood up, gathering up all the extra robe into my arms, and then went to the door to get the coffee. I had to carry my robe to avoid tripping over it.,

I walked down the hall. There had to be a room around here with coffee. Brian Senior was getting ready in some other part of the venue, and they definitely had coffee for all the people who had to deal with him today.

I heard the laugh behind me. Hunter was standing at the other end of the hallway, leaning against the wall, a bag of bagels on a table next to him. "Is that outfit for real?" he asked, clearly trying to choke back a laugh.

I should have known. I was doomed to run into Hunter as soon as I walked outside in this ridiculous robe. "Don't get me started. Someone convinced my mom that these were nice looking robes to get ready in. I hate it," I said.

"You look like the Easter Bunny got electrocuted," he said. He reached out and flicked a piece of fluff on my shoulder.

Sometimes it was amazing that Hunter was the guy who managed to pick up anyone he wanted at school. What a smooth line.

I dropped the extra robes back down onto the floor. "I swear they picked the least flattering color for me on purpose. I would have been totally fine getting ready in old running clothes if they didn't want me messing up my dress."

"It's kind of cute. In a pretty unattractive way," he said, grinning at me.

I rolled my eyes at him. That had to be the single most backhanded compliment that he could give me. "You're really making me feel better here."

"I can tell you that no one would look good in that robe, but you look better than anyone else would," he said, wrapping me in a hug and kissing my forehead.

I closed my eyes for a second, relaxing into the hug. I was going to make it through today. This wasn't going to be as bad as I was mentally making it out to be. I was going to be fine. Just fine.

Hunter released me from the hug and passed me a to go cup. "This is for you. I know you like to have a thousand things of sugar in your coffee, so I think I got enough in there."

Thank goodness. I would have preferred vanilla syrup,

but this was going to be drinkable. "Thank you. I owe you one. I owe you a million."

He grinned and gave me another kiss on the forehead. "I figured you needed carbs and sugar."

He was very right. "I told my mom that I was going to find her coffee. We're getting ready down the hall there," I said, pointing towards the room.

"I would never have expected your mom to make you wear that robe," Hunter said, picking up the back of my robe as we started the walk down the hall.

"Trust me, I'm so confused. My mom isn't normally someone who cares about stuff like that, and all of a sudden, we're wearing fuzzy robes and drinking champagne and doing makeup," I said.

I took a sip of the coffee Hunter had brought. It was way too sweet, but I wasn't going to tell him that. I was just happy that he was here.

"Sorry for not getting here earlier, but my mom would have killed me for showing up when I was still sweaty. And I thought your mom might lose it if I showed up directly from practice," he said as we reached the coffee station in the hall.

"It would have been kind of funny if you'd shown up straight from practice and needed a shower. All the people who are here and freaking out about my hair not looking perfect would have had something else to worry about," I replied. I filled up a coffee cup for my mom. "Come with me."

"Of course," he said, still holding my robes in a bundle

in his arms. "I do have a suit in the car, so you know. I wasn't planning to wear this to the wedding."

"You could have. It would have been hilarious." Brian Senior would not have known what to do with Hunter in a t-shirt and shorts, but he wouldn't have been able to figure out what to say. Not when Hunter actually won games, unlike Brian Junior, who hadn't gotten off the bench for soccer all year.

It was a bad sign that I was here on my mom's wedding day and already planning how to one up Brian Senior. But he deserved it.

"Are you ready for this?" I asked, glancing over at him before we opened the door into the getting ready room.

I knocked, and the wedding planner came out. She glanced at me, then at Hunter very obviously. "This is supposed to be where the women are getting ready, Kinsey."

That was such bullshit. "This isn't gender segregated. I can bring my boyfriend here if I want. And also, I don't care about your stupid rules."

Hunter rested his hand on my back for a second, as though he could tell that I was not ready to take shit today. He was going to jump into action if I started to lose it at the wedding planner. Good call, Hunter.

The wedding planner stared at me. "Excuse me?"

Okay, that was a little bit much for the situation. I swallowed. "I'm bringing my mom coffee. And Hunter is coming with me."

I stepped in, Hunter following right behind me. "That

was a lot," he said. "She seems like she could be a little bit annoying, given how much you snapped at her."

"A little bit?" I took another sip of my coffee. It was growing on me. Maybe I was just sugar deprived. "It's been awful. I keep getting bossed around by a wedding planner who wants me to look like the Easter Bunny with a drug problem."

He snorted. "It's not the most flattering thing you've ever worn. But you're still cute."

I elbowed him in the side. "Be nice. I have the bagels," he reminded me, nudging me with his shoulder.

That was a winning point. Elise looked up from where she was sitting on the couch, her eyes traveling from me to Hunter and back again. "Do I smell bagels?"

The fact that that was the first thing that she'd noticed was making me like her a little bit more.

Hunter looked at me, raising an eyebrow. Almost like he was letting me decide how nice I wanted to be. Fortunately for Elise, I was feeling generous. "Yeah, do you want one?"

"Please?" she asked, looking directly at me and not at Hunter. She was really redeeming herself here.

"You pick. I'm going to go give my mom this coffee," I said, looking up at Hunter. He nodded slightly towards me. "But make sure to leave a cinnamon raisin for me."

"Don't worry. I got you an everything and a cinnamon raisin in case you can't make up your mind," Hunter said, his hand grazing my side. "I know you."

I wasn't indecisive. I just liked having multiple bagel options, because bagels were a rare treat for me.

I crossed the room and knocked on the door to the room where my mom was doing her hair. "Is everyone dressed?" I called.

"Yes, come in!" my mom's voice came back.

I pushed open the door and passed her the coffee. "I got your coffee, Mom."

"Thanks so much," she said, reaching towards me and taking it from me. The hairdresser behind her stared at the coffee, probably in jealousy. "I really appreciate you being here today, Kinsey."

"Of course," I said, looking at her. I blinked back a tear for a second, then stopped myself. "Of course I was going to be here."

She looked at me for a second and then nodded again. Maybe it wasn't obvious any more. I could have chosen to be so many other places. I could have refused to come. But I was here, and I was faking it the best I could.

"I'm going to go put my dress on," I said finally. A good excuse to get out of this robe and be able to walk again, at least. "I think I'm going to skip hair and makeup."

"That's okay with me," she said, looking up at me. "You're beautiful without it, Kinsey. Really."

I did want to roll my eyes at my mom, but I decided against it at the last second. "You too, Mom."

I walked back out into the room where Hunter and Elise were sitting. Elise was slowly eating a bagel and staring at her phone, and Hunter was doing the same. He looked up and grinned when I walked back in.

Maybe she had just tried to make conversation last

night. Maybe I was judging her way too harshly, and I needed to calm myself down and take a step back.

"I have to get my dress on," I said, looking from Elise to Hunter. "It might take me a few minutes, because I have to get out of this robe first."

"Let me know if you need help," Hunter said, taking a step towards me and passing me a bagel. "And I put the cream cheese on for you."

I took the bagel from him, resisting the urge to throw my arms around him in front of Elise. Something was bubbling up in me, the knowledge that I couldn't have done any of this without Hunter's support.

I went into one of the changing rooms, pulling my dress down from its hanger and staring at it. It was the dress that I'd gotten earlier this summer, shopping with my mom. That hadn't even been two months, that shopping trip, and everything felt different now.

I stepped into the dress, pulling it up. It wasn't tight, but there was no way that I was going to be able to reach around and zip it up.

I stuck my head around the side of the door. "Hunter?"

"Need help?" he asked, immediately sticking his phone back into his pocket and walking over.

"Do you mind zipping up my dress?" I asked, holding it together in case Elise looked over. I might not hate her right now, but I was not flashing her.

He shut the door behind him, staring at me. He swallowed. "Kins. You look beautiful."

I looked back at him, my heart feeling too big for my chest. There weren't enough words to say everything I wanted to say. The feeling that was overwhelming me, making it hard to breathe – this wasn't just liking him. This had to be love.

I didn't want to live in a world without Hunter. I wanted him to be part of my story forever. I wanted *us*.

I swallowed again. His hand skimmed my back, pulling up the zipper on my dress.

I caught my breath as he stepped back. His eyes never left my face, and he stared right into my eyes. "Kinsey."

"I love you," I blurted out. My heart started pounding. The words were so big and still not enough for everything I felt.

Hunter's arms were around me. He pulled me into him, resting my head on his chest. "I love you too."

I pulled him as close as I could, trying to say everything that I couldn't put into words.

Whatever was coming, it was going to be okay. I had Hunter. I could do anything with him beside me.

His hand cupped my chin, and I leaned my head back to kiss him. He pressed his lips to mine.

It was our first kiss all over again. But it was even better this time. It was the kiss that said that this was just the start of our story, the start of something bigger and better than I could have imagined. This was our love story.

He pulled back from the kiss, resting his forehead on mine. "I'm yours, Kins. We'll get through it together."

I stared up at him, trying to find the right words to say.

But before I could say anything, someone started pounding on the door. "Open up, I need my dress," Elise yelled.

I started laughing, burying my head in Hunter's shoulder. "Her timing is perfect," he said, wrapping his hand in my hair.

"Seriously!" she called again. "I don't know what you two are doing, but I need my dress!"

"We should go before she rips the door down," I said, resting against him for another second.

"That would be something," he said, squeezing me tighter. "You ready?"

"Ready," I said, taking a deep breath. He kissed my forehead before I turned towards the door and pushed it open.

It wasn't just Elise outside. Ellery and Lily were standing there, both holding bagels. "You look awesome," Ellery said, looking over at me, then very obviously at Hunter.

"She does," Hunter said, looping his arm around my back.

"We weren't going to leave you here by yourself," Ellery said. "Even if Hunter beat us here."

"You can't get rid of us, even if Brian Senior comes out and threatens us with carb-free bagels," Lily added.

I looked at them, then back at Hunter, whose arm was still wrapped around me. He smiled down at me, pulling me tighter.

No matter what this year was going to throw at us, I had them now. Lily and Ellery and Hunter. Hunter most of all.

"I love you all."

ABOUT THE AUTHOR

Caroline Hopkins has been writing since high school, when she discovered that writing stories was much more fun than taking notes. She loves a good romance, coffee in every form, and listening to too much Taylor Swift. She lives in New York City with a very spoiled cat and far too many books.

Find her online at carolinehopkinswrites.com.

Summer Off Script

Sutton Someday

9 781961 878129